"Oh, really? My presence unnerves you?" And he took a step closer, until there was very little space between them at all. "Is it just me, I wonder? Or are you flustered by other men, as well?"

"Not you at all, my lord. It is just that I am unaccustomed to such attention. While teaching."

He laughed softly, and the hairs on the back of her neck rose as he whispered, "You are lying again, and not very skillfully."

"I swear I am not." But her voice became breathy as she said it, with a tone that was all wrong for the earnest denial she should mount.

"I will agree that you are not accustomed to teaching. But, looking as you do, I find it hard to believe that you are unaccustomed to masculine attention." He was making no effort to hide an interest that she suspected had little to do with her knowledge of geography. "A simple governess would not dress the way you do."

He stood very close to her. Too close, for she could feel the heat of his body or ⬚⬚⬚⬚⬚⬚⬚⬚⬚ ⬚⬚⬚⬚⬚⬚ ps I shall not have to r⬚⬚⬚⬚⬚⬚⬚⬚⬚⬚⬚⬚⬚⬚⬚cide to remove yourself. F⬚⬚⬚⬚⬚⬚⬚⬚⬚⬚⬚⬚⬚us for you to remain und⬚⬚

* * *

Dangerous Lord, Innocent Governess
Harlequin® Historical #1048—July 2011

Author Note

Somewhere in the writing of *Miss Winthorpe's Elopement,* it became clear to me that I was only telling half the story. The more I wrote, the more I became convinced that there was another whole book that would explain the behavior of Tim Colton and his wife, Clare.

Perhaps Clare secretly had a heart of gold. Perhaps things weren't as they appeared between her and the Duke of Bellston. Perhaps she only needed love, and if I gave them a little time Tim and Clare could work out their differences and live happily ever after.

Or perhaps not.

And as I wrote, I discovered that I'd been leaving myself little clues as to how unhappy they really were together, and what might happen between the two of them once they were alone in Wales.

Once I stopped fighting the truth, the book all but wrote itself. My research became a weird mix: the nineteenth century, British horticulture, conservatory design and old-fashioned gothic romances. The result was the story you are about to read.

CHRISTINE MERRILL

Dangerous Lord, Innocent Governess

 **Harlequin**®

TORONTO NEW YORK LONDON
AMSTERDAM PARIS SYDNEY HAMBURG
STOCKHOLM ATHENS TOKYO MILAN MADRID
PRAGUE WARSAW BUDAPEST AUCKLAND

Recycling programs
for this product may
not exist in your area.

ISBN-13: 978-0-373-29648-4

DANGEROUS LORD, INNOCENT GOVERNESS

Copyright © 2009 by Christine Merrill

First North American Publication 2011

This edition published by arrangement with Harlequin Books S.A.

For questions and comments about the quality of this book
please contact us at Customer_eCare@Harlequin.ca.

www.Harlequin.com

Printed in U.S.A.

To Jo Carr. May it always be this easy.

Chapter One

'Her Grace will see you now.'

Daphne Collingham followed the servant to the door of the sitting room, and took an involuntary breath as she was announced. Was it always this intimidating to seek employment? She certainly hoped she would never have reason to know.

Once her mission here was finished, she could return to her real life in London. And she would miss none of the Season: the parties, the balls and the tiresome chore of hunting up a husband who would meet with her father's approval. But for now she must remember that she was a humble governess, whose only intent was to make a future in caring for the children of the Colton household.

She tried not to shudder at the idea.

Perhaps it was worse for her because she knew that her petition was a sham. And while it might be rather nerve racking to meet a duchess on a social occasion, it was much more so when the duchess stood as gate-keeper to a place one wanted to enter. Even more so when one was still trying to memorise an employment history that one had bought off a stranger on a north-bound coach.

The Duchess rose as Daphne entered, which was entirely unnecessary, given their difference in class, and reached out to take her hand. 'Miss Collins.'

'Your Grace,' she responded with what she hoped was appropriate subservience.

The Duchess sank back on to the divan, and gestured her to a nearby chair. The woman in front of her looked more like a schoolteacher than the wife of a peer. But looks could be deceiving. Daphne hoped that the Duchess believed the same, for she doubted very much that she was managing to look the part of a prospective governess. Her curtsy alone should have given her away. It would have suited in a drawing room, she suspected. But she had practised curtsying like a governess in front of a mirror at the inn, and could not seem to manage it.

The Duchess narrowed her eyes as Daphne bowed to her, as though she had recognised the deficiency. It had not been unfriendly. Merely a sign that the fact had been noted, recorded and filed appropriately. The Duchess of Bellston suspected she would prove difficult.

But now, the woman was examining her references, and smiling. 'These seem to be in order. Although they refer to you as Daphne. I understood, from your original letter, that your Christian name was Mary.'

'There was already a Mary in the last house, your Grace. So they called me by my middle name, Daphne. I've grown to prefer it.'

The Duchess nodded. 'Daphne. Very pretty. And it suits you much better than Mary.'

She certainly hoped so.

The Duchess was reading more carefully. 'These are most exceptional.'

'Thank you.' She had laboured long to erase the name of their previous owner, and insert her own. The fact that they were exceptional forgeries needn't enter into the conversation.

'You have been in service long?' There was a definite upturn at the end of the sentence, as though the Duchess had her doubts. Probably the fault of that damned curtsy.

'When one enjoys one's work, the time passes quickly.'

'And you do enjoy your chosen profession, and are not doing it solely from duty, or a need to make a way for yourself?'

'I adore children.' And there was the biggest lie of all. For while she hoped that she would manage to adore her own, she had never found the children of others to be better than a necessary evil.

'Excellent,' said the Duchess, eager to believe her. 'For that is just what this family needs.' She looked at Daphne with the same searching expression she had used upon the paperwork. 'The residents of this house have undergone a loss, and the children's behaviour has been somewhat…' she paused significantly '…difficult.'

'Difficult?' Oh, dear. It had never occurred to her that the children would be part of the problem.

The Duchess smiled encouragement. 'But it will be nothing to someone as experienced as you. It is just that they will need more than rote learning and a firm hand. They need understanding. And affection, of course.'

What they needed was justice. But Daphne nodded enthusiastically at the Duchess's words. 'The poor dears. One can never replace a mother, of course. But if it is possible to provide stability, and a woman's touch?' She gave a deprecating shrug. 'One tries.'

The Duchess let out a visible sigh of relief. 'I think we are in agreement. While I place a high value on education, the Coltons are bright children, and naturally inquisitive. Advanced for their years.'

Daphne nodded, as though she understood. It was strange that a woman who was little better than a neighbour should take such interest in another man's children. Perhaps she thought it her duty, as lady of the land. Or perhaps there was some other, more ominous reason that she felt a need to insinuate herself into the household.

The Duchess continued. 'They will find their own way. They need less help in that area than they need a sense that they are safe and cared for.'

As long as their father was present, there was little Daphne could do to ensure their safety. But she nodded again.

The Duchess rose and straightened her skirts. 'If you will just wait here, while I speak to Lord Colton, the butler will be along shortly with some refreshment for you. When I return we will go to meet the children.' She said it with confidence, as though the hiring was a foregone conclusion, even without the consent of the master of the house. Then she turned and left the room. Daphne could hear her on the other side of the partly closed door, speaking with a servant about tea and cakes.

She let out the breath she had been holding. The first hurdle was cleared. When she had met the real Miss Collins, while travelling to Wales for a family visit, Daphne had thought it amazing good luck. Here was a woman heading straight to the place that she had really wanted to see: the home of her beloved cousin, Clarissa. And since the true governess was heartily sick of tending the children of others, it had not been hard for a persuasive young lady to talk her out of her identity.

It had cost Daphne two of her favourite gowns, a garnet brooch and the spending money she had been given for her visit. But the total was more than a year's salary for Miss Collins, and would give her an opportunity for a well-deserved rest. She could have her dreary life back, once Daphne was done with it, and no one would be the wiser.

Daphne got quietly up from her chair, and moved to the doorway. She stayed well in the shadow of the door, listening for the Duchess's steps as they turned down the corridor to the left. Her slippers clicked quietly against the marble in an efficient staccato, pausing after a few seconds. There was the sound of her voice, distant and barely intelligible, requesting entrance.

It was impossible to hear the response.

Daphne eased the door open, expecting to hear a squeak of hinge. But it moved noiselessly. It hardly mattered, for when she poked her head into the hall, there was no one to hear any sound she might make. If she was quick, she could begin her investigations, and be back in the room before a servant appeared with the tea tray. No one need be the wiser. She followed the direction of the Duchess's steps, taking care that her shoes made no noise at all as she moved, and counted off the paces she had heard the Duchess take. As she progressed, she could hear the sound of voices from an open doorway, increasing in volume as she approached.

'And just what gives you the right, Penny, to meddle in this at all?' It was a man's voice, brusque and irritable.

Daphne slowed her steps to listen.

'Do I need permission to help a friend, when I know he is in need?' The Duchess's voice had lost the edge of efficiency. It was warmer. Perhaps there was something more than friendship between the two. Daphne inched along the wall that held the door and glanced across the hall.

There was a large, gilt-framed mirror on the wall opposite her, meant to bring light to the dark corridor from the conservatory at the end of the hall. As she moved closer to the open door, she could see the reflection of the study where the two were speaking.

After a frigid pause, the man responded to the Duchess. 'Yes, your Grace, you do require permission.'

'Your Grace?' She could see the hurt on the woman's

face, as her reflection crept into view. 'Suddenly we are to be formal, Lord Colton?'

'I see no reason to pretend that engaging servants to spy upon me is an act of friendship.'

'That is not what I am doing,' the Duchess protested. And Daphne flinched. He had guessed her own purpose without meeting her, even if he was wrong about the Duchess's part in it. 'I am concerned for the welfare of the children.'

'If you were motivated by concern, you would leave them in peace. And me as well.'

She had inched forward to the point where she could see most of the room and the Duchess in profile before the desk, and the man seated in front of her. She was not sure what she expected, but it was not what she saw. Clare had described her husband as weak, anaemic, cruel. In her own mind, Daphne had seen him as a great, grey spider, pale and thin but deceptively strong, and with influence far beyond the reach of his thin grasping fingers.

But that did not fit the real Timothy Colton at all. Dark brown hair falling forward on to the healthy complexion of a man who enjoyed the sun. His shoulders did not speak of great height, but they were straight and unbent. He was quite ordinary. And if she was honest about it, rather handsome.

It seemed her adversary was nothing more than a man.

The Duchess leaned forward, on to the desk, trying to catch his gaze, which was directed sullenly downward.

'Perhaps solitude is the best way for you to deal with your grief. But must the children suffer?'

He raised his face to hers. 'Grief? Is that what you think my problem is?' He gave a bleak laugh. 'I am glad that Clarissa is gone. In time, so will the children be, if they are not already.' There was no hesitation as he spoke, no sign that he might feel guilt over speaking so about his wife of twelve years.

Daphne felt a fresh wave of hatred for the man seated behind the desk.

The Duchess whispered, almost as though she feared that there was a listener. 'We are quite aware of your feelings on the subject. It would be easier for all of us if you were not so plain about it.'

'Is that what this is about, then? An attempt to make things appear more normal than they are? Your husband is the magistrate. He would have been better off had he admitted the truth, and dealt with this when he had the chance, just after she died. I would not have faulted him for it. You can hardly blame me if you find that maintaining the lie is difficult.'

So it was just as she suspected. Her cousin's death was not the accident that everyone pretended.

The Duchess straightened, and her tone became chill. 'It does not matter to me, Tim, if you wish to wallow in your misery. I care only for the children. It will not be as easy for them as you seem to think. A female presence will be a comfort to them, if you allow it.'

'The only comfort they are likely to have will be gained far away from this mausoleum. Edmund is old enough for school, as is Lily.'

'You mean to send them away, do you?'

'I want what is best for them. And that is to be far away from the memory of their mother's last day. And far away from me.'

'Even Sophie?'

She saw the man stiffen in his chair. 'I will find a place for Sophie. She is my daughter, after all. And no concern of yours. I do not need your help, your sympathy, your friendship or your misguided attempts to make right a thing that can never be repaired.' Then he looked up out into the hall, and into the mirror. 'And I do not need a governess.'

His eyes met hers in the mirror, and for a moment, she knew what it was to face death. They were the soulless black eyes of a murderer, and they stared into her as though he had known that she was there the whole time.

She turned and fled back to the drawing room, not caring how much noise she made.

Tim Colton leaned back in his chair and folded his arms. The Duchess gave no indication that she heard the prying governess clattering off down the hall. She seemed near to explosion. 'You do need a governess, Tim Colton, if you mean to act like a spoiled child. Perhaps Miss Collins will be able to persuade you, since I cannot, that your behaviour is doing injury to the children you seek to protect. She will be an employee in this household, no matter what your opinion on the subject might be. If you resist me in this, I shall go to my husband, just as you ask. He will have you locked

in your room until you can stand before the House of
Lords and explain yourself. When you are gone, we will
pack the children off to stay with their mother's family.
Does that suit you?'

'You know it does not.' And in his own ears, his
voice sounded sullen. A spoiled child's muttering, just
as she had said. He had best gain control of himself, or
the children would end up with the Collinghams. And
the last thing he wished was for them to grow up to be
just like their mother.

'Then we are agreed. I shall go back to Miss Collins
and arrange for her salary. You shall put on your coat,
comb your hair and come to meet your new servant.'
She turned and swept from the room.

Tim sat at his desk, head cradled in his hands. Penny
had made another effort to arrange his life. He supposed
he was expected to be grateful for it, but felt nothing
more than numb.

Perhaps she was right in it. If he was as concerned
for his children as he claimed, then surely he did not
wish to cause them more pain than he had already. And
at this late date, an airing of the family secrets would
do more harm than good.

With any luck, this latest governess would last no
longer in the house than the previous one had, or the
ones before that. They had all found the children 'difficult' and the master of the house 'disturbing', although
he doubted that they had admitted that last fact to Penny.
But on the rare occasions when they spoke to him
directly, he could see that they had guessed the truth.

It was in their eyes, and in the great care they took never to be alone with him.

Once Miss Collins fled, things would return to quiet and solitude. A few months would bring them to the start of the spring term. He would pack Edmund and Lily off to the best schools he could find. And for a time, he would be alone with Sophie.

He felt his heart wrench again, wondering how much lonelier it would be when he was left to parent the silent little girl, without the buffering of the two older children. Then he pushed it to the back of his mind, and rose from his desk to greet the new governess.

As he pulled on a jacket and ran a hand through his hair, he thought of the reflection of Miss Collins in the hallway mirror. He had seen her, from the corner of his eye, moving slowly into focus, trying to glean the details of a conversation she had no part in. Was she curious as to the fate of her employment? It spoke of a desperation that was absent from the previous candidates. If the job was so important to her, then it might be difficult to dislodge her from it.

Or it could be something else. Something far more sinister. Spies listened at doors. If she came to this house to learn and not to teach, then he had another problem altogether.

As he neared the sitting room, he could hear the sound of voices through the open door. Penny was arranging the particulars. He was hardly needed. If he was lucky, he might have no further contact with the girl after this brief introduction. He stepped into the open doorway and froze in surprise, unprepared for what he saw.

The reflection in the mirror had not done her justice. It had been watery and unclear. Other than her eyes, which were curiously intense, he had not noticed anything singular about her. But in person?

He caught his breath. She was a beauty, and the failed attempt at simple clothing and stern coiffure did nothing to hide the fact. Her hair was a rich chestnut, and framed a face that was softly rounded, with full red lips and startlingly green eyes. He could imagine the curves of her body under the stiff fabric of her gown, for she had none of the sharp angles he'd come to associate with women of her class. There was nothing to hint at a privation that might have urged her to take a position. Nor did she have the pinched, disapproving look of one secretly envious of her charges' wealth.

He gripped the door frame in surprise as a wave of lust swept over him. It had been a long time since he'd been with a woman. Too long, if he had begun to harbour thoughts about the servants, especially someone brought into his house to care for his children.

But as he looked at her again, he could not resist the thought that she might be better suited for the bedroom than the classroom.

Take her there, and see.

The thought chilled him, although his blood ran hot at the sight of the girl. It did not do to give too much weight to the odd thought that might cross one's mind, in a moment of weakness.

Is it weakness or strength, to act on your desires instead of hiding from them? You were never such a coward, before.

More madman than coward, if he was hearing voices. And even more mad to listen. If what one desired was wrong, one must not succumb.

Too late for that. You are already lost. If you want the girl, wait until the house is asleep. Then go to her and take her.

No. He closed his eyes so he could no longer see the object of temptation, and willed his pulse to slow. But it only became easier to imagine the skin hidden under the plain dress, and the smooth feel of it against his, the soft lips startled open by his kiss, and the tightness of her body as he came into her.

The voice in his head gave a sigh of satisfaction. *Open your eyes and look at her, coward.*

He could feel his will weakening as he allowed himself to be persuaded. Surely she did not seek the life of a governess, unless all matrimonial options had failed. She must have resigned herself to never knowing the touch of a man. If she was lonely, and as frustrated as he was, then was seduction such a great crime?

You have done worse.

Everything inside him froze. He had done worse. And worse yet, he had escaped punishment for his crime. One could justify anything, if one could live with one's self after doing the unthinkable.

Penny turned and saw him, standing in the entrance, and gave a hurrumph of frustration at his lack of manners. 'There you are, Timothy. Come into the room and meet Miss Collins.'

'Miss Collins.' He bowed, stiffly, from the waist.

The young woman stood as he entered, and responded

with a curtsy, and a cool and professional smile. 'Lord Colton.'

'I understand you have been retained by the Duchess to see to the care of my children. It is so nice to finally meet my new employee.' He gave her a pointed look to tell her he had seen her hiding in the hall, and was annoyed by it and the Duchess's handling of the whole affair.

'And to finally meet my employer.' She responded with a look that seemed to convey her opinion of a man who cared so little for his own family that he would leave such an important decision to a neighbour.

Their eyes locked, as though in battle. For a moment, he was convinced that she had heard the voices in his head as clearly as he did himself, for she looked both disapproving and disgusted, though it was only their first meeting. Perhaps he deserved her censure. But it angered him, all the same. So he held her gaze far longer than was proper, until he was sure that she knew who was master and who was servant. At last, she broke away and cast her eyes downward. He gave a small nod of satisfaction, and said, 'Welcome to my home. And now, if you will excuse me?' And he left the room with Penny dumbfounded and his pride intact.

'That man,' muttered the Duchess in frustration and gave a small stamp of her foot.

'Indeed.' Daphne swallowed, trying to control the strange feeling she had had, as her cousin's husband had smiled at her. He had stared at her far too long, until the look in his eyes had gone from sullen to seductive. He had looked at her as a wolf might look at a lamb.

She was sure that the Duchess had not seen the worst of it, thinking the man had been rude and not threatening. For when she turned to Daphne, she had a grim smile that said she would not be crossed in this, no matter how stubborn the master of the house might be. 'Lord Colton has proved difficult on the subject of his children's care.'

'They are his children,' Daphne said softly, rather surprised at how little the Duchess seemed to care about the fact.

'Of course,' the Duchess responded. 'But recent events have left him all but unfit to care for them. As a close friend of the family, I feel a responsibility to help him through this difficult time.'

'You knew Lady Colton?' Daphne smiled eagerly. She might have an ally, if the woman had also known Clare.

'I knew her. Yes.' And now the Duchess's look was one of distaste. She offered nothing more, before changing the subject. 'But come, you must be eager to see the nursery wing and meet your charges.' She rose quickly and preceded Daphne to the door and out into the hall, as though the merest mention of the children's mother hung in the air like a bad smell.

As they walked up the main stairs, Daphne paused for a moment and glanced behind her. So this was where it had happened. She could almost imagine her cousin, who had been so full of life, lying dead below her on the floor of the entry. She shook off the image to further examine the scene of the crime. Smooth marble treads, and an equally smooth banister that might have denied an adequate grip to the woman who had struggled here.

She glanced at the floor to see faint proof that a rug had been present and was now removed. So the poor carpet had taken the blame. A loose corner, a trip and a fall. Perfectly ordinary. Most unfortunate.

But Daphne believed none of it. Clare had used the stairs for twelve years without so much as a stumble. There was nothing to be afraid of, if someone was not here to push you down. When she was finished in this house, everyone would know the truth and Clare would be avenged.

The Duchess did not notice her pause, absorbed by her own thoughts, which did not concern the unfortunate death of the mistress of the house. She gave a helpless little shrug. 'I might as well tell you, before we go any further, that there is a small problem that I have been unable to deal with.'

'Really.' There were many problems with this house, and none of them small. Daphne wondered what would incite the Duchess to comment, if the death of Clare had not.

'In my letter to you, I promised something I could not give. The bedroom just off the nursery is the one intended for the governess. Convenient to the class-room, and next to little Sophie should she need you in the night.'

Daphne nodded.

'The oldest girl, Lily, has taken the room as her own.

I have been unable to dislodge her from it. The two older children care deeply for the littlest girl. And in the absence of a regular governess they have taken the duties of Sophie's care upon themselves.' For a moment, the Duchess looked distressed, nearly to tears over the plight of the children.

Forgetting her station, Daphne reached out a hand to the woman, laying an arm over her shoulders. 'It will be all right, I'm sure.' It was comforting to see that the Duchess cared so deeply for the children, for it made her actions in the Colton house seem much less suspicious.

The Duchess sniffed, as though fighting back her emotion. 'Thank you for understanding.' She walked to the end of the hall and opened the door to the servants' stairs, looking up a flight. 'There is a small room at the top of the house. Only fit for a maid, really. But it is very close to the children. And yet, very private. There is nothing at all on this side of the house but the attics, and the one little place under the eaves. And it is only until you can persuade Lily to return to her own room.'

Daphne looked up the narrow, unlit staircase, to the lone door at the top. 'I'm sure it will be adequate.' It would be dreadful. But it was only for a few weeks. And living so simply would help her remember her position.

'Shall we go and meet the children now? I have sent word that they are to wait for us in the schoolroom.' She led the way past two bedrooms, which must be Sophie's and the one Lily had usurped, to a small but well-stocked classroom. There were desks and tables, with a larger desk at one end for her, maps and pictures upon the walls and many shelves for books.

Remembering how she had felt as a child when cooped up in a similar room, Daphne was overcome with a sudden desire to slip away from the Duchess, to lead her in hide and seek or some other diversion. Anything that might prolong the time before she must pick up a primer.

The children lined up obediently in front of her, by order of age. Daphne felt a surprising lump form in her throat. They were all the picture of her beloved Clare. Red hair, pale complexions, fine features and large green eyes. Some day, the two girls would be beauties, and the boy would be a handsome rakehell.

The rush of emotion surprised her. She felt a sudden, genuine fondness for the children that she had not expected. She did not normally enjoy the company of the young. But these were the only part of her cousin that still remained. She had to overcome the urge to talk to them of the woman they both knew, and to reveal her relation to them. Surely it would be a comfort to them all to know that Clare was not forgotten?

But then she looked again. The light behind their eyes was the same suspicious glint she had seen in the man behind the desk on the floor below. They had also inherited the stubborn set of his jaw. Without speaking a word to each other, she watched them close ranks against her. They might smile and appear co-operative. And her heart might soften for the poor little orphans that Clare had left behind. But that should not give her reason to expect their help in discovering the truth of what had happened to their mother, or in bringing their father to justice.

She smiled an encouraging, schoolteacher's smile at them, and said, 'Hello, children. My name is Miss Collins. I have come a long way to be with you.'

The boy looked at her with scepticism. 'You are from London, are you not? We make the trip from London to Wales and back, twice a year. And while it is a great nuisance to be on the road, it is not as if you have come from Australia, is it?'

'Edmund!' the Duchess admonished.

Daphne chose to ignore the insolence, and redoubled her smile. 'As far as Australia? I suppose it is not. Do you find Australia of particular interest? For we could learn about it, if you wish.'

'No.' He glanced at the Duchess, who looked angry enough to box his ears. He corrected himself. 'No, thank you, Miss Collins.'

'Very well.' She turned to the older girl. 'And you are Lily, are you not?'

'Lilium Lancifolium. Father named me. For my hair.' When she saw Daphne's blank look, she gave a sigh of resignation at the demonstrated ignorance of the new governess. 'Tiger Lily.'

'Oh. How utterly charming.' Utterly appalling, more like. What kind of man gifted his first child with such a name? And, worse yet, a girl, who would someday have to carry that name to the alter with her. Clare's frustration with the man had not been without grounds.

Daphne turned to the youngest child. 'And you must be little Sophie. I have heard so much about you, and am most eager to know you better.' She held out a hand of greeting to the girl.

The littlest girl said nothing, and her eyes grew round, not with delight, but with fear. The two older children stepped in front of her, as though forming a barrier of protection. 'Sophie does not like strangers,' said Edmund.

'Well, I hope that she will not think me a stranger for long.' Daphne crouched down so that she might appear less tall to the little girl. 'It is all right, Sophie. You do not have to speak, if you do not wish. I know when I was little I found it most tiresome that adults were always insisting I curtsy, and recite, and sit in stiff chairs listening to boring lessons. I'd have been much happier if they'd left me alone in the garden with my drawings.'

The little girl seemed taken aback by this. Then she smiled and shifted eagerly from foot to foot, tugging at her older sister's skirts.

In response, Lily shook her head and said, 'Sophie is not allowed to draw.'

'Not allowed?' Daphne stood up quickly. 'What sort of person would take pencils and paper away from a little girl?'

Edmund responded, 'Our last governess—'

'Is not here.' Daphne put her hands on her hips, surprised at her own reaction. She had not meant to care in the least about the activities of the children. But she found herself with a strong opinion about their upbringing, and on the very first day. 'You...' she waved her hand '...older children...' it took a moment before she remembered that calling them by name would be best

'…Edmund and Lily. Look through your books and see if you can find an explanation of the word *tyranny*. For that is what we call unjust punishments delivered by despots who abuse their power. And, Sophie, come with me, and we will find you drawing supplies.'

The older children stood, stunned, as though unsure if she'd meant the instruction or was merely being face-tious. But the younger child led her directly to a locked cabinet, and looked hopefully at her.

'They are in here, are they?' Daphne fumbled for the keys the Duchess had given her at the conclusion of the interview, which fit the doors to the nursery and school-rooms, the desk and its various drawers. But she could find none that would fit the little cabinet. The girl's face fell in disappointment. She patted her lightly on the head. 'Fear not, little Sophie. It is locked today. But I promise, as soon as I have talked to the housekeeper, I will remedy the situation, and you shall have your art supplies again.'

All the children looked doubtfully at her now, as though they were convinced that she would be unable to provide what she had promised.

But the Duchess was smiling at her, as though much relieved at the sudden turn of events. 'Children, let me borrow Miss Collins to finish arranging the particulars. Then she shall have all her keys and you shall have your paints and pencils.' She led Daphne back out into the hall, and squeezed her arm in encouragement. 'Well done, Miss Collins. Barely a minute in the room, and you have already found a way to help the children. You are brilliant. And a total justification of my desire to advertise in London for a woman with exemplary references, instead of dealing with the problem in the haphazard manner this family is accustomed to. I am sure you will do miracles here. You are just what is needed.'

Daphne could only pray that the woman was right.

Chapter Two

The rest of the day passed in a whirl. The Duchess helped her to find more keys, made sure that her things were sent to the little room in the attic and arranged for her salary. When it was nearing supper time, she left to return to her own home, which was only a few miles away. Daphne felt her absence. It was almost as if she had made a friend of the woman, she had been so solicitous.

But now she must strike out on her own, and find the evening meal. Which led to the question—where did the governess usually eat? She struggled to think if she had ever seen one at her own family's table, or dining with the family in the home of friends. But it was possible, even if they had been there, she would not have noticed. She doubted that they were encouraged to call attention to themselves.

She strolled down the passages of the ground-floor

rooms, and found the dining room closed and dark. Wherever the Colton family ate, it was not a formal thing. But if servants were not waiting at table, then they must be below stairs, having a meal of their own. She went to the same stairway that would lead to her room if she followed it upwards to the end. She took the stairs downwards instead, and came out into a large open room with a long oak table set for supper. The servants were already gathered around it.

She came forwards and sat down at a place somewhere about the middle, offering a cheery 'hello' to the person next to her, who appeared to be a parlourmaid.

The room fell silent for a moment, and the housekeeper looked down the table toward her. Without a word, the woman went to the sideboard for a fresh plate, for the person Daphne must have displaced. This was handed down the table, and there was much shifting and giggling as the servants around her reorganized themselves according to their rank. It appeared that servants had a hierarchy every bit as structured as that of a fine dinner party above stairs. And Daphne had wandered in and disrupted things with her ignorance.

Once things were settled again, the housekeeper, Mrs Sims, announced, 'Everyone, this is Miss Collins. She is the new governess that her Grace hired for the children.'

The staff nodded, as though they did not find the Duchess's interference to be nearly so unusual as the presence of a governess at the servants' table.

The housekeeper favoured her with another nod. 'In the future, Miss Collins, you are welcome to eat in your room or with the children. No one here will think you are putting on airs.' She said it rather as a command, not a request.

It rather put a crimp in her plans to gather intelligence below stairs. 'Thank you, Mrs Sims. I was rather at a loss today as to what was expected. But I am sure this shall be all right, tonight at least. I wished to meet you all.' She smiled around the table.

And was met by blank looks in return, and mumbled introductions, up and down the table.

'Where did the previous governess eat?' she asked by way of conversation.

'Which one might you mean? There have been three since the lady of the house died. And many more before that. They all ate in the little dining room in the nursery wing.'

'So many.' It did not bode well for her stay here. 'What happened to them? I mean, why did they leave?' For the first sounded far too suspicious.

Mrs Sims frowned. 'Of late, the children are difficult. But you will see that soon enough.'

And there was mention of the difficulties again. But in her brief meeting with them, they had not seemed like little tartars. 'I am sure they are nothing I cannot handle,' she lied, really having no idea how she might get on with a house full of children.

'Then you are more stalwart than the others, and more power to you,' said the butler, with a small laugh. 'The first could not control them. And the second found them disturbing. The third...' he gave a snort of disgust

'…had problems with little Sophie. Thought the poor little mite was the very devil incarnate.'

'Sophie?' Having met the girl, this was more than hard to believe.

'The master caught Miss Fisk punishing the girl. She had been forcing Sophie to kneel and pray for hours on end, until her little knees were almost raw with it. And the older children too frightened to say anything about it.' The housekeeper shook her head in disapproval. 'And that was the last we saw of Miss Fisk. Lord Colton turned her out of the house in the driving rain, and threw her possessions after her. He said he had no care at all for her safety or comfort, if she did not care for the comfort of his children.'

'Served her right,' announced the upper footman. 'To do that to a wee one.'

'You'll think so, if he finds reason to turn you out, I suppose?' asked another.

The boy smirked. 'I don't plan to give him reason. I have no problem with the children.'

'Or the neighbours,' said another, and several men at the table chuckled.

'The neighbours?' Daphne pricked her ears. 'Do you mean the Duke and Duchess?'

The housekeeper glared at the men. 'There are some things, if they cannot be mentioned in seriousness, are better not mentioned at all.'

The butler supplied, in his dry quiet voice, 'Relations are strained between our household and the manor.'

'But Lord Colton seemed to get on well enough with the Duchess.'

'There is nothing strange about that, if you are imply-ing so.' The housekeeper sniffed. 'The master has no designs in her direction.'

'No,' said one of the house maids with a giggle, 'his troubles were all with the Duke. Her Grace wishes to pretend that nothing is wrong, of course. But she was not here for the worst of it. If she had seen the way the Duke behaved with Lady Colton…'

Now this was interesting. Daphne leaned forwards. 'Did he…make inappropriate advances?'

A footman snickered, and then caught himself, after a glare from the butler.

But a maid laughed and said, 'It was hard to see just who was advancing on who.'

'Remember where your loyalties lie, Maggie,' murmured Mrs Sims. 'You do not work at Bellston Manor.'

Maggie snorted in response. 'I'd be welcome enough there, if I chose to go. My sister is a chambermaid at Bellston. And she has nothing but fine words to say of his Grace and his new Duchess, now that our mistress…' the girl crossed herself quickly before continuing '…is no longer there to interfere.' She looked at Daphne, pointing with her fork. 'When her ladyship was alive, I worked above stairs, helping the lady's maid with the ribbons. And let me tell you, I saw plenty. Enough to know that his lordship is hardly to blame for the way things turned out in the end.'

'Then you should know as well the reason we no longer see his Grace as a guest in the house.' The butler was stiff with disapproval.

Daphne's eyes widened in fascination as the conversation continued around the table.

'It is a wonder that Lord Colton did not take his anger out in a way that would be better served,' said a footman, 'on the field of honour.'

'Don't be a ninny. One does not call out a duke, no matter the offence.' The upper footman nodded wisely. 'There's rules about that. I'm sure.'

'In any case, weren't all the man's fault.'

The housekeeper sniffed again, as though she wished to bring an end to the conversation.

'Just sayin'. There are others to blame.'

The housekeeper tapped lightly on her glass with her knife. 'We do not speak of such things at this table, or elsewhere in the house. What's done is done and there is no point in placing blame for it.'

The table fell to uneasy silence, enjoying a meal of beef that was every bit as good as that which she had eaten at home above stairs. Daphne suspected that such meals had gone a long way in buying the loyalty of the servants, none of whom seemed to mind that the master had murdered the mistress.

One by one, the servants finished their meals and the butler excused them from the table to return to their duties. But Daphne took her time, waiting until all but the butler and housekeeper were gone. If there was information to be had, then surely they must know, for it seemed that they knew everything that went on in the house.

But before she could enquire, the housekeeper spoke

first. 'Why did you choose to eat below stairs, Miss Collins?'

'I thought, since I am a servant, it was appropriate.'

The housekeeper gave her a look to let her know that she had tripped up yet again. 'A servant now, perhaps. But a lady above all, who must be accustomed to a better place in the household than the servants' table.' Mrs Sims looked at her with disapproval. 'And a lady with a most unfortunate tendency to gossip. It is not something we encourage in this house.'

'I am sorry. I was only curious. If I am in possession of all the facts, I might be best able to help the children.'

The butler responded, 'I doubt there is anyone in possession of all the facts, so your quest is quite fruitless. But I can tell you this: the less said about their mother, the better. She was a hoyden, who got what she deserved.'

Daphne let out a little gasp. 'Surely not. The poor woman, God rest her soul.'

The housekeeper drew herself up with disapproval. 'You think that knowing the truth will help the little ones? Then here it is, or all you need to know of it. What happened to our mistress was the result of too much carrying on. The children are lucky to be rid of her, however it happened.'

So Mrs Sims suspected something was strange about the death. But the housekeeper's assessment was most unjust. 'I hardly think it is fair to believe such things, when you yourself admit that no one knows all the facts in the situation. In the last house I was employed, everyone thought much the same of the only daughter. They were all most censorious, when she was guilty of the smallest breaches of etiquette. She strayed from the common paths in Vauxhall with one of her suitors. And before she knew it, she was packed off to the country in disgrace. I suspect she was no worse than Lady Colton.'

'Do you now?' The housekeeper shook her head. 'Then you are most naïve. If the young girl you mention was already straying on to dark paths with young men, then *I* suspect it was for more tickle than slap. Perhaps the late Lady Colton would have called it innocent fun and not the death of the girl's reputation. In fact, I am sure that my lady and the girl would have got on well together. Clarissa Colton would have approved, for the young lady you describe would have been taking a first step toward becoming what she had become: a lady with no discernible morals. It pains me to say it. But her ladyship had no sense of decency whatsoever. No respect for herself, and certainly none for her husband.'

It stung to hear such a blunt assessment of her character. For the housekeeper seemed to agree with Daphne's parents that her trips to Vauxhall could have put her beyond the pale. And Mrs Sims had predicted Clare's reaction to the thing well enough—she had said that there was no harm in it at all. She came to her cousin's defence. 'Perhaps, if I were married to Lord Colton, a man so distant, so cruel and so totally lost to gentleness, my behaviour would be much the same.'

'If you were married to him?' The housekeeper let out

a derisive laugh. 'Quite far above yourself, aren't you, Miss Collins? His lordship is not good enough.' She glanced toward the conservatory, as though she could see the master of the house through the walls separating them. Then she said softly, 'I have worked in this house for almost forty years. I have known Lord Colton since he was a boy. And there was nothing wrong with his character before that woman got her hooks into him. A bit of youthful high spirits, perhaps. A slight tendency to excess drink, and with it, a short temper. Things that would have passed, with time. But under the influence of his wife, he grew steadily worse.'

'So his misbehaviour is youthful high spirits. But the occasional straying of a girl will permanently damage her character.'

The housekeeper gave her a look that proved she thought her a complete fool. 'Yes. Because, as you can see, his problems did not render him incapable of making a match.'

'But I do not see that they have made him a good choice for a husband,' Daphne snapped in return. 'In my experience so far, he is a foul-tempered, reclusive man who cares so little for his children that he allows the neighbours to choose their governess.'

Mrs Sims frowned. 'He cares more for the children than you know. And if you care for them as well, you will see to it that the boy grows up to be the man that his father is, and the girls learn to be better than their mother, and get no strange ideas about the harmlessness of straying down dark paths in Vauxhall Gardens. Good evening, Miss Collins.'

Daphne had the strange feeling that she was being held responsible for the wayward actions of her imaginary charge, and that Mrs Sims's estimation of her skills had gone down by a wide margin.

Which made the truth seem all the stranger. What might Mrs Sims have said if Daphne'd admitted that she was the girl, and that her parents had no idea that she had elected to come to Clare's home, instead of her dear aunt in Anglesey? She was supposed to remain there until such time as her behaviour was forgotten, her reputation restored and her head emptied of Clarissa Colton's nonsensical advice.

She walked slowly up the stairs to her room. In retrospect, she had to admit that the outing to Vauxhall had been a mistake. She had been so blue, in the wake of Clare's death. And her beau, Simon, had assured her that moping at home was no way to honour her cousin's memory. But once she was alone with him in the dark, she suspected that Simon cared less for her feelings than his own. Her London social life had ended in a flurry of open-mouthed kisses, wayward hands and a slap that had brought her friends running to her aid. And then running just as fast to spread rumours of what they had interrupted.

As she looked at the three flights of stairs in front of her, she wished her parents could see what penance she had set for herself. Several weeks of hard work, with not a single ball, *musicale* or country outing to break the monotony. It had been exhausting just meeting the family and making arrangements for the position.

She suspected it was likely to be more difficult, once

she began the duties she had been hired for. Although she knew nothing of teaching, she must begin proper lessons directly, or someone would become suspicious.

Unless there was no one who cared enough to suspect her. If the governess here normally ate with the children, in the absence of a governess, did anyone eat with them at all? It seemed unlikely that their father would come upstairs and take his meal if there were perfectly good rooms for that purpose on the ground floor. And she had been introduced to no nurses or servants who had charge over them.

It appeared that they were left to their own devices. She knew little of children, other than that she had recently been one. And in her experience, too much freedom meant an opportunity for mischief, and the fostering of wilful ideas that would make the job of governess to the Coltons a difficult one.

Her candle trembled a little as she climbed the last flight of stairs, and she regretted not investigating her sleeping quarters in daylight. With its lack of windows, the narrow stairwell would be intimidating, both day and night. She certainly hoped that the room above had some natural illumination, for to be climbing from darkness into further darkness would lead to unnecessary imaginings that would make for a difficult first night.

She opened the door, and was relieved to see a bright square of moonlight from the small window opposite her. She walked across to it, and looked up into a brilliant full moon, which seemed almost close enough to touch. The ground below was distant. The shrubs and trees casting shadows that were sharp as daylight in the white light from above, giving the whole an unworldly quality, as though a day scene were rendered in black and white. She turned and looked at the room behind her, which was lit the same way.

If she were a real teacher, she might know how great an insult she was paid by these accommodations. She was all but sleeping in the attic. Half the ceiling of the room slanted, to make the space unusable for one so tall as she. Her trunk had been pushed to that side, next to the small writing desk, which held a dried-up inkwell and the stub of a candle. On the other side there was a bed, pushed in front of a door that must lead to further attic rooms. That they'd placed furniture in front of it was the only assurance given that she would not have other servants tramping through her private space when bearing things to storage. There was no proper wardrobe, only pegs for her dresses. A small mirror hung upon the wall. And that was all. If she wished for a chair for the writing desk, she would need to steal one from another room, just as she suspected the intended chair had been stolen from hers.

She sat down upon the bed and tested the mattress. It was lumpy and narrow, and certainly not what she was used to. But if one was tired enough, one could sleep anywhere. She was already at that weird combination of exhaustion and wakefulness that one got sometimes when overtired. Enervated, but not sleepy. Perhaps a book from the library would provide the necessary soporific. The light in the room was almost bright enough to read by even without a candle, and she had no curtain to block it out.

She took up her candle again, and came back down the flights of stairs to the brightly lit ground floor, and the familiar feeling of warmth and civilisation. She found a volume that she did not think too dreary from the rather intellectual holdings of the Colton library. She wished that Clare had been alive to greet her when she arrived. Then she could stay here reading before going up the stairs to a fine guest room, secure in her place as a visitor in this house, and not an intruder.

When she turned to go back to her room, it suddenly occurred to her that two choices were open to her. She had taken the servants' stairs to the ground. Surely, as governess, she was closer to family than serving maid, and entitled to use the main stairs? It would mean a flight in the open, postponing the stifling darkness that led to her room.

But it would also mean a trip down the nursery hall, past the children's rooms, before she reached the stairs to her room. She suspected it was her duty to check on them, and make sure that they were all snug in bed, resting for the next day.

Her duty. If she were really the governess, her time would not be her own. She would be responsible for the watching of the children, morning and night. The needs of the family must always come before her own.

Until such time as she revealed the truth about Clare's death. Then she need answer to no one, least of all the murderous Lord Timothy Colton. Tomorrow would be soon enough to begin the charade of watching his children. Tonight, she would have one last night of her own, no matter how mean the comforts might be.

So she went to the end of the hall and opened the door to the servants' stairs. The stairwell was narrow, and the rise steep. The first flight was just as black as the stairway to her room. She took a firm grip on her candle, tucked the book tightly under her arm so that she could grasp the handrail for safety, and began her ascent.

She could not help the chill feeling and the shiver that went through her, alone in the dark with only her candle for company. The hall doors were shut tight on all the landings, cutting the regular pathway of the servants off from the rest of the house, as though they were mice in the walls, and not a part of the household at all.

She started as she heard a door above her open, and someone else beginning a descent. The person was beyond the bend in the stairs, so she could not yet see who it was. It was ridiculous to worry, but she was suddenly taken with the notion that when she arrived at the next landing, there would be no one on the stairs above her. The ghostly footsteps would walk through her, with only a passing feeling of icy air.

What a foolish notion. More likely, it would be a footman on his way to the kitchen, or someone else sent on an errand. She would round the next corner and find nothing unusual. But she could not resist calling a hoarse 'hello?' into the darkness.

The space around her got suddenly darker, as though a candle around the corner, barely able to cut the gloom of the stairwell, had been extinguished.

Did the person above her mean to keep their identity a secret? There was no point in it, for she would come upon them with her own candle in just a few more steps.

But the footsteps had stopped as well.

She could feel her own steps falter at the realisation, before plucking up her nerves and continuing her climb. She rounded the bend in the stairs and kept climbing, eyes averted, before working up the nerve to look up at the silhouette of a man, looming on the flight above her. He was not moving, just waiting in stillness for her to pass him.

This was not normal behaviour, was it? For though it might make sense to wait while another passed, it made no sense at all to do so in silence. It turned a chance meeting into a threatening situation. Or perhaps it was only her imagination. She proceeded up the stairs, hand on the rail and eyes focused on the shadowy face of the man in front of her, watching the features sharpen in focus with each step she took.

Then she gasped. 'Lord Colton.'

'Miss Collins.' He did not move. And although she had not thought him a particularly large man, he seemed to fill the stairwell in front of her, blocking her progress. 'What a surprise to find you creeping about the house so late at night.'

His tone was insulting, and she caught herself before responding in kind, remembering that he was her employer, not her equal. 'Merely coming back from the library with a book for my room. It is sometimes difficult to sleep in a strange place.'

'And since you are educated, you sought solace in a book.' In the flickering candlelight, his smile looked like a sneer.

She nodded.

'Very well. But you had best be careful on your way. Stairs can be dangerous.'

What did he mean by that? Was it a threat? And why threaten her, for he hardly knew her? What was he doing on the servants' stairs at all? He had even less reason to be there than her.

She glared back at him, not caring what he might think. 'I assure you, my lord, I am most careful when it comes to stairs. And since lightning does not strike twice in the same place, a second fall in this house would be a most unusual circumstance indeed.' And then, without waiting for dismissal, she released the handrail that they were both holding, and went to pass him and continue her ascent.

There was not enough space to go around without brushing against him, and she steeled herself for the moment when their bodies would touch.

And suddenly he reached out to steady her, his hand on her waist. The touch was like a jolt of electricity, cutting through the fear she felt of him. For a moment, she was sure that he was debating whether to embrace her, or give the downward shove that would cause another fatal accident.

Then the moment passed, and he was helping her to find the handrail and go on her way. She continued up the stairs, hurrying her pace, all the time aware that his downward steps did not resume.

* * *

Tim waited on the stairs, frozen in place, listening to her progress. She must be in the small room in the attic, for he could hear her, passing the second-floor landing and continuing upwards. It was a lonely spot at the back of the house, far away from prying eyes and ears. No one would know if he turned and followed her.

But he did not want that, did he? For only a moment before…

He hurried down the stairs to the ground floor, shutting himself up in the study and reaching for the brandy decanter. One drink would not matter, surely. Just to steady his nerves. He poured, and drank eagerly, praying for the numbness that would come with the first sip.

For a moment, when he had heard her call out, he had been convinced it was Clare. Although he had not noticed it at the time of introduction, there was a similarity in tone, just as there was in colouring. And her voice had startled him so that the trembling of his hand had put out the candle. He'd stood, rooted to the spot, hearing those approaching footsteps, waiting for the figure that would round the corner: the vengeful spirit of his wife.

And he had not been disappointed. There were her accusing green eyes staring up at him, as though daring him to run. He had all but given up the main staircase. For that had been where he expected to see her, when she finally came for him. But the sight of her approaching on the back stairs had been totally unexpected and utterly terrifying.

When he realised that it was a mistake of the light

and his overwrought nerves, his response had been a jumble of emotions. Anger at being so foolish. And suspicion of her behaviour, which had been quite ordinary and probably an appropriate match to the strangeness of his.

And then, there had been that hint of desire, as he'd stood close enough to feel the warmth of her body and smell her scent. Longing that a touch might lead to something more than a chance meeting on the stairs.

He looked down in to the half-full glass of brandy, momentarily surprised to find it in his hand. Then he smiled and set it aside. He gave a nervous, involuntary chuckle, and ran a hand over his eyes in embarrassment. It did not say much for the state of his nerves if he could manage to work himself into such a state over nothing. There were no ghosts on the front stairs, or the back. Although she was most attractive, the governess's resemblance to Clare was superficial, at best.

The cause of all his problems was a penchant for brandy and redheads. Once he learned to leave them both alone, the remainder of his life would go easier. And he sank back into the chair, and laid his head on the desk to rest, too weak from the realisation to take either set of stairs to his room.

Chapter Three

Daphne awoke with the dawn, the rays of morning light streaming upon her bed with aggressive good cheer, making sleep impossible. It was just as well. For she suspected the real Miss Collins would have risen intentionally at this time, so that she might be washed and dressed and down the stairs to breakfast. She would be ready to start lessons before the children were half out of bed.

Daphne had never been an early riser. The best she was likely to manage was prompt, but surly. She pasted a smile upon her face and put on one of the sensible gowns that she had bought off the real Miss Collins. Then she came down the stairs to the nursery wing, walking down the hall until she found the open door to the children's dining room.

The sight of it made her smile; it was attractively decorated but informal, rather like the breakfast room in her own home back in London. The woman who had been introduced to her on the previous evening as Cook was setting eggs and ham and tea things on a side table. It was most unusual to see her doing work that would be better suited to a footman. But she gave Miss Collins a defiant look, that seemed to say, What if I am? Someone must watch out for them.

The children filed in from the hall, and Cook greeted them pleasantly, making sure that their plates were full and that everyone had enough of what they wanted. She extended her offers to Miss Collins, as though relieved to see that there would be an adult present at the meal, before excusing herself and returning to the kitchen.

Daphne smiled hopefully at the three children across the table from her, and attempted polite breakfast talk. Had they slept well? Was it not a beautiful day? Did they have enough to eat? And were they sure that they did not want a second helping of anything? Absolutely sure? Because she had no problems with delaying the lesson, and they should not feel a need to rush their morning meal.

It would have been a blessing to her if they could manage to delay lessons indefinitely. She had no more interest in sitting in a classroom as teacher than she had managed to display when she had been a student.

The children answered all questions in polite monosyllables, as though they had decided her presence was to be tolerated for the moment. But they intended to make no effort at a closer relationship than was absolutely necessary.

Eventually, her attempts at conversation were

exhausted, as was the breakfast food. She suggested that they wash their hands and make their way to the classroom, where the real business of the day could begin.

They were almost eerily agreeable to it, as though faintly relieved to be able to do something they preferred over socialising with the governess. They took what appeared to be their regular seats in the room, and folded their hands on their empty desks, waiting to be impressed.

'Very well then,' she said, and waited for something to fill the blank void in her mind as to what would happen next. Perhaps it was best to discover what the children already knew, before attempting to educate them further. 'Please, children, gather the books you have been working in and show me your progress.'

They remained unmoved, still in their seats, staring out at her.

So she reached for the nearest book, a maths primer that had given her much trouble when she was their age. She opened it, paging through the equations. 'This would probably be yours, wouldn't it, Lily?' She arched an eyebrow, for she had seen the girl's name written clearly inside the front cover. 'Show me how far you have got.' And please Lord, let it be not far, for Daphne had given up on that particular subject before she was halfway through the text.

The girl took the book sullenly and flipped through pages until she was nearly at the end.

Daphne gave a nervous laugh. 'My, my. How well

you are doing. Perhaps I will allow you to tutor your brother.'

Lily gave her a disgusted look. 'He has been this far and further for at least six months.'

Daphne narrowed her eyes. 'Then perhaps I shall allow him to tutor you. Edmund!' She smiled and turned suddenly upon the boy, to catch him making faces at his sister.

He had the grace to look embarrassed at being caught, and then his expression turned as sullen as his sister's.

'Lily says you are good at maths. Is that your best subject?'

The boy raised his chin and said, 'I prefer reading.'

'Do you? Well, we can not always do what we prefer, but I wish for our time together to be enjoyable. What is it you like to read? We will see if we can incorporate it into our studies.'

He went to the shelf and brought down a book that was almost as big as himself, and held it out to her. 'Plutarch.'

She smiled feebly. 'In Greek.'

He nodded. And she could tell by his smile that he knew he had bested her.

She turned to Lily. 'And I suppose you enjoy Plutarch as well?'

'Yes. But not so well as Edmund.'

'Then we must see what can be done to encourage you.' She pointed to the front of the room. 'Edmund. Today, you may read to us. I wish to hear you declaim. Choose your favourite passage.' She walked to the back of the room and took a seat.

The boy began in a clear, unwavering voice, reading with what she supposed was accurate and enthusiastic inflection. But the prose was, quite literally, all Greek to her. She had no idea how to correct him, or if it was even necessary. So she chose a polite and interested expression, similar to the one Lily was wearing, and folded her arms across her chest. It would be possible to spend at least an hour of the school day, if the passage was long enough. By then, she would think of some other trick with which to keep them occupied.

There was a slight pause in the reading, and Edmund said something, still in Greek.

There was another slight pause, which she suspected was just long enough for the older girl to translate something she did not expect to hear in the reading. And then she stifled a laugh.

So they had realised she knew little Greek and were going to have fun at the expense of the governess. 'Please return to the text that is printed before you.'

She must have guessed correctly, for Edmund responded with a look of surprise, and fear that she had understood whatever rude thing he had said.

She glanced over at the younger girl, Sophie. Unlike the other two, the child was doing her best to be obedient. She sat quietly, staring down at the hands folded in her lap, and shooting glances out the window, when she thought no one was looking. The poor thing clearly wanted and needed to run and play, but was afraid to call attention and risk punishment.

Yesterday, it had appeared that the girl liked to draw. Perhaps with paper and pencils, and a little peace, she would find a way to express herself. 'You do not have to sit through the lessons if they are too advanced for you, Sophie.' She spoke softly so as not to alarm the girl. 'I'm sure your turn will come with Plutarch, before too long. But for now? Perhaps you would prefer to draw instead. I promised you your art things, didn't I? And now I've got the keys, I can give them to you.'

She opened the cabinet in the corner and found a rather nice selection of pens, brushes, paints and crayons, and paper of a quality that made her almost envious of the little girl. Then she prepared a place at the table near the window, where the light would be good for drawing.

Sophie smiled in relief, and climbed up on to the chair, taking the pencil eagerly and stroking it and the paper as though they were more precious than china dolls.

Then Daphne went back to allowing the boy to teach her his Greek. Edmund continued to recite, this time with a tired voice that said that he understood well what she was trying to do, and that the whole thing bored him to tears.

There was a limit to this, she thought, before it became plain to everyone that she had no idea what she was doing in a classroom. When she had hatched the plan, she had thought that she might occupy the children for a few weeks before they caught on to her ruse. But if they had tumbled to her within hours?

The Duchess was right. They were as sharp as needles. Too clever for their own good. But since the house made little effort to hide its secrets, perhaps she would not be here long.

And what was to happen to the children, if that was so? They seemed just as stubborn about remaining in the house as their father did in sending them to school. But if their father would admit to his crime, and accept punishment for it?

Then they would have to go somewhere, wouldn't they? They could not remain in the house alone. Perhaps the Duchess would see to their education. She had no children of her own, and she seemed most fond of them.

What happened to them did not really matter, she reminded herself. For they were no concern of hers.

But perhaps they were. They were Clare's children, as well as Lord Colton's. There was a family connection to her. Perhaps she could persuade her father to take them in. Clare's parents could not do the job. They'd seemed to care little enough for what had happened to the mother, once she was off their hands. Why should they want a good home for their grandchildren?

If she meant to disrupt their lives further in the name of justice, she held some responsibility in seeing that they were cared for. She must give the matter more thought.

Edmund reached the end of his passage and returned to his seat.

'Very good,' she said. 'You read well. Let us see how you write.' She went to the shelf, and pulled down another book, and gave him a page from Homer to translate. 'And, Lily, why don't you work on your maths?

Since you seem to be managing well, you may work at your own pace.' Then she wandered to the window to check on Sophie. 'Have you finished your drawing, little one?'

The girl nodded eagerly, and held the paper out to her.

And Daphne dropped it in revulsion as she got a look at the subject.

It was Clare. Or what had been Clare. There was no mistaking the fact, for the rendering was skilful, even in the hands of a five-year-old. It was a woman's body, dead at the foot of the staircase, arms and legs at odd angles, and a head that was curiously misshapen.

Daphne crumpled the paper and threw it to the floor.

Sophie drew back in alarm, sure that she had done wrong and trembling as she awaited punishment.

The older girl gave her a look of bitter triumph. 'It serves you right for giving her the pencils. Our first governess ran screaming to Papa. The next one called her a devil. And the last one tried to beat the devil out of her, until Papa caught her at it and sent her away.'

Daphne took a deep breath and scooped up the paper from the floor, straightening out the wrinkles and laying it back on the table. 'Since I did not assign her a subject, I have little right to complain about the finished work.' She tried to ignore the subject matter and focus on the execution. Then she looked down at Sophie. 'I would not normally give lessons so advanced to one as small as you. But it is clear from looking at it that you have more than normal abilities for a child of your age.' She crouched down beside the girl and urged her back into her seat.

Sophie looked at her in confusion, tears in her eyes, still half-expecting punishment.

'It is all right,' Daphne said. 'You needn't worry. I love to draw as well. And I know how comforting it can be to sit with pen and paper, especially when one has something on one's mind. Unless I tell you otherwise, you may draw whatever you wish. Is that all right?'

The girl gave a hesitant nod.

Daphne steeled herself to look again at the wrinkled sketch. 'You have a good eye for detail and your proportions are fair. But no one has taught you about light and how to draw it.'

The girl gave her a puzzled look.

She smiled back encouragingly. 'You might think that there is nothing to see in empty air. But it is possible for the artist to show the light, by showing the shadows. Let us put figure drawing aside for now, and start with something simple, like an apple.'

She took a blank sheet of paper, and drew a rough fruit, then showed Sophie how to choose a direction for the sun, and put in shading and highlights with a bit of chalk. Then she offered the paper back to the girl. 'Now you try. Begin with round things, like apples. And then try something with angles, like the bookcase or the window frame.'

Sophie looked at her with growing amazement, as though these were the first words she had understood in hours. And then she smiled and took the pencil back in her hand, placed a fresh sheet of paper on the table and bit her lip in determination, bending eagerly over her work.

Daphne watched the older children, who were exchanging looks of surprise and confusion, as though she had interrupted the perfectly intelligible Greek with a language they could not understand. She turned to them, hands on her hips. 'I suppose this is as good a time as any to see how you children draw. Lily, show me your watercolour book.'

'I do not have one.' The girl was almost stammering in embarrassment.

Daphne fought down the feeling of triumph. 'You do not draw?'

'It is hardly necessary, for if one knows maths and languages...' Edmund said in a starchy tone.

'Your father knows those things, I am sure. And how to draw, as well. He enjoys gardening, does he not?'

'He is a botanist,' said Lily, as though deeply offended by the slight.

Daphne waved it aside, not much caring about the difference. 'Then he must know enough drawing to render the plants he works on.'

The older children's eyes grew round, as though they had never considered the fact.

'And I doubt he would like to hear that you are dismissing any element of your education as frivolous. We must work to correct our ignorance, rather than making excuses for it.' And now it was her turn to be surprised. That last had sounded rather like something her school mistresses had said to her. Perhaps all that was necessary to turn oneself into an educator was to starch one's bodice and put on a stern expression.

She smiled at the children so as not to appear too forbidding, remembering the minimal effect such lectures had had on her. 'For now, you may continue with the lessons you have. But in future, we shall see that you gain some talent for art.' She smiled at Sophie, who was dutifully drawing an apple from memory. 'After I have got the more advanced student properly settled.'

The little girl turned to her with such a look of surprise on her face that it almost made her forget her role and laugh. But then Sophie smiled, as though the words were better than rubies to her. With such talented siblings, she had never been the star pupil.

And if what the older children had said was true, she had endured far worse since Clare had died. So it helped her to draw horrible pictures to help recover from her mother's death. Was there really any harm in it? Daphne picked up the sheet of paper, considered throwing it on the fire, and then smoothed it and set it aside. If it was destroyed, the poor girl would only draw it again.

She stared down at the image of her cousin, crumpled in death. The girl had drawn it from memory, just as she had the apple. Had no one the sense to keep her away, so that she did not have to see such a horrible sight? But the picture was very informative, for it showed just what she had expected: Clare lying on her back as though she had toppled backwards, and not fallen face first as one likely would if the death were accidental.

Without realising it, Sophie might help to prove her mother's murder.

Chapter Four

Daphne took the picture and placed it between the pages of her own sketchbook. It was too disturbing to hang on the schoolroom wall, but the information in it was too important to discard. She would conceal it for now, then take it to her room where she might examine it in detail. She encouraged the children to work on what they wished, and gave only the barest supervision, assuming that they would come to little harm reading from their texts.

At lunch time, Cook delivered trays of food to the nursery dining room, and they paused in their lessons to eat. The same seemed to hold for tea, and would happen at supper just as Mrs Sims described. The household had given the children no reason to come below stairs at all, if they did not wish to. She wondered if the intent was to keep them away from their father. For if it was, it told the real truth about the loyalty of the servants to their master. They would support him, of course. They took his side in what had happened to his wife, and frowned on gossip about it.

But they feared him, feared for the children and kept them far out of his path.

When a maid had come to clear away the tea things, and they were almost ready to return to the classroom, she noticed a shadow from the doorway that fell across the room.

Lord Colton was there, observing them. She had not heard him approach, and could not shake the feeling that he had been standing there for quite some time, unnoticed. It put her on her guard. Though she doubted he had seen or heard anything of interest, it was disquieting to think him so adept at spying.

'Miss Collins.' He gave the same curt bow he had given her on the previous day, and she feared he was ready for another disquieting battle of wills.

Before he could catch it, she broke her gaze, and gave another curtsy, eyes downcast to hide her discomfort. 'Lord Colton.'

'How are the children today?'

'Very well, my lord.' She hoped that she was not expected to go into detail on their progress, for she had nothing to add.

'We shall see about that. For if I find otherwise, I will turn you out, no matter what the Duchess might say.'

She flinched at the suddenness of the threat. And when he saw her reaction, and that she was showing none of the bravado of yesterday, he gave a faint laugh and went to greet his children.

She felt her muscles tense in instinctive defence of them. They were stubborn little beasts, to be sure. But what could one expect, when they had a monster for a father? What poison had he poured in their ears about their mother? And what abuses had they undergone to leave them so suspiciously quiet?

Colton's smile changed as he approached the children. As he looked at them, the lines seemed to smooth from his forehead, and his lips were turned upwards not in a cynical parody of mirth or seduction, but with joyful anticipation. The tension in his body disappeared, making his movements easy. He seemed to become younger with each step, almost as if he were a denizen of the nursery wing and not the master of the whole house.

He came to the boy first, bending down, smiling and offering his hand, which his son took and gave a pale imitation of a manly clasp. The father asked how the studies were progressing, and the boy answered that they were satisfactory. And then Colton said something in what sounded like Latin, and the boy answered quickly and easily, as though in his native tongue.

They conversed thus, for a few minutes, and the child cast a sidelong look in her direction. They were talking about the new governess again, were they? If she lasted long enough to make a difference here, she would take an opportunity to teach the children some manners. It was quite rude to switch languages, and take advantage of the ignorance of others. Even more so when the other was your teacher and had so much ignorance to abuse.

The boy said something adamant, his jaw set in a stubborn parody of his father's.

The older man shrugged. With a half-smile, he glanced in Daphne's direction and shook his head. Then he turned to the older girl and dropped to one knee so that he could greet her face to face.

'Bonjour, Papa.' She gave him a shy kiss upon the cheek, but her smile had a wicked glint to it. She continued in French, as though she wished to prove that she could best her brother in something.

Her father answered her in the same language, and they proceeded to discuss the day. Daphne had less trouble with this, for she knew more than a little French, although the girl did speak quickly for one so young. Apparently, the day was *bon*, as was the new teacher. Although the girl was equally adamant that such guidance was not necessary, and that they would show him how well they could manage, if left to their own devices.

Her father answered with a *c'est la vie*. If *Tante Penny* wished it, then what were they to do? The children must prove that they could take care of themselves by giving no more trouble to the new teacher, for he knew what mischief they were capable of. While he did not wish her here, neither did he wish to see Miss Collins running to his study in fits, or, worse yet, to the neighbours, because his children were being naughty. But if the governess were to try any of the evil tricks that the last one had, they were to send word. He would come and deal with her, and there would be no more trouble. He looked up at Daphne, to make sure that she had understood the warning.

She looked back at him, and raised her chin a fraction of an inch to show that she did not fear him. She had to admit, if the last woman had been as bad as the servants said, the family had a reason to be less than trusting of her.

But while Lord Colton obviously disliked her, his conversation was surprisingly innocent, and he was even tempered with both children. It came as rather a surprise, for she had expected some sign of the problems there. Perhaps the children did not understand what had happened to their mother, or their father's part in it. He must be a master actor, to be so calm and pleasant with them that they felt nothing of what he had done.

And then he turned again, dropped to both knees and held his arms wide. 'And where is my little Sophie? Come here, darling, and give your papa a hug.'

She turned and looked, expecting to find the strange, haunted child warming to the sight of her father, as the other two had done. But instead, she heard a quick scurrying behind her, and felt the tug upon her skirts. When she looked down, she saw Sophie's little face turned up to hers, the tear-stained cheeks pressed tight to the fabric of her dress, fingers white and claw-like, twisted into the cloth so tightly that Daphne was afraid that there would be holes worn in it, when she managed to get the girl to release her.

And the little eyes were shut tight, screwed closed,

as the mouth murmured something silently, over and over again, like a prayer.

'Sophie, sweetheart, come here and tell me about your day.' She would have expected the tone to be more demanding, in response to such obvious disobedience. But instead it was even softer, and more gentle then it had been the first time. 'Did you draw a picture? You love to draw.' There was a wistfulness to the tone, and Lord Colton cleared his throat, and addressed Daphne directly, as though she might not have heard. 'She very much loves to draw, and is surprisingly proficient, for a girl of such small years.'

The little girl burrowed further into her skirts, clinging even tighter, as though each word from her father's mouth was a blow upon her back.

Daphne looked helplessly at the master of the house, afraid that he would demand that she pry the poor creature loose, and turn her over to him. Then she put her hand upon the head of the child in a gentle caress, and felt the girl snuggle against it, eager for protection.

Still on his knees, her employer dropped his hands to his sides in a gesture of defeat. 'No hug today then, little Sophie? Tomorrow, perhaps. I will wait.' If she wished to see the man punished for his deeds, perhaps it had already happened. He was brought to his knees before her, and his daughter's rejection was sufficient to leave him broken, his shoulders slumped, his expression downcast. As he rose to his feet, he seemed a much older man than he had when entering the room.

'It is good to see you all doing well.' He glanced at Daphne as though she were a canker in a rose. 'And so,

I will leave you in the capable hands of Miss Collins.' It appeared she had bested him, without even realising they were competing. Lord Colton turned to leave.

The two older children took a step forwards, as though to stop him, but then froze in their tracks, afraid to signal.

And young Sophie was the strangest of all. For though she was obviously terrified of the man when he came close to her, she watched his retreating back with a hunger greater than the others. Daphne could feel the girl tensing, ready to spring after the man in the doorway, to throw herself upon him like a little animal.

But if she wanted her father to stay, why would she not just say so? It was clear that he wanted to be with her, and the other children as well. It was only Sophie's rejection that was keeping them away.

Daphne shook her head, confused at her response to the scene. She was not here to make it easier to reconcile father and daughter. She was here to get the horrid man away from them, so that they had a chance at a normal life.

Chapter Five

Daphne rose the next day when the sun crept over the horizon, just as she had the day before. So this was to be her routine, while in the Colton house. Rise at dawn, take all meals above stairs with the children, and have what little time to herself she could, after she had readied them for bed. They had gone to their rooms easily enough after the previous night's meal. And she had taken time straightening the classroom and lingering in the dining room over a cup of tea.

Before going up to bed she had passed Sophie's room, trusting that the older children would not need her help. And through the door, she had heard faint sounds of the girl whimpering in her dreams. But when Daphne had opened the door to come to her aid, she had found a candle burning on the nightstand, and Lily, sitting on the edge of the bed, her hand on the little girl's shoulder. She'd looked up at Daphne, as though annoyed at the intrusion, and whispered, 'She will be all right in a moment. But it is best not to wake her.'

Daphne nodded. Not her choice of action, perhaps. She would have shaken the girl awake immediately. But there was nothing about the sister's actions that seemed rooted in malice. In fact, it appeared that Lily often took the role of comforter, and showed no desire to give it over to a stranger. Daphne had trusted her to do what was best and gone to her room.

Once there, she'd removed Sophie's sketch from her own book and hidden it under the folded gowns in her trunk. Should someone enter the room, it would not do to let them think she was too interested in the subject. But should she need to provide proof of what she had found, it would be invaluable.

That morning, she went to breakfast with the children, and from there to the classroom. The Duchess had been right. They were quite capable of teaching themselves. In some subjects they were clever enough to teach her. She let them proceed, helping with such few questions as they had, trying to do as little damage to their educations as possible.

But if she wasn't actually needed in the schoolroom, there was no reason she could not slip away for a short time, to begin her search of the rest of the house. She excused herself under the guise of going to the library for a book. And with one last glance at the bowed heads, she shut the schoolroom door and hurried down the hall.

She looked into the children's rooms first. There was nothing out of the ordinary in Lily's or Sophie's room, other than that the connecting door appeared to stand open at all times, in testament to the sisters' close bond. Further down the hall was Edmund's room, orderly but boyish. And beside it the cold, dark room that would be Lily's, still with some of her things scattered around, as if waiting for her to return.

She moved more slowly now. Somewhere down the hall was the master suite, and there was a risk of blundering into Lord Colton. Although at this hour he should be below in the conservatory, where she suspected he spent most of his days. She turned the knob on the door at the head of the stairs, and found his room, quiet and empty. It was ordered to the last degree, with no ornaments on the dressers, no item out of place in wardrobe or drawers. There was no wrinkle in the cover on the bed, no mashed pillow or lump in the mattress to hint that the owner of the bed might sleep restlessly, from guilt or any other reason.

If she had not known better, she would have suspected that the person whose room this was did not reside in the house. It was almost too neat to be inhabited. It was a blank. A cipher. And it was unlikely that he might be hiding anything in it. If he meant to write a journal of confession, there was not even a writing table on which to do it.

Perhaps Clare's room would be different. She glanced to the wall that had the connecting door. If the servants had not already cleared the room, there might be some evidence of the state of her cousin's mind in the days before her demise.

But when she put her hand to the knob, it did not

turn. Locked. She sighed in exasperation and exited cautiously into the hall, ready to enter from there.

Also locked.

Every room on the floor was open to her, including the master's bedroom. The only place she could not search was the room of her beloved Clare. In her mind, it became the room she most wanted to see. For there would be no reason to lock it if there was not something to hide.

She walked back down the hall to the nursery, frustrated by her defeat.

When she returned to her desk, the tea things had arrived. The children were busy, red heads bowed over the tray, pouring her a cup. They looked up as she entered with such innocent smiles that she was immediately suspicious.

So she smiled back at them, as guileless as they were, and said, 'You are preparing my tea things. That is very kind of you.' She took the cup they offered, watching the intent way they observed her, waiting for her to take the first drink.

She sat down on the small settee in the corner, and paused, with the cup halfway to her mouth, noting the rapt expression on the faces of the older two children.

'But it is hardly fair that I should be able to take tea, while you have nothing.' She set the cup down upon the tray, and, without looking at the contents, offered it to Edmund. 'You should drink before me, for you are the heir and I am but a servant.'

The boy looked at the cup with alarm.

She smiled. 'Here. Take it.' She held the cup out to him again.

He picked it up, tentatively, and sipped.

She held up a hand. 'Just swish it about your mouth for a bit.'

The boy made a terrible face, looking like he would gag rather than take another sip.

She waited for a second. 'Now spit it back into the cup, please.'

He hurried to do as he was bade.

'And smile.'

The boy opened his mouth to show a face full of bright purple teeth.

She smiled in satisfaction. 'Just as I thought. You put ink into my tea, as a trick. And you never stopped to think what might be in the ink, or that it might hurt me.'

'A little would not hurt,' Lily insisted. 'You would have spat it out. It tastes horrid.'

'Suppose I had not spat out the tea after getting a comical blue smile. Suppose I had swallowed it. Who knows what it is made of, or what harm it might have done? Do you wish to go to your father and admit that you poisoned the governess?'

Without warning, little Sophie started to cry with great gulping sobs. And both the older children looked not just guilty, but disproportionately frightened.

Daphne reached out and scooped the little one into her lap. 'There now, Sophie. No harm has been done. I am all right, as will your brother be, once he has rinsed the colour from his teeth.'

'Will you tell Father?' the older girl asked, in a hoarse whisper. 'We never meant to hurt you. We never meant to hurt anyone. Do not make him send us away.'

And Sophie cried even harder.

The situation was rapidly getting out of hand, and Daphne suspected that the real Miss Collins would have been better equipped for it. But she would manage as best she could. She put an arm around the helpless Sophie, and gestured that the older girl should sit close beside them. She glanced back at Edmund in a way that she hoped was neither angry nor judgemental, and said, 'Take some water from the pitcher and wash out your mouth. Then bring the cakes and come sit with us.'

When the children had surrounded her on the couch, she cuddled Sophie until the crying stopped, and let Edmund pass the teacakes back and forth amongst them. 'Now, there. See? I am not such a great ogre, am I? And I am not about to be a ninny and run downstairs to trouble your father with schoolroom foolishness, if you will leave off tormenting me. I have three older brothers, who most enjoyed playing pranks on their little sister. I doubt there is a trick you will try on me that I have not already experienced. But now that I am grown I had hoped that I would not be bothered with ink in my tea cup and worms in my writing desk.'

'Worms?' Edmund asked, obviously fascinated.

She nodded. 'Great long ones from the garden. My older brother Thomas shut the poor things up with the sealing wax, meaning to surprise me.' She grinned at the memory. 'I dare say it was an even bigger surprise to him when he found them in his cucumber sandwich later in the afternoon. Half of them, actually. That quite put him off worms, and cucumber sandwiches as well. To this day, he lifts the bread before he eats.'

Both the girls laughed, and Edmund followed, after a brief indignant look.

'Now, you are afraid, are you, that your father means to send you away?'

They returned solemn nods.

'You know that it is almost time for Edmund to go away to school? Possibly even past time.'

'I will not leave my sisters,' he said, looking not so much at the older girl as he did at Sophie.

'Then it is in your best interest to keep your current governess happy, rather than frightening her away. If you have someone to monitor your education here, your leavetaking can be prolonged.'

'We do not like strangers,' Edmund said stubbornly.

'You have little choice in the matter,' she answered him. 'Someone must do the job. But a stranger is not the same as an enemy, unless you wish to make me one. It might go easier for all of us if you keep me as an ally. For I mean you no harm.'

There, that was vague enough.

'And even if you must go away to school, your sisters will be in good hands.'

Of which she had no proof at all. She felt a pang of guilt. There was no telling what chaos she might make of their little lives, if she succeeded in her plans.

The children seemed to consider, and there were sly looks passed one to another. At last Lily, as the oldest, spoke for the group. 'We wish, above all else, to remain here, just as we are.'

'And while I wish you to be well educated, I am also most concerned for your happiness. I doubt that an unhappy child makes a better pupil.'

'If you could explain to Father…'

'I hardly know him well enough to make demands, or even suggestions about your education. But in time, I will try to speak to your father on the subject. I cannot guarantee that you won't be sent to board elsewhere. That is often the way of things. But I will do my best to see that your wishes are considered, rather than just the conventions of society.'

The children seemed to relax a little at this. They were looking at her differently, as though seeing her for the first time. She offered them her hands, and said, 'Do we have a bargain?'

Little Sophie announced, 'It is a bargain, Miss Collins.' They were the most words that Daphne had heard from the girl since she had arrived. They came as rather a surprise, for Daphne had begun to suspect that the girl was mute. But the phrase was spoken loud and clear enough, as though she did not wish for her meaning to be mistaken.

The other two children looked equally surprised, but shrugged their shoulders and took Daphne's hands, shaking them in agreement.

'Very good. Then I think it is time that we went back to lessons. If you can help me with the maps, we shall spend the rest of the afternoon on geography.' For she suspected that she could not make nearly such a hash of it as she might on languages or maths. Any fool with a pointer and an atlas ought to be able to manage the subject without embarrassing themselves.

She'd barely begun her lesson when the master of the house entered the room, quietly, so as not to disturb her pupils.

But of course he did. At the sight of him the children lost all interest in what she was saying. They turned to look back, smiles on their faces, although Sophie's was hesitant. It was as though she enjoyed looking upon him, but enjoyed even more that it was from a distance, as one might like to view a tiger in a cage.

Daphne made to stop, for there was little point in continuing the lesson with him standing at the back of the room, arms folded across his chest.

'No, pray continue, Miss Collins. I am very interested in the education of my children.'

Oh, dear. The last thing she needed was for him to take an interest in her teaching, since she had little interest in it herself. But she soldiered on through the lesson, pointing out locations on the big map of the world, and sharing what little she knew of them. The minutes seemed to drag by. But, finally, she heard a hall clock chiming the hour. It seemed as good a time as any to release the children to their father.

The greetings went very much as they had done on the previous day, with the older two speaking formally to him, and Sophie hanging back, tangled in Daphne's skirts.

'Go, now, and prepare for dinner. And remember to wash your hands and faces,' she called after them, thinking she sounded very much like her own governess.

'Miss Collins.'

When she turned, her employer was still in the room, staring at her with a hard expression. And she became suddenly conscious of how alone they were. 'My lord?'

'I would like a word with you. In my study.' He turned and walked from the room, not waiting to see if she followed. It surprised her to see him turn right instead of left, eschewing the main staircase, to take the servants' stairs to the ground floor. But the door to his study was very near to the bottom of them, as was his conservatory. Perhaps that explained his choice.

Once in the hall, he opened the door to his study, and allowed her to precede him, shutting it tightly behind them. Then he turned upon her, and said, 'Explain yourself.' He gave no further clue as to what he might mean. But, if possible, his expression became even more forbidding.

She struggled to think what she might have done that he'd found objectionable. There were probably a hundred things. She was unable to settle upon any one that was worse than the others. Since she did not wish to give away any more than she had to, she said, 'In what sense?'

'You are no more a governess than I am. I wish you to explain what it is that you are doing, here in my house, caring for my children.'

'I do not understand, my lord.' She carefully wiped any trace of guilt from her face, and replaced it with a look that she hoped was suitably puzzled. 'Were my references not to your liking?'

'It matters little whether I liked your papers or no, since the decision to hire you was totally that of my neighbour. And I suspect, should I look closely at your letters of reference, I would find them to be in your own hand.'

'Sir!' This was too close to the truth, so she fell back on outrage as her only defence.

He paced the room, hands waving in agitation. 'I could forgive a small mistake made when teaching maths. For who among us does not, on occasion, transpose a number, or forget to carry a one? And a mistake in French or Latin could be passed off as colloquial, were I to be in a charitable frame of mind.'

He turned suddenly, and pointed at her. 'But do not tell me you are qualified as a teacher, if you cannot find our colonies on a map.'

'Whatever do you mean, my lord?'

He snatched a ruler from his desk and brought it down with a sharp crack against the surface of the globe on the table top. 'This, Miss Collins, if you wish to know, is the former colony known as New York. And the location to which you were pointing—' he brought the pointer down again, with another loud slap '—is Canada. Which is, if I am to believe *The Times*, still a colony of Britain. And this—' he slashed with the pointer '—is the border between the two.'

She leaned forwards, and peered at the map. 'So it is,' she said weakly.

'The principal export of the area is not tobacco, which needs a much more temperate climate to thrive.'

'Well, you should know, for you have a much more complete knowledge of horticulture than I.'

He glanced at the ruler, and for a moment she feared he meant to use it upon her in anger. But he threw it aside and turned to face her.

Without thinking she took a step back, and felt her shoulders bang squarely into the wall behind her.

He smiled, realising her fear, and took another step to close the distance between them. Then he said, so softly that she doubted anyone would hear, 'Can you explain the errors you have made?'

She could hardly blame her own governesses for her inattention when the subjects had been covered in lessons. And so she muttered, 'It is just that I become nervous when I am observed.'

'Oh, really. My presence unnerves you?' And he took a step closer, until there was very little space between them at all. 'Is it just me, I wonder? Or are you flustered by other men as well?'

'Not you at all, my lord. It is just that I am unaccustomed to such attention. While teaching.'

He laughed softly, and the hairs on the back of her neck rose as he whispered, 'You are lying again and not very skilfully.'

'I swear, I am not.' But her voice became breathy as she said it, with a tone that was all wrong for the earnest denial she should mount.

'I will agree that you are not accustomed to teaching. But, looking as you do, I find it hard to believe that you are unaccustomed to masculine attention.' He was making no effort to hide an interest that she suspected had little to do with her knowledge of geography. 'A simple governess would not dress the way you do.'

She glanced down at her gown, which was one of her own, a simple day dress of pale green muslin. 'There is nothing exceptionable or immodest about what I am wearing.'

'Other than it does not belong to a servant. Is it yours, or did you steal it, I wonder?'

Now that she was ensconced in the household, she'd felt it safe to put aside the simple frocks she'd borrowed from Miss Collins, and return to wearing her own clothes. But apparently she'd been wrong, for it had made him suspicious. 'It was a gift. From a previous mistress. A cast-off.'

'But brand new.' He reached out a finger to touch the fabric at her throat. 'But what is this you have stuffed into the front of it?'

She should slap the man for such impudence. But she suspected he was only trying to frighten her, and it would not do to let him succeed. So she muttered, 'Chemisette.'

He took a pinch of the cotton, and plucked at it, and she could feel the ties give way, as he drew the neckpiece out of the gown. She found the little ruffled blouse to be oppressive and unnecessary, and there was some part of her that rejoiced at its removal. As the air touched her skin she had a flash of memory from her forbidden walks in the dark paths of Vauxhall Gardens. The sense of anticipation, and the furtive rush of desire.

Colton saw the look in her eyes, and smiled. 'You prefer it this way, don't you? It is the way you normally wear it. With your throat bare and your bodice low, so that men may admire your breasts.'

He was staring at her, and she felt her nipples tighten in response.

He nodded as though aware of her reaction. 'The gown is yours, but the modesty is false.' He looked into her eyes again. 'Tell me, now. Why did you come to my house? Nothing about you is as it seems, Miss Collins. And if you do not give me the truth, you cannot blame me for assuming the worst about you.'

She snatched the fabric from his hand, crumpling the starched cloth in frustration. 'I came to help your children, since you seem unwilling or unable to do so.' It was not a complete truth, but neither was it a total lie. Then, she risked a threat of her own. 'And if you try to remove me from my post, I shall tell the Duchess. And she shall take action.'

He stood very close to her. Too close, for she could feel the heat of his body on the bare skin of her throat. His voice was hoarse when he answered, and barely above a whisper. 'Perhaps I shall not have to remove you. It will be better if you decide to remove yourself. For you must realise that it is dangerous for you to remain under this roof with me. Time will tell if you truly care so much for my children that you are willing to risk your honour to teach them.'

And, for a moment, she knew how Timothy Colton

had been able to escape justice. For when he stared at her with those bottomless dark eyes, his threats against her felt more like promises of illicit pleasure from a man who did not care for law or sin. The sort of man who would have what he wanted, and the whole world be damned. She put her hand to his chest and pushed him away, breaking the spell of his gaze. 'I care for your children, Lord Colton, and my honour as well. But I do not now, nor will I ever, care for you. Not for your title, your money or your designs upon me.'

And then she turned and fled the room, before he could see that she was lying, yet again.

As the door closed, Tim reached out to grab his desk for support. It was as though her sudden absence had left him physically weakened. He should not have even invited her into this room, where they were alone and the door was closed. And he certainly should not have touched her. He had meant to give her a stern warning, or dismiss her without one. For though the children seemed to have no complaints, what good was a teacher who knew less than her students?

But in the absence of prying eyes, his mind had filled with strange fantasies. He had wanted to see the skin of her throat, and the bared swell of her breasts above the gown. And the foolish girl had done nothing to stop him. She had trusted her virtue to his fragile self-control.

He wished he could write to Penny and explain the problem. If she would not permit him the care of his own children, then at least she could show mercy and remove Miss Collins from his house. Send him another woman who was less attractive, older, more timid. Someone who did not stare into his soul with her cat-like green eyes, as though daring him to kiss her.

He stared at the door that she'd slammed behind her and let his lust settle into a bone-deep longing. He was not thinking rationally if he'd consider, even for a moment, admitting to the Duchess that he was unable to master his reactions to Miss Collins.

But it did not matter how he felt. After what had happened with Clare, he did not deserve female company. Better to lock himself in the conservatory, far away from temptation and the new governess. For he'd come to believe that the two things were one and the same.

Chapter Six

Daphne opened the window, desperate to catch the last breath of summer air. She could see by the falling leaves that the season was almost done with its change. After the interview of the previous day, she had decided to postpone searching the ground floor for a time. It would be best to stay away from Timothy Colton, until his interest waned. She had returned to wearing Miss Collins's cast-off clothes to forestall any further harassment. But the stiffness and starchiness of them felt unnatural against her skin, just as Miss Collins's job did on her mind. Why must they stay in the boring old schoolroom, when there was so little time left to play before winter came?

After the night's rain, the room was stuffy and damp in a way that the garden would not be, for the sun had dried the grass and was burning off the last mist in the valleys that she could see in the distance. She longed to take out her own sketch pad and draw it, just as Sophie would.

And then she smiled. She had had thoughts just such as that often enough when she was a child. And there was always a nurse or governess with a stern expression to lay those thoughts to rest and send her back to her books.

But for now, she was in charge of the classroom, and there was no reason things could not be different.

'Come, children. To the garden. It is too fine a day to be trapped inside.'

They seemed to hunker down in their desks, as though they expected her to pull them out into the sunshine, against their will. 'We should stay here,' Lily said firmly. They were looking at her as though she had failed yet another test, proving herself to be less a true schoolteacher. But what sort of children were they, that they preferred the schoolroom to the trees, on the last fine day of autumn?

Daphne smiled. 'We can take our books with us and manage just as well, sitting under a tree. You do have a garden, I am sure. For I saw it as I was entering the house.'

'It is very fine, although better in summer,' said Edmund, smiling as a point of pride. 'Father has an amazing selection. Rare plants from America. And the roses of course, in all colours. And the herbs, but everyone has those.'

'Not as we do,' said Lily, warming to the idea. 'There is an entire section of it, plants brought from China. Lilies, for me. And poppies. And a lotus in a pond with fish. And there is a little pagoda that Father had built, just for us to play in.'

Edmund grinned. 'Mother said it was a waste to have the only folly in the garden be expressly for us. But Father is of the opinion that such buildings are perfect for children, but quite nonsensical for adults.'

Lily lifted her chin proudly. 'He says that it is not necessary to improve upon the beauty of nature by sticking a building in front of it.'

'What your father said is quite true. If one has a sense of the arrangement for the plants themselves, then one hardly needs more than a bench on which to sit and enjoy them.' It stuck in her throat to agree with the man. But in this, at least, he was right. And if it helped to gain the co-operation of the children, then she would ally herself to the devil. 'You sound very proud of your father's work. And very knowledgeable. You must give me a tour of the grounds.'

'It is hardly proper schooling to be wandering in the garden.' Edmund had remembered his place, and was trying to sound as stern as any schoolmaster, and convince himself that fun could have no part in learning.

She smiled at him. 'Is that your opinion, Master Ed, or some philosopher's? I suspect that the sunshine of Greece was sufficient for Plato to teach.'

'Please?' The sound of little Sophie's voice surprised them all. 'May we go to the garden?'

They all turned to look at her, and she seemed to shrink for a moment, as though she realised that speaking above a whisper had called unwelcome attention to herself. And then she squared her little shoulders and spoke again. 'May we play?'

And there was such a look of desperate hope on her little face that Daphne knew it would be impossible for Edmund to object. 'There. See? Your little sister wishes it as well. There can be no harm in one day of sunshine, can there? You can show me the plants, and then you may sit under a tree, and learn philosophy as it was first taught, with plenty of fresh air. Come.' She opened the door, and gestured them out into the hall, then closed it behind them and headed for the main stairs.

She had managed to detach them from the room, but they lagged even further behind, once they realised the path she had chosen. 'We always take the back stairs,' said Lily.

'This is shorter.'

'But we always take the back.' Her voice managed to be both firm and shrill. Daphne turned and stared at the wide-eyed little girl. Was it fear of the accident site that made her balk, months later?

She turned to them, each in turn, and saw the same nervous expressions. It would not do to upset them. But did it do them a service to foster an irrational fear? She shook her head. 'Today, I think it better that we take the main stairs. Directly down, out the front doors and on to the path to the garden. Much shorter than going all round the house. You will be outside and playing in no time.'

She smiled to show them that it was all right. 'If you are afraid, then I shall go first.' Little Sophie was cowering behind her sister, as though the thought of it was equal to the worst terror of her young life.

So Daphne reached out a hand to her. 'Come. Sophie and I will show you. Sophie, you take the banister, and I will hold your other hand. My family assures me that I am as hard to move as a marble statue, once I get an idea into my head. You will be protected on both sides.'

The girl hesitated for a moment, while desire and fear warred within her. And then she stepped forwards, and wrapped her fingers around the banister until they were as white as the stone. With the other hand, she took Daphne's fingers in a death grip, and closed her eyes.

It made things tricky, if the child meant to take the stairs without looking. But who was she to argue? So she took a step forwards that almost lifted the little girl off her feet. The child's hand loosened on the rail enough to slide, and her little feet hurried to keep up with Daphne's.

She kept up a running commentary, to put the girl at her ease. 'See? Or you would, if your eyes were not closed. Not difficult at all. Only stairs, just like the ones at the back, but safer because they are not so narrow and steep. And you do not need a candle to light the way.'

And then they were in the hall, safe and sound. Sophie opened her eyes in wonder. She turned back to her brother and sister, and her smile was so radiant that for a moment Daphne felt like a true governess, one that might know nothing of Socrates, but still managed to teach a very important lesson.

The older children hurried the last few steps with a relieved sigh, and ran ahead to open the door in front of them. She smiled to them in encouragement. 'Go on. You can find the garden better than I. Race. As fast as you can go. Without dropping your books, of course.' She tried to be stern, with little success.

The children shot past her and out the door.

She turned to follow them. But the words 'Miss Collins!' echoed behind her, bringing her to a full stop.

She turned to see Lord Colton standing perfectly still in the hallway behind her. 'My lord?' The fact that he could approach without her noticing made his continual scrutiny most disturbing. She took a step away from him, fearing that he might try to re-enact the scene of the previous day.

But the weird, seductive light in his eyes was overwhelmed by anger, and his lips were bloodless white, until he spoke. 'If you are to spend any time in this house, you will learn that I value the safety of my children over all. I will not have them upset, or put at risk in an effort on your part to prove some foolish point.'

She bristled in return, her fear of him forgotten. 'I did nothing to jeopardise the safety of the children. We merely walked down a flight of stairs.'

'The stairs are dangerous,' he sputtered, obviously uncomfortable.

It gave her a strange feeling of power to see him out of countenance. 'And I say they are not. There is nothing about them that puts a person at risk. If one is careful, the chance of an accidental fall is so small as to be moot.' She glared at him, hoping that he could see her knowledge of the truth, and her contempt for him, plain in her eyes.

'If you think it matters what *you* think in this situation, then you have an imperfect understanding of your role here. I wish for the children to use the back stairs, as they seem perfectly content in doing.' He took a step closer, until he seemed to tower over her.

He was trying to bully her again, as he had done yesterday. And she would have none of it. 'You say you are interested in your children's welfare. And yet you wish for them to use the steep, unlit stairs at the back of the house.' She smiled at him for proving her point so well. 'Then perhaps their safety does not matter so much as you think.' And she swept past him, and out of the door.

The gardens were as magnificent as the children had promised, and it took only a short time for her surroundings to calm her, and blot out the unpleasant altercation in the entry hall. Most of the flowers were finished blooming. But when she wished to know how they had looked at the height of the season, she had merely to ask. Sophie would sit with her pastels, and produce hurried sketches that were riots of colour, yet impressively harmonious in their composition.

'In summer, it must be truly splendid,' Daphne breathed, for she could not help herself.

Edmund frowned. 'Do you really think so? Mother wished for a garden more like the ones she saw in London. She was most vexed.'

'Many designers prefer a more artificial landscape, and their clients are willing to pay a great price to obey them. Your mother was interested in fashion, and the appearance of wealth. She would have followed their example.' Daphne waved a hand. 'She would have no patience for subtleties like this.' And she stopped herself, wishing she could take back an opinion about the late Clarissa Colton that, while perfectly true, was quite unflattering. And it should have been quite beyond the knowledge of Miss Collins, governess and stranger to the family. 'Or so I assume,' she added, hoping the children did not notice her slip.

'She had no patience for us,' Edmund blurted.

'I'm sure that was not true,' Daphne corrected automatically. But in her heart, she recalled the Clare Colton she had known, and feared the children were right.

'It was true,' Lily said in a voice so small and sad that for a moment she sounded more like Sophie. She reached out and took Daphne by the hand, leading her to the China garden, to see the pagoda. But instead of going to the front so that she could stoop and enter with the children, Lily led her to the back. She pointed to scratches in the red enamel work. 'When Mother learned that this was to be built for us, but that Father had included nothing for her, there was a frightful row. He said she could do what she liked inside the house, and with the town house and grounds in London. But that the glasshouses, the conservatory and the grounds here in Wales were his, to do as he liked. And that was that.' Lily ran her finger over the scratches. 'So she found a spade.'

In Daphne's mind it was easy to imagine hot-tempered Clare swinging furiously at the little playhouse, taking her anger out upon it. And she wondered if that had been the worst of it, for Edmund's eyes had gone very round, looking at the scratches, as though seeing the same thing.

Without thinking about it, she reached out to both of them, gathering one child under each arm. She said, in a resolute voice, 'Your mother was very foolish to behave in such a way. And to take her anger out upon you or your things was very wrong indeed.'

Lily sighed. 'She would not have done it had it been for Sophie alone. She said we were Father's children, but Sophie was all hers.'

Daphne cursed Clare under her breath. She wanted to remember her cousin as blithe and beautiful. Why had it been so easy to forget that, on occasion, she could be shallow and cruel? To see the truth on the faces of the children was truly sobering.

She crouched beside them, as their father had done. 'Still more nonsense. You are every bit as charming as your little sister, and just as much a part of your mother.' She pulled them into a hug, and ruffled their bright red hair. 'And far too clever for the likes of me to be teaching, although you must have realised that by now.'

'But we won't tell,' whispered Lily, and Edmund gave a solemn shake of his head. 'We like you much better than our last governess.'

'And I like you, as well.' She smiled at them. 'And I will not think anything of it, if you want to take a short break from your studies to play in the fine pagoda that your father has made for you. Winter will be here soon. Enjoy the garden while you can.'

The two older children did not need a second offer.

With a last glance of relief, they took off after their little sister in a game of hide and seek amongst the flower beds.

Daphne smiled to herself. Perhaps she had some skill as a governess after all. For she had been right to bring the children here. Removing them from the house for an afternoon had certainly done Sophie good. Her sketches were proof of that. She was using all the colours, not just the black and red that she had used to render Clare, and drawing with lines that were smooth and flowing, not jagged and tense. It was good to know that she had happy memories as well, of blooming trees and flowers.

And the pictures were exceptional, not just in execution, but in the subject matter. The variety was amazing, with samples from all over the world. Despite his obvious faults, Lord Colton did seem to have an eye for the ordering of the plants. He had managed to lay colour against colour, just as a painter might, and blend textures of bark and leaf, until she felt she could spend hours here in fascination. Nor had he neglected education. The plants were neatly tagged with genus and habitat as proof that they would live in harmony in the places from which they had come. It was a feast for an artist and scientist alike.

And without intending it, she felt a fleeting admiration for the man that had orchestrated it. It was so peaceful here. Was it even possible for the creator of such beauty to give himself over to violence?

She glanced in the direction of the conservatory, for the garden wrapped around the wing that had the glasshouse. She suspected it was a magnificent view, even from within the house. From inside the conservatory one would be able to look out on to the terraced garden and have an illusion that there were no walls at all, but that one was suspended in a glass bubble in the middle of Eden.

Or perhaps a glass cage. For there, framed in one of the large arched windows, was the master of the house. His palms were pressed flat to the glass, body straining as though in confinement. He was smiling as he watched the children at play, but it was not a happy thing to see. Then he noticed her observation of him and stared for a moment into her eyes. All expression on his face faded. And he turned and disappeared into the foliage on his side of the barrier.

Chapter Seven

When the sun began to set it grew cooler, and it was clear that they would need to come in for their evening meal. Daphne shepherded the children back to the nursery. She saw to it that they were properly washed and dressed and had the cook send them their evening meal.

It made her smile to listen to their chattering, for the fresh air had put life into them. Even Sophie was talking, infrequently, but in an almost normal tone. But as quickly as it had come the energy seemed to fade, and she knew that it meant an early bedtime.

Which left her alone. Once the children had gone, it occurred to her that she had heard no more from the master of the house on the subject of her interference with the children. It was almost a pity, for she wished he could have seen the ease with which they climbed the main stairs on their return to the house. They scampered up the steps as though they were not there, just as children should. She had had to give them the perfectly ordinary caution to walk when inside the house. They'd laughed and slowed, but given no thought to the possibility of accident or the fate that had befallen their mother. It had been as if she'd broken down a wall, and set them free from one of the cells their father had trapped them in. Now that they had tasted freedom, she doubted that it would be an easy thing for him to banish them again to the back stairs.

She viewed it as a small victory against the tyrant. She marched up the stairs to her room, full of satisfaction. Of course, she had done nothing to find the truth, as yet. But to help Clare's children was to do some justice for the woman.

Although the stories that the children had told about their mother were almost as disturbing as the problems with their father. It was a shame to think that they had not been their mother's first consideration. But to be honest with herself, she had never thought of Clare as a mother of three. In all the time they had spent in shopping, riding in the park with Clare's many admirers and attending parties and balls, she had mentioned the children so seldom that Daphne had needed to consult with Miss Collins to verify their names and ages.

While she might care for them in memory of Clare, she could not shake the feeling that her cousin would have discouraged the interest as unnecessary. But she decided to put the feeling aside as she climbed the stairs to her room, and focus on the day's success instead of what Clare might or might not have intended. It did no good to think on it, for the state of her cousin's mind at the time of her death was a thing that could not be known.

She opened her door, and sensed a change almost immediately. Her room was filled with a spicy sweet scent of flowers. And there on the night stand was a crystal vase filled with red gilly flowers, baby's breath, lilies of the valley and a sprinkling of hyacinths. She could not help the smile on her face, for the bouquet was magnificent. There were so many cut flowers in the house. She had seen orchids and roses in bowls scattered about the main rooms as though they had no worth.

But these flowers were simple and unassuming, perfectly appropriate for the tiny servant's room she occupied. She stepped forwards and buried her face in them, letting the feeling of the afternoon garden come rushing back to her. Then she felt along the table, searching for a note of explanation.

And stopped. A note was hardly necessary, for there could be only one person who had arranged for the flowers. When she had asked about a particularly fine display in the hall, Mrs Sims had said that they'd come from one of the glasshouses in the grounds. And that everything in the house was cut and displayed at the recommendation of her master.

Timothy Colton was the only one who could have sent the flowers to her.

She looked again at the arrangement. The flowers were an unusual mix of seasons. They looked well together, but were not common companions. Perhaps he had a meaning in choosing so. There was a language of flowers, was there not? It would render a note unnecessary, if he'd spoken to her using the plants. And if the garden was any indication, he was as comfortable speaking through them as Sophie was in talking with pictures.

She gave a last, lingering sniff to the heart of them, and then retreated down the stairs to the library. For if any house might have a book to explain the meaning, she was sure that this one must.

He had made it easy for her. The needed volume lay open on the main table, ready for her consultation. She looked down at the page before her. Baby's breath meant sincerity. That was encouraging, for whatever he wished to say was truly felt. Lilies of the valley were humility, which was also good. And the hyacinths? She flipped hurriedly through the pages.

Hyacinths said 'forgive me'. She covered her hand with her mouth to hide the smile. It was a bouquet of apology for his behaviour towards her in the hall. He was displaying humility before a servant, but with no loss of face and without the need to admit aloud that he had been wrong. She could not decide whether to be insulted by the subterfuge or to admire the cleverness of it. If he wished, he could always deny that there was any meaning at all. It was not as if he had given her roses. There could be nothing more innocent than gilly flowers.

Which must have a meaning as well, she supposed. She flipped to the *G* page, and did not find what she was seeking, and so tried again under the other name, carnation, and found a whole list, with each colour having a different meaning.

And her finger stopped upon red. Admiration. He felt admiration, for her?

She returned to the hall, shutting the library door behind her. Apology. Humility. And sincere admiration. Why could it not have come from any other man in the world? From Simon, perhaps, whose loutish behaviour had got her banished from London. If his few moments of stolen passion had been accompanied by a floral apology, and some sign that it had meant anything at all to him to be alone with her? That he had done what he had done because he sincerely admired her?

A tear traced down her cheek, and she wiped it away. Her friends in London felt nothing but embarrassment in knowing her, as was demonstrated by their distance before her departure. No one had come to see her off. And she doubted, even now, that they had given much thought to her absence.

But Timothy Colton had known her only a short while, and they had spoken only a handful of times, most of them marred by threats and strange behaviour. And yet, she did not doubt for a moment the truth of the flowers, or think his feelings were less than he claimed.

She hurried back toward her room, but stopped on the stairs, gripping the handrail. She was giving him too much credit in this. And there had been a fleeting moment of pure pleasure, on discovering the meaning of the flowers, and knowing their source. Was it so easy to forget the reason for this visit? The man was a murderer.

But not cold-blooded, a tiny voice reminded her. What had happened must have been a crime of passion. She could see in his treatment of the children that he was not a man given to common displays of violence.

But that did not matter. He had killed Clare.

But Clare was the one in the house prone to childish tantrums and violent behaviour, if the children were to be believed.

If Tim had acted against her, perhaps she had given him good reason. Had she done something that he had seen as a threat to his children? Whatever the reason, he had been deeply wounded by his actions, as had the whole family. The children were desperately afraid of being separated from their father, no matter what he had done. And he longed to keep them close.

She had thought she could blunder into the house, denounce the man and leave with a light heart, knowing that justice had been done. But what would that do to the children? How would the truth help anyone?

She was trembling in confusion as she climbed the last stairs to her room. Anything she had done, anything she did and anything she might do—all paths would lead to more pain for this family. And knowing that Lord Colton had tender feelings for her made it all the more complicated.

She could forgive her body's reactions to him. He was a handsome man, virile and with an element of darkness that made him all the more attractive. It was no different from falling for a rake or a rogue. The knowledge of danger made the flirtation more exciting. But her time in London should have taught her better. She must not let her mind wander into sympathy for him or allow herself to be flattered by a bouquet. A few flowers would not wipe away the stain of murder.

And perhaps she was being foolish. Admiration could mean many things. Some of them were quite simple and not the least bit romantic. He might simply be acknowledging a job well done in the garden today—his admiration of the way she had dealt with the children's fears. He might have given her the flowers without another thought about her, or the foolish romantic meaning she might construe.

She came back to her room, and saw the bouquet again, a lone spot of beauty in the otherwise grim room.

Her room.

She sat on the bed, shocked by a rush of emotions. Suddenly, she was sure that no servant's hand had touched the vase. Tim had prepared the thing himself. And then he had climbed the last lonely flight of stairs and placed it there for her to find. He would feel no compunction about it. It was his house, after all. All the rooms were his.

But she knew it was more than that. The message was clear, and there was nothing innocent about it. He had entered her room without her knowledge or permission, and left flowers so that she might know what he had done. Whatever she might think he meant by admiration, it meant more than just common praise. The man who had killed her cousin desired her. Although the meaning of the bouquet was harmless, the delivery spoke of possession, and of a man who would not be swayed by barriers of propriety if he wanted her.

She remembered the darkness in his eyes, and the way it seemed to swallow her as she looked into them. When he came for her, would she be able to resist him? And would she want to try?

Tim dug his hands into the soil on the potting table, feeling the tension leave his body and peace flow in with the scent of earth. Why couldn't everything be as simple? Sun, soil and water. And plants were happy. But people?

He was never sure. He could not shake the feeling that his lovely new employee hated him. It was not as if he hadn't given her every reason to. He had not treated her well, for he had not meant for her to stay.

But this was something more. She had disliked him from the first meeting. It was as though she'd come into the house with the feelings. And yet she seemed unfazed by his behaviour. No matter how he tried to frighten her, she remained defiant in a way that the other governesses had not. He had forbidden her to take the course of action she had taken this afternoon, and she had ignored him as though his opinions did not matter.

He smiled grimly to himself. She had been right, of course. The children were doing well under her care. In the garden, they had looked better than they had in months. And the sight of them together had moved him, for a moment, to wonder what it might be like for them to have a mother, not a nurse.

He shook his head. He'd been thinking the same such nonsense when he'd cut and arranged the flowers. But it had been worse than that, when he'd taken them to her room. If he'd intended a simple 'thank you', he could have delivered it to the classroom. Or sent a maid with it.

But he had wanted to do the thing in secret. And he'd wanted to see where she slept.

He had never been to the tiny room under the eaves. It was little better than an attic, and not at all as he imagined the governess's room to be. But with Lily in the bedroom most convenient to the nursery, the governess had made do with second best.

The small space had been full of the scent of her. He could understand why the children might thrive under her care, for there was something else in the air, as well. A lively intelligence? A lack of care? A singleness of purpose that was the same he felt when at work? He had looked about her room and felt an overwhelming sense of peace.

But quick upon it came the feeling of desire. He remembered the fire in her eyes when she looked at him as she flouted his authority and dared him to respond. She'd had opportunity enough to tell him that he was behaving improperly, or at least to show fear in the face of his advance the previous day. But she had stood her ground as though willing to see how far his emotions might take them. Perhaps she secretly wanted his kiss as much as he wanted to kiss her. How easy it would be to lie down upon the bed to await her return!

Then he would strip her bare and crush the flowers against her skin to release their scent and to mark her with the meaning of his gift. He would make love to her with all the passion and turbulence he felt in his soul. And she would give him the peace that she had shared with the children. She would set him free.

He could imagine her, under him, neck arched to receive his kisses, legs spread to receive his body, unafraid to cry out in passion, alone at the top of the house where no one might hear what they were doing.

He had left the room, frightened by the image, hurrying down the stairs until he was back in the conservatory. Once there, he shut it tight against the outside world. There were reasons to fear discovery.

What he imagined was wrong. He wished to treat a young lady of good character, a servant under his protection, as though she were a mistress, wanton and experienced, and eager for his touch. It showed how far his own character had fallen. If he had come to believe that all women were no better than Clare had been, hungry and whorish, then in the end he would treat the next woman in his life in the same manner he had treated his wife, with loathing and contempt. And the relationship would come to the same bitter end.

Chapter Eight

The next day at breakfast the children greeted her as formally as ever they had. It was as if a curtain had dropped over the success of the previous afternoon, and it was all but forgotten. Daphne cursed herself for thinking their problems would be so easily solved. While the children might be better than they had been on her arrival, their behaviour was nowhere near the boisterousness that she might call normal. And it did not help that yesterday's sunshine had disappeared, replaced by fog.

After almost a week of her pathetic attempts at teaching, Edmund and Lily seemed to have contented themselves with being self-taught. They got out their books without argument, helping each other through any difficulties. Daphne arranged Sophie's usual table for drawing, and gave her pencil and charcoals, showing her how to smudge the coal to get lights and shadows, before wiping her hands and going to the sofa. Without thinking, she took her own sketchbook in her lap and made a rough drawing of a park, shrouded in mist. She added shadows, and phantoms hiding behind crooked trees. The grimness of the subject suited her current mood.

Perhaps this afternoon she could find the time to begin her search of the downstairs. Lord Colton had nothing of interest in his room. If there was anything out of order, it would be below, in the study, perhaps. Or the conservatory, where he spent so much time. But how was she to go into his sanctum without arising suspicion?

Perhaps she should thank him for the carnations. But it might mean being alone with him in the study again. And the man she had met, when last she was called there, was not at all like the one who had attempted to speak with flowers. It was most confusing.

Sophie tugged upon her skirt, trying to gain her attention, and held papers out to Daphne, with a half-smile and eyes eager for approval.

'You have finished already?' Daphne smiled back. 'Such a clever girl you are. Let us see what you have done.' She got up from her seat and walked across the room to Sophie's table.

Sophie held the drawings out before her, and Daphne remembered, too late, that she had not given the girl a theme. Sophie had drawn her parents in a way that shocked the viewer with their dissimilarity.

The one of her father was an accurate enough rendition, although the nose was a trifle too large. He was smiling, as she had often seen him do when greeting the children. He was in shirtsleeves, probably just come from the conservatory, for Sophie had even managed to capture a smudge of dirt on the white of his cuff. His arms were outstretched and welcoming, as though he meant to scoop the viewer into them and hold them close.

For a moment, Daphne forgot all trepidations and smiled back at the picture, just as Sophie was doing.

But the one of Clare left no such feeling of peace. She supposed it was some progress that the woman in the picture did not lie dead at the foot of the stairs. Instead, she was very much alive. She was wearing a gown that Daphne recognised from their time in London. She had admired it greatly. But it had never occurred to her how inappropriate it might be, if one were mothering small children. In the picture, Clare's red hair was piled high on her head, and jewels glittered at her neck and ears. Her hands were gloved, and seemed to hover at her skirts, as though she had been caught in the act of pulling them out of reach of mud on the street. Her lips were twisted in a cold smile that conveyed utter disdain. Sophie had captured her beauty, but also her unapproachability.

But there was something else about the picture, something unaccountably wrong. At first, Clare seemed out of scale with the picture of her husband. In the drawing, she seemed overtall, her features elongated in a way that accentuated the haughty brow. It was then Daphne realised that the perspective was not so much wrong as merely different. Although she could not see his legs in the picture, Tim must have been on his knees, for he was just as he would look to a five-year-old who was meeting him on eye level as he crouched to give a hug.

But Clare had towered over her small daughter. She made no effort to hide her height or to relate to the girl on her level. The angle of view had created strange shadows, making Clare's face not just aloof, but openly hostile.

The expression, coupled with the set of the hands, and the knowledge that it all came through the eyes of a child... It made Daphne suspect that Sophie had approached too close, with hands that were less than immaculate, and been sent packing for it.

She glanced again at Lord Colton's dirty shirt, rumpled hair and easy smile.

Sophie reached out to touch the picture, wistfully. The coal smudged her fingers, and she glanced at the drawing of her mother, as though she had been caught anew, and found wanting. She hurriedly wiped her hands upon her pinafore, then looked at the smudges she'd made, and gave Daphne a look of hopeless resignation.

Daphne laughed at the girl and reached into her pocket for a handkerchief, hurrying to set her at ease. 'Drawing is messy work, isn't it? But it cannot be helped.' She took Sophie's hands in hers, wiping. Then she bent low so she could look into the girl's face. 'Your drawings are very good. You have learned much since I've been here. I am very proud of you.'

Without warning, Sophie threw her arms around

Daphne's neck and almost pulled her off balance, giving her a hug and a rather wet kiss upon the cheek.

Daphne hugged her in return and then gave her a kiss on the top of her head. She was momentarily overcome by the sweet smell of little girl and the desire to be able to sit with her, holding her tight whenever she wanted.

She realised her mistake almost immediately, releasing the girl and taking an involuntary step back. It was wrong. She had never loved children, nor had she meant to change her feelings about them. She would be gone soon, back to her normal life. Some day, perhaps she would have her own. But these were not hers to hold. She was to care for them. Not about them. And she absolutely must not develop a sense of attachment. For who knew what would happen, if she succeeded in her plans?

Sophie sensed the rejection and stepped away herself with a look that said she realised she had been bad again, and was sorry.

And impulsively, Daphne threw her fears aside and pulled the girl back to hug her again. She would sort out the details later. But for now, things would be as they were, and all would be happy. 'Do not worry, Sophie. You only startled me for a moment. Thank you very much for the lovely hug. And do not worry about dirty handprints and smudged drawings. Accidents happen all the time. No one is to blame.'

The girl gave her the most amazed look, as though the concept of an accident was a foreign one. And then she gave Daphne another hug, this one guaranteed to leave a dirty handprint on Daphne's neck. Sophie stood back and waited for the response.

Daphne laughed. 'Now that was not an accident at all. That was deliberate, you silly girl. But it came with another very nice hug and it is not terribly difficult to wash my neck. I hardly think it merits punishment. Do you?'

Sophie stood, as though considering for a moment, and then gave a solemn nod, which, as Daphne watched it, turned slowly into a smile.

'Very good. Now go wash your hands in the basin, and we shan't have to worry about it.'

By afternoon, the fog had turned to rain. It made steady streams on the window panes, and the children dozed over their books. Daphne was dozing in her chair as well. Even Sophie, who normally had no trouble entertaining herself with paper and pen, was drawing listless spirals, but showing no interest in them.

Daphne glanced at the drowsy children. If there were some way to keep them occupied, while she investigated the conservatory… And if she could distract Lord Colton as well…

A thought occurred to her. If it worked, it would be almost too perfect. She shut her book with a snap and smiled at the children. 'Enough of this. You cannot learn anything if you are barely awake. Let us have an adventure.'

The children looked at her sceptically.

'We will go downstairs, into the conservatory, and ask your father what he is working on.'

'We cannot,' Lily said, without even thinking.

'Why?'

'He is working and does not need us interfering.'

Edmund added, 'We will track the dirt everywhere and spoil our clothes.'

'Urchins,' said Sophie, in a sharp tone that made the older children start guiltily as though hearing the voice of a parent.

'Has your father told you that?' Daphne asked, feeling a sudden wave of annoyance at the man. It was little wonder that his relationship with his children was in shambles.

'The door is closed,' said Edmund firmly, as though that answered all.

'I suspect it is to keep the plants from taking a chill,' Daphne answered reasonably. 'We will go and ask him, shall we? Bring your books. And your drawing things,' she added, looking at Sophie.

The girl hopped off her stool, eager to leave the schoolroom.

The other children followed with less enthusiasm as she led them down to the east wing of the ground floor.

Although it was still raining and she could hear the low splattering of water against the multitude of glass panes, light was streaming through the glass doors at the end of the hall. She threw them open, and shepherded the children inside, then waited for Lord Colton's response. She could but hope that the presence of his family would distract him from any of the tricks he tried when she met him alone. He would be too eager for their attention to pay Daphne any mind. And he would hardly expect her to acknowledge his gift of flowers while they were there.

At the sound of their entry, he looked up from his work with a quiet curiosity, and said, 'To what do I owe the honour of this visit?'

'The children are bored with regular classes, and I felt that they might learn much more readily while in communion with nature as they did yesterday, even if it is held captive in a glasshouse.'

He grinned. 'Capital idea. I know I often gain knowledge by keeping a healthy sense of exploration.'

The children blinked at him in surprise, as though it had never occurred to them to visit their father before.

Colton ducked his head slightly, embarrassed by his enthusiasm. Then he muttered, 'If you wish, you may help me with my planting. There are aprons enough, hanging by the basin.'

Lily started forwards, and passed too close to a pot, sending it teetering on edge and dumping the plant on to the marble table. When she rushed to set it up again, a flower broke off in her hand. The expression on her face was near tears, and Sophie took a hurried step behind Daphne, clinging to her skirts.

Daphne waited for the explosion she was sure must come. There had to be something to justify the children's fear. But instead, their father gave a small sigh, righted the pot and scooped the dirt back in, bedding the plant again and pressing the soil down upon its roots. Then he smiled, picked up the flower, and tucked it behind his daughter's ear. 'You needn't look so worried,

Lily. It is a living thing. It can make a new blossom, just as easily as you can grow a fingernail. Come, let me show you its sisters.' And he took her gently by the hand and led her to a rack of similar plants in various stages of bloom.

Sophie peeked out from behind her skirt, watching the progress of the other children through the conservatory.

'Would you like to follow too?' Daphne asked helpfully.

Sophie gave a small shake of her head.

'Very well, then.' She picked the girl up in her arms, and deposited her on a bench near the windows. 'Why don't you draw some of the plants? Choose whatever subject you like. But be sure to take note of the direction of the light. Later, after you have drawn the shape, perhaps I will let you experiment with water colours.'

Sophie gave her a delighted smile and opened her sketchbook.

Daphne resisted the urge to settle herself beside the girl and enjoy the warmth of the room and the steamy smell of earth mixed with green things. It was very different here than the rest of the house, which seemed to hold itself in cold formality, aloof from the cosy work space that had been fashioned here. She wandered through the rows of plants. There were flowers, both plain and exotic. She found common greenery more appropriate in a field and vegetable plants labelled with their planting and sprouting dates. At the end of each table was a log book, kept in a neat hand, that explained the purpose of the planting, the expected results and the progress of any experiments.

It was all as orderly as the bedroom had been and quite harmless. There was nothing that might further her investigations, no concealed mystery, no sign that the owner wished them gone. She wondered what the children had been so afraid of. The only secret was that it was by far the most welcoming room in the house. It must be a blessed relief to them after the weeks they'd spent in mourning above stairs.

The older children were working close beside their father, red heads bent over the table. He spoke of the various parts of a seed, then took a pocket knife, and carefully dissected the specimen they had been admiring, handing the children a magnifying lens so that they might see. They crowded him on either side and appeared to hang on every word. But Daphne wondered if it was not more than that. They were leaning close enough to touch him. In response, he laid his hands upon their shoulders, drawing them into a semblance of a hug. He seemed more relaxed than she had seen him and it surprised her. Here, he was an eager young scientist and not the brooding lord of the manor who was so critical of her teaching.

She watched him. Being close to him here did not threaten her peace, as he did in the rest of the house. Or, at least, he disturbed her in a different way. Outside the glass doors, she had found him handsome, the frown on his face accentuating the fine structure, calling attention to the brows, the chin and the width of his shoulders. When he'd accosted her in the hall she'd felt a dark frightening pull, as though she was not sure what he meant for her should she get too close.

But here he was gentleness itself. As he worked, she could admire his smile and the light of discovery in his eyes. The strength was still there. But she could see the careful, tender way he held the plants, and her gaze was drawn to his hands, long-fingered, supple and none too fastidious. She saw dirt under his nails and the stain of plants. It surprised her that she was imagining the touch of those hands, all languid relaxation and the heat of sunshine. And how easy it would be to give in to him here.

She shook her head in disgust. Her parents would be frustrated to know that this trip had done nothing to teach her temperance and moderation. In fact, she had grown even less resolute. While she should not imagine herself yielding to anyone, Timothy Colton should be the last man on earth to occupy a place in such fantasies.

Sophie tugged on her hand and held up a pencil sketch of a nearby fern, and she smiled in response. 'Oh, my. That is very good work, Sophie. Let us show your father.'

The girl looked alarmed and gave a small shake of her head.

She smiled in comfort. 'It is all right. He will like it, I am sure. Come. See.' She walked to the planting bench and said quietly, 'Lord Colton?'

He started, as though unused to his own name, and then smiled up at her, brushing the hair out of his eyes in a gesture that was very similar to his son's. 'What is it?'

'Sophie has drawn you a picture.' It was a slight exaggeration, but she doubted it mattered. She held the paper out to him.

'*Equisetum telmateia*, from the Latin for horse.' He reached out to an odd-looking plant and plucked one of the long, fernlike leaves. 'It looks very like a horse's tail. You have captured it well, my darling Sophie.' Then he turned the leaf to her, tickling her nose with the frond until she giggled. He handed her the leaf. 'May I trade you a horse's tail for a horse's tail? For I would very much like to keep your fine drawing here, to inspire me in my work.'

The little girl's eyes widened in surprise and her smile lit up her face. And then she reached up, very cautiously, and gave her father a hug.

He was completely unmanned. His eyes opened wide as well, and then he closed them tightly. And, for a moment, Daphne was convinced that she could see tears on his lashes as he reached out to wrap his arms around his daughter. 'You must come to visit me here often. If you have enjoyed yourself,' he added hurriedly. He opened his eyes. 'All of you. Come whenever you like. I would not interrupt your studies, of course. But there is much that can be learned from nature, if you are interested.'

'You want us here?' Lily sounded more sceptical than surprised, as though there was some kind of trap involved in the simple offer.

'I always have.'

'But Mother said...' and then the girl stopped.

Colton's face darkened for a moment, and then

smoothed to glasslike serenity, and he spoke to her as though she were an adult. 'Perhaps your mother was mistaken in my wishes. You have always been welcome to enter my work area. I assumed your lack of visits was due to a lack of interest on your part. Now we know better.'

Lily gave a hesitant nod.

'And now you must go and wash your hands before your dinner. Hurry along. I understand that Cook has something exceptional planned.' He hesitated for a moment, and then said, in an offhanded way, 'You could eat with me in the dining room if you wish. It would save Cook a trip to the nursery. And Miss Collins should dine with us as well. She might enjoy dressing for dinner on occasion.'

The girls' eyes lit up, and they murmured that they would find it most interesting to dine formally, as long as Miss Collins did not object.

She assured them that she did not. 'But it will require that you wash especially well. Let us go upstairs, and I will call a maid to help you.' But as Daphne went to shepherd the children out of the conservatory, Lord Colton called her back.

'Miss Collins, if I might speak with you for a moment.'

'Of course, my lord.'

'Shut the door behind you, please.'

She nodded. He was still using the mild voice, the one he had used with the children. It would be most ineffectual, if he meant to reprimand her using such a tone.

But the door had barely latched before he'd swooped down on her, scooped her up in his arms and carried her away from it, pulling her back into the conservatory until they were shielded from the glass doors to the hallway. And then, his hands were on her face, and his lips upon hers, in a sweet, laughing, relieved kiss. 'Thank you,' he breathed.

'What?' She could barely catch her breath for the contact was there and gone so quickly that she had hardly realised what was happening. But surely, it had not been her imagination? He had kissed her, for his arms were still about her body, holding her tenderly to him.

'Thank you for bringing them to me. For bringing them back to me. Thank you.' He smoothed her hair and kissed her again, this time upon the forehead.

'Bringing them back? But they were here all along.'

'You have seen how they behave with me, when we are in the schoolroom?' He pressed his face to hers, and kissed her cheek. 'It was not always thus. Since Clarissa...' a shudder ran through him '...they fear me.'

'I know.' It did no good to lie about it.

'I would do anything, if I could take it back. If there were a way to be close to them, as I once was. But I had given up hope of it.' He smiled down at her. 'And then you came, and brought them here. They would not have come for me.'

'You are being foolish. Surely...'

He placed a finger over her lips. 'I have tried. Everything I can think of. They are as secure in the nursery room as if they are in a fortress. Just as I feel safest when I am here. It upsets them when I come to visit them there, but it upset them even more when I insisted they dine with me, or spend time with me in the evenings, in the library or sitting room. We have grown so distant that we might as well be living in different houses. And yet they seem just as resistant to the idea of leaving for boarding school.' He frowned. 'Whether they love me or hate me, they cannot live for ever in that little room.'

'It will be all right,' she said, wondering if that were true. She doubted they could forgive the murder of their mother after just a few trips to the conservatory.

Murder, she reminded herself. That was why she was here, and this was a murderer, holding her close and pressing his lips to her skin. She should be repulsed by him, not attracted. She should be shuddering in revulsion at the touch of him. But instead she was trembling with emotions that she had not experienced before.

He was so gentle, with the plants, with the children, and sometimes even with her, that it was hard to keep a hold on the truth. For Timothy Colton was not what she had expected when she had come to this house. Perhaps she had been wrong all along, and the death truly had been an accidental fall.

'It will be all right.' He murmured her words back to her, as though to reassure her. 'When you say the words, Miss Collins, I almost believe it.' And then he laughed. 'Miss Collins, though you have been here for nearly a week, I do not even know your given name.'

'Daphne,' she whispered.

'Daphne,' he whispered back. 'A nymph fair enough to tempt Apollo. You are well named, then.'

'She became a laurel tree to escape him.' Daphne whispered the only piece of the legend she could remember.

He smiled. 'Then it is only natural that I should find you in my glasshouse.' And he kissed her again. He was exquisitely gentle, as though giving her credit for more innocence than she felt. He used the barest touches to part her lips, the lightest stroke of his tongue against hers and a featherlight touch of his hands on her waist.

She felt a stirring inside her. Perhaps it was passion. Or perhaps only a desire that he hold her this way for ever, kissing her with that same reverent intensity. Then she would not have to think about the past or the future. Only the moment. And the moment was incredibly sweet.

When he pulled away, he smiled. 'Did you appreciate the flowers?'

'Flowers?' Appreciate. And his choice of words triggered a blush.

He dropped his hands to his sides. 'Oh, dear. I thought, when you came here, that you had understood my message. And that the visit was related...' And now, he looked quite thoroughly embarrassed. 'Please forgive me, for my actions were incredibly forward, if you did not mean... And even if you did, I should not have...' His words trailed away, and he put his hand to his temple and closed his eyes as though he would wish himself out of the room.

She stared in amazement. The man in the study who threatened her honour had been naught but a paper tiger. The man before her now had given a few gentle kisses, and was embarrassed at his own forwardness.

She touched her fingers to her lips. Perhaps he was not all paper. For there was resolve behind the gentleness. When he chose to, he had proved himself to be quite commanding. 'I liked your flowers very much. But I had forgotten how a visit to the conservatory might appear to you.'

And now he looked horrified that he had kissed her and was preparing another apology. Was this the man she was convinced was a killer?

She gave him her best society smile, that had captured the attention of half the men in London, and got her into so much trouble that she was sent off to rusticate. She hoped, if used judiciously on a single gentleman, that it would not do any harm. 'But I am not overly bothered by your misunderstanding me.'

'That is good.' His smile was more of a grin and really quite charming. 'A great relief, actually. I was momentarily overcome with the progress you had made with the children. And your presence as well—' He stopped. 'And you do not mind if we all dine together, this evening?'

'I should think it the most natural thing in the world.'

'Very well, then. Until this evening.' He bowed to her with none of the stiffness he had shown on her arrival. She curtsied in response, and it came off as a rather playful bob, and nothing like what was appropriate for one's employer.

But she doubted that it would matter much longer.

Tim watched, through the glass doors, as she went down the hall and up the main stairs towards the nursery suite. The turn of events had been surprising, but most welcome. Clearly, the woman was an experienced governess in many things that mattered more than giving lessons and maintaining order. He had never been so glad to be mistaken in his life. He owed her more apologies than his simple bouquet had offered. There were not enough flowers in the house to convey his shame at the way he had treated her. And, in retrospect, the scene in the study had been beyond mortifying.

And a dark voice within him whispered, *'You no longer want her?'*

Of course he did. For she was most beautiful. He had not forgotten the lure of her flesh, nor ceased to imagine their joining. But there were other methods to achieve the ultimate goal than brute force. He could court her in a normal way, slowly and gently. She got on well with the children, which was very important. He could behave as a gentleman and make her a proper offer. If she found him worthy, then she might accept. And there would be no impediment to making the kind of marriage he had always wanted.

'No impediment, now you have got rid of Clarissa.'

He pushed his knuckles against his temples, as

though the pressure could silence the words ringing in his head.

'Are you going to tell her what kind of man you are, before the wedding? Or do you mean to surprise her some night when she has angered you?'

He could feel the cold sweat upon his forehead as he struggled with the memories of his first wife. He would never hurt Daphne. She was nothing like Clare.

'The woman is different, but you have not changed. If it could happen once...'

He shook his head, because he did not want to believe. He had always been so sure of his temper. Positive that intellect conquered impulse, and moderation was more powerful than violence. And then, everything had changed.

And now, he could not be sure of anything, ever again.

Chapter Nine

Dinner was a strained affair, and not at all what she had been expecting after the time in the conservatory. Daphne took care with her appearance, not wishing to seem too eager to please her employer. There was always a chance that she had misunderstood the depth of his interest, for he had the most mercurial nature of any man she had met.

But he had kissed her.

She closed her eyes, remembering the feel of his lips. They had not been the most passionate kisses she had received. But then, most girls her age had not been kissed at all. She should have no cause for comparison. After the sudden salute upon the lips, he had got control of himself and tried very hard to give her a near-perfect first kiss. He was hardly to blame if someone else had got there before him.

She put on a gown of sea-green silk that was beautiful but demure, and prepared herself for an evening of shy looks down the table. And remembering that she was still the governess, she made sure the children were scrubbed and ready before leading them in procession down the stairs and into the dining room.

The room was beautiful. The food was perfect. And the children excited, but polite and on their best behaviour.

It was only the host who was wrong. He had taken the time to dress to perfection in a coat of black superfine, a waistcoat of deep blue brocade and a shirt so white as to be blinding in comparison. Although she was no expert, she could see that his cravat was a masterpiece. His valet must have left the floor strewn with spoiled linen before getting it right.

But the man in the suit was as different as his clothes. He was not the hot-tempered Lord Colton that she had met upon arrival, nor the warm Timothy Colton of the afternoon. This man was as cool towards her as a stranger might have been. He would not meet her eyes, seeming to be most concerned with the children and their happiness.

He treated Daphne as though she were the governess. Invisible. Just as she had wanted from the first. The fact might have been laughable had it not been so frustratingly unexpected.

The children felt the change as well, and grew more quiet and reserved as the meal went on. Her host threw aside his napkin in frustration long before the dessert course and retired, claiming illness. She and the children finished the meal in silence and returned to the nursery to prepare for bed.

It was a disaster that undid much of the progress of the last few days. Daphne frowned. Perhaps it was all too much, too soon. It had left the children overwhelmed. But she was hard pressed not to lay the failure at the feet of the one responsible: Lord Timothy Colton. It had been his sudden foul mood that had spoiled everything. The children decided to take the next day's meals back in the nursery, and returned to their usual study habits. There was very little she could do about it.

She attempted to beard the lion in his den, going down to the conservatory without the children to demand an explanation. But she found only the occasional gardener, or under-gardener, tending to the plants at the instruction of his lordship. The man in question was by turns riding, resting, walking the grounds or missing. He was avoiding both her and the children.

Had something happened to change him profoundly, between four in the afternoon and six in the evening?

She doubted it. The thing that had changed them all had happened months ago, on the night that Clare had died. Unless she managed to exorcise the malevolence, there was little chance of lasting happiness for any of them. So she returned to her original intention of solving the mystery. There were still rooms unsearched, and questions unanswered.

After lunch on the next day, she made sure the children were settled and took herself to the ground floor.

It was there that Mrs Sims found her, one hand upon a desk drawer knob in the library.

'Was there something you needed, Miss Collins?' The woman seemed surprised to find her there.

Daphne struggled a moment for a plausible answer, moving her hand out from beneath the desk. 'I'd come to see if there was another pot of ink that I might borrow, to write some letters. The one in the schoolroom is thinner than I normally use. But while I am here, there is something that you might help with. It is almost embarrassing to ask, after all this time.'

'There is no need to be embarrassed, Miss Collins. I will help, if I can.'

Daphne gave her a relieved smile. 'It is a small thing, really. I have spent so much time above stairs with the children that I am barely acquainted with the common rooms. A stranger who had stopped to see the grounds would know more about the house than I do.'

Mrs Sims smiled in return, to find the request so small. 'You would like a tour of the house.'

'If you are not too busy. The children are so good with their studies, and so obedient. They do not need me for several hours at least.'

Mrs Sims was obviously surprised at their transformed character. But then she said, 'You have done much to help them. They are good children by nature, just as their father was.' And she launched into a story of how things used to be, when the children haunted the library they were standing in, rather than hiding above.

They moved from library, to drawing room, to

morning room, and in each Mrs Sims seemed to have a story about the master or the children and how things used to be. Daphne observed carefully, but had to admit that there was little to see. The rooms were orderly. Nothing about them made her suspect that she would find secrets in the drawers, concealed panels or any other gothic nonsense.

The only thing absent from Mrs Sims's narrative was mention of the previous mistress. Apparently, the decoration of the rooms had been done by Lord Colton's mother, classically but simply. In her twelve years Clare had left it unchanged. Daphne remembered the Colton town house, which she had visited frequently. It had been in the first stare of fashion, and Clare always seemed to be changing the silk on the walls, the rugs or the furniture, to reflect any passing trend or fancy.

Of course, in all the visits Daphne had not met Lord Colton, or heard anything but unflattering commentary about him, his house and Wales in general. None of those things was as important to Clare as the fact that she be seen in the best places, with the best people, dressed in the height of fashion.

Mrs Sims was walking Daphne back towards the nursery, and they passed the bedroom that she was sure must have belonged to Clare. She could imagine what she would see there. It would be decorated as the town house had been, totally out of step with the stately pace of the rest of the house, to suit the changing taste of the occupant. But there was no good way to request a tour of it.

She glanced at the waist of the housekeeper, walking

just ahead of her. The ring of keys hanging there probably contained the solution to her problem. And as if it was a sign from heaven, the knot holding them in place appeared to be loose.

The temptation was too much to resist. 'Mrs Sims?'

The woman stopped and turned back to her with a questioning look.

Daphne pointed to a large oil on the wall. 'I have been walking past this portrait, every morning, and wondering who it might be. Did Lord Colton have a brother?'

Mrs Sims launched into another, rather animated description of the subject, Tim's father, who had been plain Mr Colton, living here until his death. It had been the death of a distant cousin that had brought the title…

Daphne stood just behind the woman, as though admiring the portrait over her shoulder. She gave the slightest tug on the ribbon that held the keyring. She could feel the keys beneath her fingers begin to slip. And with a move worthy of a London cutpurse, she collected them in her hand without so much as a jingle, and drew them slowly away, stuffing them into her own pocket.

The housekeeper was so involved in her story that she did not feel the change. Daphne kept up the pretence of interested questions before admitting that it was time for her to return to the children, but thanking Mrs Sims most sincerely for her wealth of information.

She stayed long enough with the children to be sure

that she was not needed, and then checked the hall
again. The old servant had returned below stairs, and
the way was clear for her to visit her cousin's room.
She looked both ways, up and down the hall, before
proceeding quietly to the room at the end. What explanation should she give, if she was seen entering? She
could think of nothing. Perhaps something concerning
the children. Although what they would want from their
late mother's room, she had no idea.

She tested the door again, and found it still locked.
Then she removed the purloined keys from the folds of
her dress. She fitted them quickly into the lock, one at a
time, until she came to the one that turned the mechan-
ism. Opening the door, she slipped inside and closed it
silently behind her.

The room was dark, for the curtains had been drawn
to keep the sun from damaging the furnishings. But
there were no holland covers over them, and no layer of
dust. It was all neatly kept with the bed smooth and well
made, as though the mistress would be returning shortly.
It was an attractive room as well, with pale green silk
on the wall to match the hangings on the bed.

Daphne swallowed a wave of sadness. They matched
the light in Clare's green eyes as well. She could imagine her cousin choosing the colours that would show her
beauty to best advantage, sitting at the dressing table
as a maid fixed ribbons in her beautiful red hair.

And then she remembered the disturbing pictures that
Sophie drew and shuddered involuntarily. Clare would
never sit at this table again. And however horrible she
might have been to the people closest to her, she had

been kind to Daphne. The death of one so full of energy resonated deeply with her, as though she had lost a part of her own life.

She glanced quickly around the room as her eyes adjusted to the dim light coming from the cracks in the curtains. Then she hurried to the wardrobe, and flung open the doors to see the gowns neatly arranged, and in the bright colours that Clare had loved so well. Each drawer she opened was the same: an intimate glance into the life of her cousin, and a reminder of how suddenly and unexpectedly it had ended.

The jewel box was still sitting on the dresser. She found it odd. Tim should have taken the thing and locked it away to avoid tempting the servants. But no, when she popped the lid the necklaces, rings and ear drops lay forgotten in sparkling perfection on the velvet.

And beneath them was a small bundle of letters, tied with a ribbon.

She untied it quickly and drew the first out, stepping closer to the window to read.

My darling Clarissa,
I know I must not see you. Even writing is wrong. But how can I bear this torture? I long for a taste of your lips, the perfection of your breasts in my hands, the feel of your body when you yield to me and your cries of passion in my ears…

Oh, dear Lord.
Her hands trembled as she read the letters, and then her body, for they were more shocking than anything

she had read or seen before. On reading them, there was
no doubt what had been occurring. It was all described
in detail for her. As she read, the room grew hot and
her clothes constricting, as though her body was licked
with the flames of someone else's passion.

Each letter, in the same masculine hand.

And each one signed, Adam.

Was Adam the Duke of Bellston's given name? It
had to be, for it proved so much. The reason for the
estrangement between the houses. The reason for Lord
Colton's jealousy. And for Clare's untimely death. It
had been wrong of Clare, so horribly foolish, to openly
betray her husband. But wrong of the Duke as well to
betray a friend.

Perhaps, if there had been love between the two, she
could understand. She read on, searching the pages for
some sign that the relationship had been more than what
it appeared. But he said nothing of love, just the torment of a man nearly demented with desire, and graphic
descriptions of their adulterous coupling.

Seeing the words felt…wrong. She knew they were
not meant for her eyes. But still, she was driven by curiosity. If there was a truth to be revealed in the letters,
she would not find it by shying away from them.

Or perhaps her desire to read was merely voyeurism.
It made her feel strange inside. Hot and trembling, and
eager. As she read them, she could not help but imagine
bare flesh and twining bodies, and to remember the feel
of the stolen kisses in Vauxhall Gardens and Simon's
stealthy hands playing at the bodice of her dress. What
would it be like to drive a man so mad with desire that

he would have reason to write her such letters? And to be so lost to decency that she would save them, and pore over them, reliving each illicit moment?

And although she knew the words were not his, her mind turned to Timothy Colton. The dark look in his eyes when he saw her. The deep, smoky sound of his laugh. His hands and lips, as they might feel upon her body if he threw restraint aside.

She took a deep breath and dragged her eyes from the letters, refolded the papers, then thrust them deep into the pocket of her skirts. The contents showed her nothing she needed, other than the name at the bottom, which was the only thing of use. She could not very well show them to the Duchess. But perhaps, if the Duke knew what she had discovered, he would be willing to treat the matter of Clare's death more seriously.

She turned to the writing desk, and pulled open the little drawer to find stationery and more letters. Things from her and from the family. And some things in Clare's hand. Notes to herself, and letters begun and then forgotten. And thrust deep into the stack, with the ink smeared, as though it had been hidden while in progress.

My darling,
My marriage has grown intolerable, and my husband near to violence. Things cannot continue as they are. I fear for my safety. I mean to come to you, with the child which I know to be yours. If you cannot give me your love, at least offer me sanctuary…

This was even more serious than what had gone before. Had she truly been with child, or was it merely a ruse to gain the Duke's attention?

And if it was true…

An angry husband. And a lover, powerful, but recently married, who would have no desire to see his reputation sullied by a woman who would not quietly disappear once he was through with her. How easy would it have been to stand by and let her husband remove the problem, and then hide the truth from gratitude?

Or worse yet, to wait until an opportunity presented itself, and then remove the problem himself. To allow suspicion to fall on the man who had been wronged. Would it be better to let him hang for his wife's death, or would guilt prevent the murderer from going so far? Just as easy to spare the life of his old friend, but allow him to remain under the cloud of suspicion. For with Timothy Colton alive, no one would ever suspect…

'What the devil…?'

Light flooded the room, catching her, and she thrust the last letter into her pocket with the others. When she turned, the interruption had come not from the hall, but from a connecting door that lead to Tim Colton's room.

He was striding towards her, face contorted with fury. 'You. I was a fool to have trusted you, to be swayed by recent events. I knew there was something wrong and chose to ignore it.' He saw her withdrawing her hand from the fold of her skirts. 'Here, thief, what did you just put in your pocket?'

She reached in quickly and grasped the ring of keys that she had taken, holding them out to him.

He caught her by the wrist. 'And what did you mean to do with those?'

'I found them,' she lied. 'On the rug in the hallway. And I meant to return them.'

'But the owner is not in this room, as you well know.' He caught her by the wrist and squeezed until the keyring dropped upon the rug. 'You had to see, didn't you? To come to this room, of all the rooms in the house.'

'The door was locked,' she said, knowing that it did not justify her behaviour.

'Because I wished it so. But you have had no respect for my wishes in the past, so why should it matter to you now?'

'It is only a room, just as the stairs are only stairs.'

'And they both hurt, do you understand? It hurts to be constantly reminded of her, and of what happened. To come across things, perfectly ordinary things, that dredge the memories to the surface. It hurts the children. And it hurts *me*.' And for a moment, it was as if she could see inside him, and the torment roiled there like black smoke, always just below the surface.

'And now that you have seen, are you satisfied? I did not keep my wife in chains, if that was what you thought. I was not hiding some dungeon behind a locked door. It is just a lady's bedroom. She had everything.' He threw open the door to the wardrobe, and swept the dresses on to the floor. 'Silk, satin, feathers and bows.' And then he turned, knocking the jewel case on to the floor to join the dresses, emeralds and pearls scattering across the carpet. 'And more jewels than a woman could wear in a lifetime. She treated it all as dross, and me as well.'

Then he turned back to her, and closed the distance between them.

She stepped backwards to get away, until the wide green bed blocked her retreat.

He grabbed her by the shoulders and pushed her back until she fell on her back into the softness of the satin counterpane. And he stood over her and laughed. 'You have found the thing she liked best about this room, although if you truly wish to know Clare, you must understand that she was never satisfied to lie alone.' He reached up and tugged at his cravat until the knot came free, then cast the thing aside. 'And now, perhaps it is time for you to take a lesson, instead of giving them.' And he fell upon her.

Her mind was swirling with a confusion of thoughts. It would be bad to be caught in this room by a murderer. But even worse if she had provoked an innocent man past the point of reason. She might have pushed a peaceful man to violence by her own actions. If she cried out now, no one would see him for what he had been, only for what he had become.

She could not do that to him, for she could not bear to think her foolish meddling would be the cause of more suffering.

His lips came down upon hers, and she opened her own to let him do as he wished. He used the opportunity to take her mouth, thrusting into it, his hand reaching to twist in her hair and force her to greater intimacy.

It was totally unlike the kiss in the conservatory had been, burning through her resistance, leaving her weak and helpless, and happy to be so.

When she did not fight him, he slowed to a gentle rhythm, exploring her, teasing, trying to provoke a response as his fingers crept into her hair, loosening pins until it fell free.

The bed was seductively soft, and he was spreading her hair upon it, combing with his fingers as though readying her for sleep. And when he released her lips, a sigh escaped them, as though she wished him to continue.

He felt her tremble under him, and whispered, 'Are you afraid? For you should be. Do you know what will happen to you if I do not stop?'

And Lord help her, she did. Every touch, every thrust, every feeling it might arouse had been laid out in the letters as though they were a primer for the act that was about to occur.

He leaned away from her, staring down as if in challenge, his smile just as cold as it had ever been, but the light in his eyes was blazing like a flame. 'Perhaps your silence is permission to continue.' He slid his hand from her hair, slowly down her throat, over her shoulder, to the swell of her breast, and stopped very deliberately, cupping the flesh in his palm.

She felt a surprising wash of warmth at the intimacy, and her body tingled to life. He must have seen the response in her eyes, for he gave a small, satisfied nod. 'What is it that you really wanted in coming to this room? Not what you are likely to get. Whatever it was, you are welcome to take it, after I am through with you. It means nothing to me.' And then he began to move his hands over her, squeezing, stroking, working with his fingertips, until she was sure he must feel the nipples, which had grown hard and sensitive under the fabric of her gown. His lips settled into the hollow of her throat, teeth and tongue against the soft flesh there, and her body gave a sudden shudder, as she began to wonder what it might be like to feel his mouth wetting the fabric of her dress, or against the bare skin. And without thinking, she brought a hand up to touch the back of his head, holding him against her. The satin of the counterpane was smooth and cool against her cheek, just as his lips were hard and hot. Her head was filling with visions of what had occurred here, and what was likely to occur, and, instead of fear, she felt a trembling eagerness. She heard the voice in her head that had always urged her on, when a sensible girl would have run for safety.

Then he found her lips again, thrusting with his tongue into her open mouth as his hands reached for her hips to clutch her to the growing hardness of his body.

Almost without thinking she rubbed against him, and let the desire stab through her, wild and uncontrollable. She kissed him back then, as roughly as he was kissing her. She bit at his lips, stroked his tongue with her own and dug her fingers into the linen of his shirt, feeling the muscles underneath bunching as they strained to pull her closer. He straddled her, pinning her to the bed. Inside her skirts, her legs had parted, ready to receive him, and he steadied her hips, holding them against his erection so that he could enjoy the way that she rocked against him.

Desire was growing in her and her body grew wet as she arched against him. But the strange friction of bodies in clothes was not enough. She wanted more from him, all of him. He could take what he wanted, whatever he wanted, as long as he ended the torment of expectation.

His hand slipped into the slit in her skirt that gave access to her pocket, and she gave a shuddering gasp, knowing that his hand was even closer to her body, bringing her closer to the relief that she knew was coming.

But then, there was a crackle of parchment, and his fingers closed on the bundle of letters and drew them out. He leaned away from her and unfolded the first, taking only a glance at it before he jumped off the bed away from her, as though contact burned him. He stared down at her in horror. 'This is what they sent you for? Could they not have just asked? Do they think so little of me that we must play games over this? Will it never end? God help me, haven't I suffered enough?' He stared down at the pages in his hand and shook his head, then he stared back at her with eyes empty of emotion. 'You needn't have bothered. Now that I have them, I will deal with the things, then I will return to deal with you.'

Then he turned and stalked from the room.

Chapter Ten

For a moment Daphne fought the urge to run after him, to seize the letters from his hand and destroy them before he read them. For no matter what he had done, did he deserve to see their contents and to know the truth in such detail?

He spoke of suffering. And suddenly, she was acutely aware of how he must have felt to know that his friend and wife were together, doing what they had done.

And if her latest suspicions were correct, and it was the Duke who was guilty of Clare's death?

Without knowing it, she had fallen in league with the very people she sought to punish. She was helping her cousin's murderer escape justice. And by raking up the past, she was torturing an innocent man.

She could not imagine the Duchess perpetrating a fraud to protect her husband. The woman seemed decent and acting out of care for the children. But without having met the Duke, it was hard to know the truth about him. He might be a veritable demon, with a wife as innocent of this crime as Clare's husband had been.

Daphne stood up, still trembling from the rise and fall of the tide of emotions within her. And looked into the mirror on the dresser, to straighten her hair and clothing.

Clare's mirror.

At one time, it might have given her girlish pleasure to visit the room of her cousin, to see the gowns she had worn, the jewellery box she had spoken of, and to try some of the things on while looking into this same mirror.

But she had seen too much of Clare today. The truth had spoiled the fantasy she'd carried with her all these months. Timothy Colton was right. Clarissa had been vain and spoilt. Her husband was not the homely dullard she had claimed. After meeting him, she found it easier to believe the housekeeper. That whatever had happened on that fateful night, he had once been an ordinary man, pushed beyond his boundaries by his wife's scandalous behaviour.

But if that was true, than what did it say of Clare's influence on her?

She closed her eyes and tried to remember how it had been, before her cousin had taken a special interest in her coming out. Her parents had been more co-operative, certainly. They had all but doted on her, and called her the sweetest of daughters. She had been the apple of her father's eye, and a delight to her brothers, no matter how they had teased her.

But then her mother had decided that she needed to cast off her hoydenish ways and learn to behave like a proper lady of the *ton*. And she had encouraged the association with Clare, saying that it would give Daphne polish. The family had welcomed the money that Clare offered to outfit her for the Season. For with three brothers to establish, there was very little left when it came time to launch their only daughter. And Daphne had relished the connection for the freedoms it brought.

But after that point, her parents seemed for ever cross with her. They did not like the fact that Clare allowed her to drink champagne, nor that she always seemed to take it in excess, talking too loudly and behaving foolishly. They did not approve of the hours she kept, nor the company, nor the gowns that Clare helped her to choose.

And now she understood why her forays into Vauxhall Gardens after Clare's death had been the last straw. She had been becoming every bit as bad as they said, and had been too wilful to see the truth.

Daphne put down the brush she had borrowed and hurried out the door, closing and locking it behind her. Then she walked down the hall, trying to keep her pace unhurried, although the calm felt unnatural to her. At any moment, Lord Colton could appear and reveal all. Ahead of her in the hall, the housekeeper was looking carefully at the ground, probably retracing her steps through the afternoon. 'Mrs Sims. At last.' She put on a triumphant smile, and held the ring of keys out to the woman, who responded with an even more relieved expression. 'I found them on the floor near the school-room, after you had gone.'

'And I have been looking all over for them. Thank you, miss, for returning them to me. I would hate for the master to find out how careless I had been.'

Daphne managed a stiff nod and insisted that it was hardly a matter of concern. She suspected, if anyone in the household had reason to fear the master's reaction to the stolen keys, the blame would not rest on the poor housekeeper.

Tim paced nervously across the rug in the Bellston receiving room, then sat and tapped his foot. The gallop to his neighbour's house had cooled his desire to deal immediately with the false governess. But it had done nothing to settle his nerves, or to prepare him for the confrontation with Adam. After all this time Tim did not know whether to be angry for what had happened, or hurt by it.

He might be willing to let the evidence of infidelity pass, as he had meant to before Clare had died. What was done could not be undone. But that Adam should use such devious methods to gain the letters was a fresh injury, perhaps more hurtful than the initial betrayal. Tim would have given up the letters freely, if the Duke had wished for them back. Even with the estrangement between them, theft should not have been necessary.

And to involve the children by placing a spy in the nursery? He shook his head in disgust. Adam knew how important the children were to him, and how fragile.

That he would toy with them to achieve what he could have got with honesty made Tim's skin crawl with revulsion.

And shame as well, that the Duke and Duchess should know his reaction to the girl. She must have been reporting to her masters how easily she had ensnared him. Despite the truths he had learned today, he still felt an undercurrent of desire for her. It defied all logic. A sane man should not be wishing to lie back down with her and finish what he had started, even knowing that it was all a sham.

From the doorway there came a nervous throat clearing that he recognised as a habit of his oldest friend. Tim turned to it and rose, offering a formal bow, and muttering, 'Your Grace.'

Adam strode into the room and answered, 'Leave off with that nonsense, Tim, and tell me what has brought you here.' He offered a hand, which Tim chose to ignore, and then said, 'I suppose it was too much to hope that this was a social visit after all this time.'

'I think you know what it is about.'

'In truth, I do not.' And his friend did look honestly puzzled. 'It is not that you are not welcome, of course. Sit, please.' Adam's gestures were as nervous as his own, as he moved to a chair by the fire. 'Brandy. No. It is too early of course. Tea? Can I—'

'I do not mean to stay for long. I came to give you these, since you seem to wish their return.' He reached into his coat and withdrew the packet, thrusting it at Adam.

The Duke took the letters from him, his puzzlement

still in evidence. And he opened them. It was clear that it took only a word or two for him to recognise his own writing, for his pale skin blanched to deathly white, and his grasp loosened, as he let the letters slip to the floor. 'Oh, dear God. I had forgotten.'

'Had you, now?' Tim folded his arms in scepticism.

'If I'd remembered…if I'd even thought the things still existed…' He held out his hands in a gesture of hopelessness. 'I'd have looked for them after she died, when I was in the house. But it did not seem important at the time.' His eyes dropped from Tim's and he stooped to gather the papers. Then he threw them into the fire, seizing a poker and jabbing at the things as though he feared that they would leap out of the flames to torment him further. When he was satisfied that they were destroyed, he looked to Tim again. 'I am sorry that I ever wrote the damn things. I was a hundred kinds of fool back then.' He stared down at the poker in his hand, his knuckles going white against the metal, and then he threw it against the flagstones of the hearth.

'If you wanted them back, you had but to ask.' Tim said it softly, surprised that he could not find more fault with the man, for he knew well what fools men made of themselves once Clare had tangled them in her net.

'Want them?' Adam laughed. 'I had hoped, now that she was gone, that it was well and truly over. And I need never think of that time again. And now, this…' He looked to Tim again. 'I am sorry.'

'The governess found them.'

'Governess? You have retained a governess?' Once

again, his friend seemed without a clue, and his befud-
dlement almost made Tim smile. Either he was blame-
less, or a much better actor then he had been when he'd
bedded Clare. It had been easy enough to see the truth
then, no matter how Adam tried to hide it.

'Your wife hired her for me.'

Adam looked alarmed by the idea. 'She acted without my knowledge or permission. After our last talk on
the day of the funeral, you made it clear that you did
not want or need my assistance.' Adam looked ever so
slightly hurt by the memory. That argument had been the
last coffin nail in their friendship. 'I told Penny to leave
you in peace. But my wife refused to believe that your
edict applied to her.' He gave a kind of helpless shrug,
as though to say that his wife was a law unto herself. 'I
have no problem with her visiting you, of course.'

'You do not?' Tim shot him another sceptical smile.
For when Adam had first married, he had been surprisingly possessive of his new bride.

'Because I know I have nothing to fear. I would trust
Penny with my life. And if she is welcome in your house,
than she may visit with my blessing.' He frowned. 'But
if she comes to meddle in your affairs, I will try to dis-
courage her from troubling you.'

Since it was doubtful that Penny could be discouraged, once she set her mind to a thing, Tim only
smiled. 'She seems to think that I cannot manage without help. And she has told me I must take it, whether I
want it or no.'

'Well, Penny would think that. She is quite preoc-
cupied with the idea of children, now that her book is

finished. Since she has none of her own, she is most interested in yours. If she is not increasing soon, I suspect that she will come to your house and teach them herself.' And Adam smiled fondly at the thought.

'So you do not think that there was any hidden motive in her sending Miss Collins to search for these?'

'Penny have a hidden motive?' And now his friend did laugh. 'My darling wife is not one to hide her feelings in subtlety and guile. Perhaps my life would be quieter, were it so. Although not as interesting, I am sure. No, Tim. If Penny had wished to see the damn things, she would have marched to your house and demanded you give them to her. Then she would have brought them back to lay at my feet, and given me no end of grief for my foolishness.'

'She knew of the letters?'

'I told her of their existence, before your wife died. Clare was threatening me with them. I thought it would be better for Penny to know the whole truth than to be surprised by it later. And then I swore that there would be no more nonsense of that sort, and that she would have no reason to doubt me. And I have been true to my word.' There was a pride in his voice, and a peace that had been absent in the days when Clare had been alive. 'If it is any consolation to you, Tim, I am a better man, now that I have Penny. If there were a way to turn back the clock, and live the past over again, it would be different between us.'

Tim sighed. 'To my eyes, it would have been much the same. Perhaps the identity of her lover would have been different, but Clare would not have changed. And I would now be sitting in another friend's drawing room, with letters very similar to the ones you destroyed.'

Adam touched his hand to his forehead, as though pained. 'You are probably right. She would have found some way to torment you. Only her death prevented her from making more trouble than she already had.' And he looked Tim square in the eye, as if to say what they were both thinking.

Do not punish yourself. We are all glad to see her gone.

Tim swallowed the shame of it. For there was comfort in remembering that, hell though his life might be, it was better without Clarissa than it had been with her. The children were better off without her. And his friend looked happier as well. Marriage had settled Adam, changing him for the better. But would he have fared as well, had Clarissa been there, attempting to insinuate herself into the union?

Adam cleared his throat again. 'About the letters. I was an idiot. I freely admit it. I cared about them only to the extent that their existence hurt those around me. If there had been any way to spare you this trip?' He shrugged. 'But I did not send a girl to your house to hunt after them, if that is what you feared. I'd like to think that, had I wanted them, I could have come to you, called upon our old friendship and asked for them openly.'

Tim felt something loosen in his chest, and a modicum of relief. 'And I'd have given them to you, of course.'

Adam seemed to relax as well. 'And now they are

gone. Neither of us need worry about the past, for it shall not be repeated, nor mentioned again.' Adam paused, and then glanced away, as though his next words meant nothing. 'I don't suppose, while you are here, that you would be interested in a game of chess? It is rather early in the day for games. And if you are busy...'

Tim replied a little stiffly, 'I had thought, after what happened to my wife, and the accompanying scandal, that you would not wish to entertain me in your home. You are the law in these parts. And I am...' He hesitated to say the word aloud.

'An old friend,' finished the Duke. 'A very old friend. Who would have been invited back into my home sooner, had I thought you would come. But now that you are here...'

Tim hesitated. There was still the damn governess to be dealt with. For if Adam had not sent her, then who?

But let the girl suffer, waiting for his arrival. Perhaps if he tarried here, she would have the good sense to run and he might never need to see her again. His reactions to her were too volatile to be predicted or encouraged. And he was tired of being passion's fool. So he shrugged to his old friend, as nonchalant as Adam had been. 'A game of chess would not go amiss. The plants will grow, even if I am not there to watch them.'

Adam grinned back at him. 'I would never know it, the way you shut yourself up in that glasshouse. Come to the study, then. The board is set, and I have nothing so pressing that I cannot set it aside for a game.'

* * *

Tim's smile faded as he walked into the entrance hall of his home. It had been a surprisingly pleasant afternoon, probably because he had got away from the past. Afternoon had turned to evening and dinner with Adam and his wife. It had grown late, and he'd been forced to ride home in darkness. It was good that he knew the old paths as well as he did, for once the sun set, there was little light from the sliver of a moon, and the growing bank of rain clouds that threatened to obscure it.

For a few hours, he'd felt almost like his old self. Then his cheerful mood had begun to fade. For he was home. There, in front of him, were the damn stairs. And, as always, the ghostly image appeared in his mind of Clare broken on the floor before him.

He turned deliberately from it, refusing to be put out of his own home by an unpleasant memory. Perhaps he did not deserve to be happy, as he once had been. But there was little he could do about it. It was foolish to start and stare at nothing, like a coward, or, worse yet, a madman, whenever he crossed his own hall.

He disguised his hesitation in care for his outer wear, tossing the coat and hat over a nearby bench so that a servant could collect it in the morning. He took a moment to brush at his clothes as he steeled his nerves. Then he turned back to the main staircase and felt his will falter as the weight on his spirit increased. The servants' stairs were just down the hall, ready and waiting for him.

But he looked up to see the governess, waiting in total stillness at the top of the stairs. She was dressed for bed, barefoot on the marble. His arrival had surprised her. She must have thought if she did not move he would not notice her.

He smiled, and remembered his discovery of her in the afternoon. *Too late for that, my dear. From now on, I will watch your every move.* She might pretend that she had the best interests of the children at heart, but what purpose did she have to search bedrooms and creep about the house when all were in bed? If Adam had not sent her, nor Penny, then who? It made no sense to think that without motive or direction, she would go unerringly to the source of so many problems and secrete it about her person.

His anger conquered his fear, and he started up the stairs, focusing on her eyes as he climbed. The truth was hidden in them, if he could manage to dislodge it. She'd lacked the sense to flee the house this afternoon, when he'd given her the chance. And now she would answer to him for what she had done.

As he stared at her, he was pleased to see her fidget. Did it bother her to be a thief and a spy? He certainly hoped so. The crime was not so grave as some. If it was only against him, he would have turned her out without a thought.

But to deceive his children, and to allow them to trust her and to become fond of her? It was an act that could not be so easily forgiven.

So he intensified his gaze upon her, and added a cold smile. He could see the hairs out of place from their tussle on the bed, and the slightly swollen look of her mouth from the kisses he had given her. She had not fought him then, had she? Probably too embarrassed by his discovery of her snooping, and wishing she could distract him from the truth. And she very nearly had.

Or, perhaps it was more than that. He could see her eyes grow large and dark at his approach, and hear a slight hitch in her breath. Was she frightened, or was that desire he saw, when he looked into those deep green eyes? And then she bit her lip in an unconscious gesture of indecision. He felt his body respond to the naïve sensuality of it. It had to be a ruse. She must know how easily she could control him and was testing the strength of her attraction.

It was to be a battle, then, to see who could uncover the truth about the other. And at what cost.

'Miss Collins,' he said, and watched her start. 'I have returned to continue our conversation. But perhaps the top of the stairs is not the best place, for you know how treacherous stairs can be.'

Chapter Eleven

Daphne felt her chest tighten with fear. Of all the places to meet him, why must it be the dark heart of the house, on the very spot where Clare had fallen? And if he was as innocent of that as she suspected, then why did he climb the stairs like a guilty man? She reached out and put her hand on the banister to steady herself.

He looked at it and laughed, stepping dangerously close to her and placing his own hand over hers. 'Frightened?'

She stared back into his eyes, wondering what had happened to the gentle man from the conservatory. 'Should I be?'

'An innocent governess would have no reason to be afraid. But then I doubt that an innocent would be sneaking around the house in her nightclothes.'

'I got up to check on the children.' That was true. For

she had felt a storm in the air, and been restless enough to come downstairs to make sure they slept well.

'The nursery is far down the hall. What reason did you have to be on the main stairs?'

The children had brought her down from her room. But the knowledge that the lord of the house had not returned from his errand was enough to keep her there. She swallowed and said nothing. But as she looked into the face of the man next to her, she suspected he knew the truth.

He sneered. 'If you wish to search my room, it is just behind you, right next to Clare's.'

'I have already done so. Since you were not in the house, I meant to go downstairs to search your study.'

He laughed, as though admiring her impudence. 'You are caught in the very act of disturbing my peace. And you show no remorse at all. Who set you upon me, and how much are they paying you? If it is money you want, I will pay you twice as much to pack your things and go.'

'There is no one else. No conspiracy to trap you.' She stared at him, searching for the man inside. 'Only me.'

'Only you.' The thought seemed to amuse him, as though he had found himself worrying at a shadow. He wrapped his fingers around her wrist, gently, as if to show her that on a moment's notice he could yank security away from her, leaving her helpless at the top of the stairs. 'Then what do you want from me? And what are you willing to do to get it? For I grow tired with you snooping through the corners of my life.'

'I want the truth. I want to know what really happened, the night your wife died.'

'Is that all?' He laughed as though she had said something funny, released her wrist and reached for a handkerchief to wipe away the tears of mirth forming in the corners of his eyes. 'And you go to such elaborate ends to gain the truth. You come into my home. Insinuate yourself into my family. Sneak from room to room, poking through our things. If you wanted the truth, you need only have asked.'

'And you would have given it to me?' Now it was her turn to smile in scepticism.

'I don't think you understand what a burden the truth can be, or the price you must pay to gain it. If you knew, you would not seek. And when you know it, I doubt you will find satisfaction.'

'But I want to know, all the same. And I will not stop until I have discovered it.'

'You want to know,' he mocked. 'Very well. Your search is over. I will tell you everything.'

A thrill went through her. For a moment, she thought she had bested him. And then she saw the look in his eyes.

'I will tell you, later. In your room. After we are finished. The time is long past when I'd have given you the truth without something in return for the trouble you have caused here.'

He was staring at her with a hungry smile that delved into her, grasping and stroking. He was waiting for her to cry off. Expecting her fear to be greater than her curiosity.

But her heart was hammering in her chest, for so many reasons. She was on the edge of a great truth, and he held the key to it all. And what was common sense, in the face of it? She should be insulted by his suggestion, just as he wished her to be. She should tell her father and her brothers. They would call the man out for it. Or run to the safety of the housekeeper, and leave on the first mail coach in the morning. She could let all know that Lord Timothy Colton was as horrible as he wished people to believe.

Or she could remain silent, tell no one and let him have what he wanted. She would finally know the answer to the question that had been haunting her for months: what had really happened to her cousin? And, more importantly, she would learn who the real Timothy Colton was and what his part had been.

When their lips met, she knew that she already belonged to him, no matter what might happen. If there was a chance that she could bring him back to being the man who had kissed her in the conservatory, then she wanted to try.

'Very well,' she said softly.

And for a moment, she saw the look in his eyes falter. Perhaps it had all been a bluff to frighten her. At his heart, he did not want her. Not in this way. But then his doubt was replaced by suspicion, and desire overcame all. 'Now is as good a time as any. Lead me there.'

'You know the way. You have been there before, have you not?'

The gleam in his eye faltered again. It was as if she had struck a wolf upon the nose, and for a moment, turned him into a dog. She turned her back to him, before she could see the wolf return, and walked ahead of him, down the landing to the servants' stairs. It was dark, and she had left her candle on a table in the hall. She did not bother to light another, feeling her way up the stairs, towards the door at the top.

She could hear his footsteps on the stairs behind her and felt the dread in her growing. Suppose she was wrong and he was the brute she had once thought. She would be giving him the chance to abuse her, as he had Clare, to use her for his own amusement. It might all be a trick, and she would be no wiser for it than before. She knew that she should turn and confront him. Tell him that she had changed her mind. If she did it before they reached the door at the top, would he retreat or simply force her backwards into her room? She suspected it was the former. For after coming to know him, she could not believe that he was as wicked as he liked to pretend.

But if she did nothing?

Once they were in the room and the door was closed it would be too late to cry off, should she find that she could not follow through with what she had promised. And yet she kept walking, listening to the steady pace of his steps behind her, glad that he could not see her tremble. When they reached the room she entered, leaving the door open behind her. She turned to face him, but could see nothing in the utter darkness of her room.

'I should not be here.' It was easier without the sight of his haunted, angry eyes. For his voice told her he was as frightened by what was happening as she was. 'Why do you not send me away?'

When she did not answer him she heard him take a sudden step forwards, and she caught her breath in a gasp.

'Do you mean to scream, then? Perhaps it will bring the servants, and I will stop. Or you could run from me and from this house, as I have asked you to do before now. It is not too late to run.' His voice was low and inviting, as he reached out and tugged at the belt that held her wrapper, pushing it open and off her shoulders, letting it fall to the floor. 'But then, you will never know the truth.'

It was wrong of him to stay, but she did not want to send him away. Now that he was so close to her, she could not seem to find her voice to say anything at all. She could smell the spicy sweetness of the flowers he had given her, still scenting the air.

But he brought his head inches from her body, inhaling deeply so that she could feel his breath changing the air against her throat. It was as though he wished for nothing more than the scent of her. And then he whispered, 'You will not speak? Very well, then. But, if you do not stop me, I will not stop myself.'

Where she should have felt fear, she felt an odd excitement. And instead of pushing him away, she arched her neck and leaned closer to offer herself to him, until his lips touched her skin.

His hand snaked around her neck and he lifted his face to hers, forcing her mouth open to accept his kiss. There was none of the tenderness from the conservatory, or even the cool lust she'd felt from him in Clarissa's bedroom, as he'd awakened desire in her.

There was just a relentless thrusting with his tongue, to prove his possession over her mouth and the rest of her. He kissed her until her body felt weak and helpless in his arms, wet and hot and as open as her mouth.

His hand dropped to the neck of her gown, and in one smooth move he ripped the thing from throat to hem, then pulled it away from her to leave her standing bare in front of him in the darkness. And then he paused. 'Scream, damn you. Don't you realise what is happening? Make me stop this.' She heard him cast the rag to the floor as he seized one of her breasts, kneading it hard. His fingers caught the nipple, rolling and pinching, and the arousal coursed like a stream through her entire body.

She realised in shock that she had reached up with her own hand to copy his movements in her other breast, to magnify the feeling. Instead of a scream, she let out a low moan of pleasure.

His hand dropped away and he was breathing heavily, as though he had just run a great distance. Then he let out a low curse and stepped away.

For a moment, she heard nothing. Then, there was the sound of her door closing, the rustle of clothing dropped on the floor and the thump of boots. She was blind in the darkness, straining to hear his approach. But there was nothing. She was alone in the dark, cold and frightened of what might occur next.

Suddenly, his mouth closed over the slope of her shoulder. She felt his teeth graze the skin and the pressure as he sucked. Then it was over and he disappeared again. The sensations raced through her body, even after the contact stopped. She reached for him, longing to bring him back to her. But her hands met empty air.

He must have been able to see better in the dark than she, for he caught her hand in his and his lips touched her fingers, his tongue flicking the tips. And then he was gone again.

Only to return and run a fingernail down her spine, from nape to hip. It made her arch her back and thrust out her breasts until they met his outstretched hands.

He was playing a game with her. She did not know the rules or the object, or who might lose from it, but it must be a game. Or torture, she realised, as his hands disappeared and his lips touched the underside of her breast. This time she cried out in frustration when the kiss ended, and it made him laugh.

She was beginning to make out vague shapes in the darkness, and could see him standing before her. So she reached out and guided his head so that his mouth covered her nipple, forcing him to settle there for a time and suckle until the trembling began in her again. Then he pulled away.

She reached out again, and he stepped away from her, and murmured, 'Close your eyes.'

She did, and was shocked again at the increased intensity of the feeling, as his fingers brushed against the place where his lips had been. Then he disappeared again. She opened her eyes, searching for him, only to feel him behind her, pulling her body tight to his, the hair of his chest cushioning her shoulder blades, his sex pressing against her, his hands travelling easily over her body. His touch was stronger now, as he cupped her breasts and stroked her belly.

It was not fair. She could not touch him in return, and she found she needed to most desperately, to kiss and stroke as well. But he wrapped an arm around her shoulders and pinned her against his body as he made free with her, letting his other hand settle between her legs.

She started back at first, for this was even more exciting than his lips on her breast. He was exploring her, fingers touching, tracing, tickling and constantly returning to the place where he knew she was most sensitive. In response, she ground herself against the hardness behind her as though her body longed to pleasure him. It made his hand press even harder against her, rubbing against her until she could barely stand it. And then his fingers thrust into her, and it was more than she had ever felt, and yet still not enough. She was grinding against him now in uncontrollable ecstasy, her body wet and trembling, and could hear herself begging him, a desperate litany of, 'Oh, please, please, please…'

Perhaps he sought to stop her pleading, for he brought a hand to cover her lips, and she seized upon it, kissing the palm. She drew the fingers between her lips, running her tongue over them, and sucking them deep into her mouth.

And then, everything happened at once. He muttered an oath in a feverish voice that was as helpless as hers, then pushed her forwards, bending her over the foot-

board of her bed. Her weight rested on the hand between
her legs, which was spreading the entrance to her body,
readying her, guiding himself. And when he felt her
shudder under his hand, he plunged into her, over and
over, holding her steady, urging her on, until her will
broke under his and her body lost the last shred of control. She shook and spasmed; every nerve in her body
seemed to explode with the feeling of him taking her.
And the trembling, grasping feeling went on, and on,
until she felt it in him as well. After a final surge, his
movements slowed, and he pulled her upright, his arm
locked around her shoulder, and his face buried against
the damp hair on her neck. He was kissing her there,
pressing his lips to the flesh, sighing in satisfaction.

And she sagged against him, adoring the feel of his
arms around her, warm and strong. Holding her up,
holding her close, his body still in hers, possessing and
possessed. He was rubbing his cheek gently against her
skin, as though he revelled in the softness of it.

But then he sighed again. It was no longer satisfaction, but despair. And the friction of his cheek on her
body was his head shaking no, no, no, as though it was
possible to ward off what he knew was coming.

She remembered their bargain, wishing that it was
possible to call it back. But it was too late.

He whispered in her ear. 'You wanted the truth. Well,
you have certainly earned it, my dear. You have beaten
me at my own game. Very well played.'

She started away from him, trying to escape the
gentle caresses, and arms that had become a prison.

But he held her close, and whispered, in the same soft

voice. 'What happened the night my wife died is just what you suspect. After years of it, I could no longer stand her taunts and her public infidelities. And so I got stinking drunk and pushed the filthy whore down the stairs.'

Then his arms dropped to his sides and he pulled away from her. And the cold and emptiness of the house seemed to rush into her, filling her with the unbearable burden of the truth.

Chapter Twelve

Tim threw on his shirt, gathered the rest of his clothing into his arms and turned to make his escape. His descent down the first flight of stairs went easy enough. But with each passing step he could feel his legs begin to give way, his stomach churning. By the time he reached the ground floor he was running, down the hall, into the conservatory, slamming the door behind him.

He dropped the bundle on to the slate floor and rushed through the room to the tiny door at the back. He threw it open, dropped to his bare knees in the garden, and proceeded to be sick behind a shrubbery.

The storm had broken while he was in the attic room. He steadied himself on his hands, letting the rain run off his hair and soak his linen, feeling the mud on his knees and between his fingers.

That had not gone well.

It would have been laughable had it not been so

utterly pathetic on the surface and so horrible at the centre. What kind of man was he, if his first experience with a woman since his wife's death had reduced him to this?

But there was so much more than that involved. He had known that coupling with some willing female was not out of the question for him, if it was discreetly done and there was no real emotion involved. But he had thought to travel down to London and avail himself of the *demi-monde*, when the need grew great enough. Instead, he had all but forced himself upon a servant. He might try to persuade himself that she had gone willingly to her fate. But at its heart, that was a lie. He had tricked her into it. He'd offered a temptation too great to resist, in exchange for her virtue. And once they were alone, he had toyed with her until she begged him to do what he had done, so that he might not feel guilt for it later.

He shook the water from his hair and hung his head again, letting the coolness wash over him, wishing it would cool his blood so that he did not wish to do the thing again. She had been smooth and tight and wonderful, twisting and pushing against him, eager to be had.

Even now he was thinking of all the ways he wished to take her: the places, the positions, the frequency. One time, and she had made him a slave to sensation, with the boundless desires and energy of youth. Before, he thought he had wanted her beyond sanity. Beyond reason. And now it seemed he wanted her even more than that.

And she had given him no sign that she would deny

him. As he'd finished, he'd heard her soft sigh of pleasure and felt the way her hand reached back to absently stroke his flank in thanks. He had done the unthinkable. But she was not afraid. She was not hurt, or angry, or shocked, or revolted. She was welcoming, her head lolling upon his shoulder, her body still close to his as though she felt protected. And without wishing it, he was aroused again.

And so he had sought to wipe it all away, to drive her from him before he treated her as he had treated the last woman he'd dared to care about. Knowing what would happen, he had pushed his lips to her ear, and told her what she claimed she wished to hear.

His stomach heaved again, and he was sick. He lifted a hand from the dirt to wipe his mouth, realised that with the mud upon it, it was likely to make things worse. So he used the back of his wet sleeve. He tipped his head up to catch the rain in his mouth, washed it clean and then spat.

Now that his conscience was as empty as his gut, he wondered if he should feel better. And surprisingly enough, he did. He had said out loud the thing everyone knew, but which no one was willing to say.

Perhaps she would run from the house, as she should have before now. Or call the magistrate. Bring the Duke and Duchess, and force them to deal with him as he should be dealt with. At least Daphne deserved justice for the way he had treated her. If she had wanted the truth so deeply, he could but hope that she had a plan to use it, once it was known.

Perhaps it was cowardly to wish her to free him of

the responsibility of ending his own life in atonement of the crime. But he was exhausted by the whole thing, so tired of living with guilt that he had become afraid to take the next step and die. Right now, she was lying in her bed, outraged at his treatment of her, shocked by his confession, angered by his departure. She could take her revenge, and it would be over.

But he remembered the gentle touch of her hands upon his body. And thought of what it would be like if things were different. Just as he had, when he had been with her—he imagined twining her fingers with his, bringing them to his lips and then leading her back to lie on her cold, hard bed. They could begin again, more slowly, learning each other's bodies, secure in the knowledge that this was just the first of many such nights.

He shut his eyes tight against the vision. It was happiness. And after what he had done, he had not earned it. Either she would denounce him in the morning, or he would send her away. But he could not keep that which he did not deserve. And he dared not risk that she might become in his care: another broken body at the foot of the stairs, victim to his drunken rage.

Daphne woke the next morning, trembling with cold, although the room was no different than it had been before. But she was different. Conscious of her body, and the air upon it. Aware of her nakedness, and her submission at the hands of her cousin's murderer.

No.

She tried to reconcile the man she had come to know

with the man she had expected and the pieces would not fit together. He'd had opportunities from the first moment to harm her. Yet he'd waited until she had given him leave to come to her room. He had begged her to stop him.

And she had not. For she'd wanted it as much as he had. When he was through, she was sure that she had not had enough. There should be more. They should hold each other in the dark room, clinging body against body until dawn broke. And when he had begun to whisper in her ear, she was expecting endearment or assurance.

Instead, he had poured out those poisonous words, like a flood to drown her passion. And she was sure that was what he had meant to do. He wanted to hurt quickly, before she had a chance to hurt him, as his wife had done. For despite what he might think, she was convinced that he was no more a murderer than she was. She was no closer to the truth than she had been on the previous day, but it was all the more urgent that she find it. While Clare might deserve justice, it was far more important that she save the living: Tim Colton and his children. They were suffering under the misunderstanding far more than she had been.

She went to the basin to refresh herself, washing carefully in preparation for the day. And she remembered his hands upon her body, the way he had coaxed her until she was mad with desire. The pleasure came upon her again, in a sudden rush that made her grab the night table for support, until the feeling had passed. But her own touch was not enough. She wanted him there to fill her, and his lips upon hers as he did it.

She glanced at her face in the mirror. Her cheeks had a healthy glow, and there was a knowing look in her eyes that had not been there on the previous day.

She put on her dress and did up her hair, hoping that the truth was not too obvious to all around her. Tim would know what it meant, of course. He might think that he could avoid what had happened. But he would have to face it, each time he looked into her eyes.

She went down the stairs to her breakfast tray in the nursery dining room, and prepared for the day with the children. She left them to work at their own projects just as she had done in the past, and found that her eyes were drawn to the window. She stared out into the garden, imagining it as it might be in spring, took up her sketch-book and drew it as she imagined. Full of life. Full of joy.

If she could find a way to end the troubles, she might be there to see it. In spring there would be flowers, she was sure. And she wondered what type were meant to express what she was feeling. There must be something quite splendid to represent the previous night.

A footman came to the door, and announced that the master wished to see her in his study. She felt a sudden flutter of alarm. Whatever was to happen between them, it was to happen now. She made sure that the children had sufficient work to occupy them and made her way to the ground floor.

He sat at the desk, barely looking up when she entered the room. There was nothing about his demeanour to say that anything unusual had happened between them, and she wondered if it was only some strange dream on her part. But then she realised that he was playing the part of the unaffected employer, just as he had done at dinner after he had first kissed her. His feelings for her frightened him. And now he would try to push her away.

He reached into the desk drawer in front of him, and removed a bag that chinked. 'As you know, Miss Collins, it was never my plan to have a governess for the children. And much as I have tried to abide by the wishes of the Duchess, my opinion on the matter has not changed. Whatever your reason for coming here, the job seems to have become something much more akin to an investigation. But now that you have discovered what you wished, I doubt you will want to remain. There is nothing further to uncover. Your services will no longer be required. I will arrange for whatever references you might need, of course. And I am willing to pay a year's salary, in addition to what the Duchess has offered you, since the inconvenience of coming here was great.'

'Inconvenience?' she said, numbly.

'Two years, then,' he said.

'You call what happened last night an inconvenience, do you?' She tried to keep the shrill tone out of her voice. Carrying on like a courtesan would not help the matter.

He flinched. 'This has nothing to do with last night.'

'Liar! You cannot even look me in the eye to say that.'

With great effort, he raised his head and met her gaze. It gave her some small satisfaction to see the guilt and shame in his eyes. If he meant to buy her off, at least he was not unaffected by it. 'I am not lying. This has less to do with what happened last night, and everything to do with what will happen in the future. If you do not go, what happened between us will most assuredly happen again.' There was defiance in his gaze as well, now. 'I wanted you. I want you still. If you stay, I will continue to take. And when I am through, it will not end well. It is far better that I send you away now, than after you have formed some false attachment to me. For it will lead nowhere.'

She laughed, her best drawing-room set-down. 'You are trying to protect my feelings, since it is too late to protect my honour. Spare yourself, my lord. I have few romantic illusions about the sort of man that turns to his servants to gratify his lust.'

Anger flashed in his eyes, and she remembered too late that he might be a dangerous man to provoke. Then his expression changed to something strange and unreadable. 'I have no illusions about my character, either. It does little good to whine that I was not in the habit of such behaviour until last night. I cannot pretend that with the act my character has suddenly transformed for the better. And I shall not lie and say that, if you remain here, you will be safe from me.

'My behaviour proves that there are no depths to which I will not sink to gain my desires. Although I detest what I have become, I cannot change it. And when I look at you, even now, I feel what little control I have slipping from me. God help me. That you were innocent does not matter. I want you still. Honour means nothing.'

And she could understand him, for she felt no different. Need for him ran through her like an ague. Taking the money on the desk and leaving was unthinkable, if it meant that she would never see him again, nor feel what he had made her feel in the dark the previous night. 'Just as my reputation means nothing to me, when I look at you. Put the money away,' she said softly. 'I will not leave.'

He stood up from his desk, and came to glare into her eyes in a way that might once have terrified her. 'If you do not go, I will put you out myself. Or worse. You know what I am capable of, should you cross me.'

'Do it, then. If you can. If you let me go, I will tell everyone what has happened.' And now she would know if he was the villain he pretended to be. She stepped near to him, reached for his hands and put them about her throat. Then she put her arms around his waist and waited for him to decide.

He froze against her, holding himself stiff and unmoved. And then there came something, from deep in his chest, that sounded almost like a sob. But when she looked up at his face, his eyes were closed, and his cheeks were dry. But she could feel him begin to shake, as though he was fighting the urge with every fibre of his being. Then he reached out and held her as well. He was gentle, so as not to disturb her gown or her hair. He would leave no embarrassing signs that he had touched her.

When he spoke, his voice was different, as though

he were a different person. 'It would be better for you if you were to go. You might be safe. No one need ever know what happened here. I swear they will not hear it from me. I would help you start again. But if you stay…' He flinched against her, and then drew her tighter. 'Oh dear God, I want you to stay. But I can promise you nothing.'

'It does not matter,' she said, surprised that she meant it.

'It does. We both know that.' He pushed her away. He turned back to the desk, and busied himself amongst its tiny drawers, removing an envelope of what looked like tea. He poured the leaves into the cup on his desk. Then he handed it to her. 'Drink this.'

She looked into his eyes, took it and drank, without hesitation, thinking too late of poison, and the sort of man that he claimed he was. 'What is it?'

'It will prevent…' he paused awkwardly '…mistakes.'

'Then you should have given it to me before today's geography lesson, for I am sure I have confused the children again.'

He managed a bitter smile. 'Not that sort of mistake. I fear you are helpless there.' He glanced at the cup, and said, in an almost scholarly voice, 'If taken regularly, there are certain herbs that inhibit gestation. If you mean to stay here, it would be best if you were to take a spoonful each morning with your tea.'

He was right to wish to avoid a bastard. And if she meant to be so foolish as to lie with a man without protection of marriage, than she need concern herself as well. He had done nothing to make her believe that there was a future in what they had done. And, some time, she might have to return home to her old life and pretend to forget what had happened between them. If that day came, it would be best that there be no outward evidence of what had occurred.

And now, the sour taste in her mouth had nothing to do with the concoction she'd drunk. She stared down into her cup. 'Very convenient that you had it handy. Did you know that I would refuse your offer? Have there been others…like me?'

'Like you?' He shook his head and stared sadly down at his desk. 'I suspect that there are no others like you. At least not that I have had the good fortune to meet. Do you mean, have I had mistresses? Yes. But not in some time. Certainly not in the house, with my family present. It was in London, years ago. And I did not need to see to their reproductive habits, for they knew more about the subject than I.'

'Then you suspected…'

'That you would stay with me?' He looked truly sad. 'I did not dare to hope. Even now, I do not know which of us is the bigger fool for continuing with this.' He glanced at the packet on the desk. 'The herbs belonged to Clare. I prepared them for her, after Sophie was born.'

'You did not want more children from her?' Which was strange, since the man adored the three he had.

'Things concerning Clare were seldom about what I wanted. We would not have had two children, had Edmund come before Lily. Although she enjoyed the getting of them, she found the whole process of carrying and birthing to be distasteful. And confinement, with no balls or friends to entertain? She informed me after Edmund that I'd got my heir and could leave her alone. She was having no more of me, if I meant to breed her like stock and keep her penned up for half the year.'

He chuckled. 'She was most put out when she came to me with news of Sophie. It was the closest I have seen to contrition. She had been careless, and had waited too long to rid herself of the problem. Now she would have to go through it all again. And she must beg me to acknowledge the child, which was a further indignity…'

He seemed genuinely amused by the story, and it was the first time that she had seen him in real mirth, when he was not speaking to his children. 'Why would you have refused?' she asked. 'You adore the girl. Don't you?' Suddenly, she was too confused to continue.

He looked at her, and the light faded from his eyes. 'You have not guessed the truth already? That is good, for I feared that as she grew it would be more evident. Apparently not.' He looked at her again. 'When Sophie was born, my wife and I had not been intimate for several years.'

'Then how…?' She'd begun before realising how naïve it would sound. If the child was not his, then it must be a result of Clare's infidelity. 'And you were not angry?'

'Resigned, more like. I knew that Clare was not with me. And I knew that she was not celibate. Only a fool would not have recognised the risk. One cannot deny nature, after all.' He looked no more interested in the idea than if it were some statistical or scientific problem. There was none of the rage she would have expected from the sort of man that might be moved to murder an unfaithful wife.

'And you claimed Sophie as your own?'

'She is my daughter in all ways that matter,' he said, effectively closing the subject. 'If ever I meant to reject her and her foolish mother, the feeling was banished at first sight of that little girl. She was as beautiful a baby as she is a child, and totally innocent of the sin of her parents. She has grown more dear to me with each passing year, and has never known another father. And I am content with that.

'But I did not want Clare to think that my patience was infinite. So once Sophie was born, I gave her the herbs and explained the advantage of regular usage. She had no more wish to be pregnant than I had to raise a collection of other men's children. There were no further problems.'

That he knew of. She wondered if he had read the letters she'd found. They might imply that there was another child on the way. Or did they refer to Sophie? Without Clare to answer, it would be impossible to tell.

'You grow quiet. Is it so shocking to you? Do you object to educating a child born on the wrong side of the sheets?' There was something in his tone that warned it had best not be the problem. 'For I wish her to be treated no differently than the other two.'

'Of course not,' she answered quickly. 'If anything,

she needs to be treated with more delicacy, and it has nothing to do with her parentage. Recent events have shocked her badly. It will do no good to try to impose discipline on an undisciplined mind at this time.'

'That is so. Your behaviour to her, your gentleness and loving attention have been quite different from what she received from the heartless woman who should have held her dear. But what else could I have expected from Clare? In all the time I knew her, she never showed a moment's care for any but herself.'

It shocked her to see the depth of bitterness and loathing for his late wife that was plain on his face. 'If you hated the girl's mother so, then why did you marry her?'

He smiled. 'The obvious reasons: she was rich and beautiful. I desired her. I was young and foolish enough to think that would be sufficient.'

He made no mention of love, even from the first. 'No wonder she grew to hate you.'

'Grew to hate me?' He smiled. 'You question my motives. But you do not think to wonder why she married me. There was never love between us. On her part, not even the physical desire was returned.'

Daphne did not respond. She did not like to think that Clarissa's behaviour over her unhappy marriage had no justification.

Tim smiled again and continued. 'I was a grave disappointment to her, you know. She and her family had such hopes for me and I failed them.'

'Disappointment? You are a baron, are you not?' It

was certainly more than she had expected, when and if she found a husband.

'A very lowly one. And that came late, after we were married. I earned a knighthood, as well.' He said it with such mock distaste that it almost made her laugh. 'For cross breeding wheat. And if you could have seen the look on my wife's face when that happened. She was horrified. She told me often enough, if she'd have wished for a husband to earn her respect, then she'd have married a cit with a fat wallet. That, at least, would have been more useful than the meagre awards I've earned with my scholarship or my poor family connections. She and her family were rather hoping that I would inherit a better title, and the land associated with it. Not hoping so much as expecting.'

'Surely not.' It made her family sound common, as though they were willing to sell their daughter for a coronet.

'I have an uncle who is a marquis. A lovely gentleman, with a weak constitution. Unmarried, at the time I met Clarissa. I told her in retrospect that if all she wanted was the title, she'd have done better for herself in seducing the old man.' He gave a short, bitter laugh. 'She told me she thought the same thing. Uncle Henry's miraculous recovery was disappointing enough. But that he should marry late in life, and father an heir?'

Tim shook his head. 'I did not mind the change in succession, for I'd given little thought to the matter before Clare pointed it out to me. She could not believe the fact. That she had bound herself to a man who was not only poor, but devoid of political ambition, was quite beyond her understanding. She was not willing to live as I am, a tenant to Bellston. But my influential friends were valuable to further her own social climbing.'

He was so very cold and matter of fact about it that it made her want to scream in frustration. It was even worse that she remembered Clare as bright, beautiful, elegant and well versed in the ways of London. She had been so witty, and always surrounded by admirers. And totally dismissive of her husband.

There had been no doubt in Daphne's mind that when she met him he would be ugly, and more than a bit of a brute. She looked again at her employer. There was nothing dull about the man. He was obviously more intelligent than her, and with a wit as quick, or quicker, than Clare's. Nor was he brutish, for his manner was easy, and his frame trim and graceful. There was none of the hesitance she expected in a man given over to learning. Had she met him in a drawing room, she would have found him an equal to any man present in looks and behaviour.

'I was a grave disappointment to her in all ways that mattered. And she was a millstone around my neck. I enjoyed her money, of course. The house was in need of repair, and I owe the success of my experiments to the wealth she brought with her when we married. The children have been a delight and a comfort to me. I was willing to bear much for their sakes, for they are my greatest achievement.'

He looked at her, and his eyes were flat and emotionless. 'But it all came with a cost. She took advantage of every chance to humiliate me, in public or private.

There was no disciplining her. If I chose to put my foot down, tried to punish her, or attempted to embarrass her, she would repay me in kind. She enjoyed watching me suffer and was more than willing to besmirch her own reputation, if it would pay me out. She even took up with my closest friend, removing what little companionship I enjoyed, and replacing it with suspicion and doubt.'

He shook his head. 'I schooled myself to hide my response to it, to pretend that none of it mattered to me. And some days, I think I even believed it myself. Other than that? The best I could manage was to keep the children away from their own mother, so that they might not see the truth. She did not mind it overmuch, for she had little patience for them. But I fear that it has harmed them permanently, to have no woman who cared for them.'

'They are unharmed, I swear,' she assured him. 'Bright, pleasant children. Co-operative and kind.'

'And is Sophie unmarked by what has happened?' He gave her a cynical smile. 'She barely speaks. And she was a little chatterbox, before I...' His throat stuck on the word. 'Before her mother died. Now she cannot stand to be in the room with me. The other children are a little better. But not as they once were. We four were a merry little family, once. Very happy, as long as Clare stayed in town. But at the last she provoked me, until I was unable to contain my rage.'

He ran a hand through his hair. 'If not for my weakness...' Then he looked up at her. 'I do not regret what I have done, so much as I regret not planning better. I can think of at least three plants in my possession right now. Untraceable poisons. I could have administered them, and been far away when they took effect. No one would have been the wiser.'

'Don't say that. You do not mean it.' She was frantic to believe the words. 'You are too good a man to be capable of premeditated murder.'

He smiled sadly at her. 'I am honoured by your belief in me, Daphne. But you do not know me so well as you think. I am who I am, and that man is not worthy of you.' He pushed the packet of herbs across the desk toward her. 'If you mean to stay, then take these with you and see that you use them. The situation is quite complicated enough, without bringing another unfortunate child into it.' Then he returned to his paperwork, and she was dismissed.

She walked slowly back to the schoolroom, tucking the packet of herbs deep into her pocket. She should be ashamed at what they symbolised. What kind of woman feared a child rather than welcoming one? But the herbs meant that he would visit her again. And for the moment, that was all that mattered. She would not think of her old life, or what would happen when she needed to return to it. For now, she would be a governess by day. And at night, she would be Timothy Colton's mistress. Each new day would be as much future as she needed.

She stopped at the door to the schoolroom, surprised at the sound of children's voices, raised in argument. It was strange, for they normally got on so well together. She had not heard a cross word between them since the day she'd arrived.

'Lily!' Edmund dropped easily into the role of leader. 'I forbid you to speak.'

'You are not the oldest, Eddy,' she muttered. 'You cannot forbid me anything. It is time. Maybe she can—'

'No. We already decided. You must not. We said nothing to the others, and we will say nothing to Miss Collins.' As she stepped around the door frame and into the room, they did not see her. They were both casting worried glances at Sophie, who was playing in a corner and oblivious to the conversation.

'But it cannot go on like this. Perhaps Father—'

'What cannot go on, children?' She stepped in between them and gave them her best no-more-nonsense smile.

They looked up at her, obviously guilty. 'Nothing.'

'Really? In my experience it is seldom necessary to be as worried about nothing as you two are. I will find out the truth eventually, you know.' She gave them a playful smile. If it was a broken window or a spoiled book, she knew of all the locations that such problems might be hidden, from personal experience.

But her friendliness had no effect on them. 'No, you will not. Because we will not tell you.' Edmund said it as though he were announcing a death, and Lily closed her eyes tightly, as though she could wish away the consequences.

Daphne went to them, going down upon her knees before them, so that she could look into their eyes. She hoped they did not suspect what had happened between her and their father. They would be far too young to understand. 'If there is something you wish to say to me, something that worries you, perhaps? You do not have to be afraid. Not of anything or anyone. No matter who it is. You will feel better, once you can share the secret.'

Lily's green eyes filled with tears. 'No, Miss Collins. Eddy is right. We promised we would not say. And telling will not help. It will ruin everything.'

So she ceased her quizzing and reached out to hug both of them.

And as they trembled in her arms, Sophie noticed nothing, sitting in her chair by the window, smiling to her papers and paints.

Chapter Thirteen

Tim went to her again, that night, after the children were in bed and the rest of the servants had retired below stairs. He had warred with himself over the visit for most of the day. Never mind that she had agreed to it, there were a hundred reasons why it was wrong. The virtue of the girl, her class, the fact that she was in the house to care for his children. She deserved better treatment. And had he still been a man of honour, it should have mattered to him.

But the stain on his soul all but laughed at the idea that he would stick at debauchery after forgiving himself for murder. If the girl was foolish enough to submit, then what compunctions need he have about using her? In the end, he let his lust overcome his judgement and focused on the vision of naked female flesh, warm and willing, waiting in the little room at the top of the house. He could lose himself there, calm the guilty voices in his head, rut himself to exhaustion and come down to sleep in his own bed. When he finally climbed the stairs and came into her room, arousal was strong in him, like a caged animal pacing behind a gate.

She sat on the edge of her bed, waiting for him. He closed the door. But he made no effort to douse the light, for he wanted to see her body. She was naked, as he had imagined her, the cold air peaking her breasts, limbs smooth and pale. He pulled off his clothing and left it in an untidy heap on the floor. Then he walked towards the bed, bare. He could feel the air raising bumps on his skin, and his hair standing up in protest. 'How can you stand the room so cold?' he asked. And then realised that, even if it mattered to her, there was no fireplace. He'd provided nothing to keep her warm. 'You should wear a nightshirt, or you will catch your death.'

She smiled. 'My only one was torn last night, and I have not yet had the time to mend it.'

He had done that to her as well. 'I will buy you another,' he blurted. 'As fine as you might wish. Sheer cotton, perhaps, or a very fine embroidered linen.'

'So that you might rip it off me again?' And she gave a small laugh. It was not the knowing sound of a courtesan, or the laugh of derision he would have got from his late wife. This was a sweet sound that seemed to say he could do whatever pleasured him, for she trusted him to bring her pleasure as well. She was looking at him through the lashes covering her slanted green eyes, trying not to appear too curious about his arousal.

And the illusion shattered in him that he could treat her as though she were a nameless stranger with no part in the matter of their coupling. She was looking at him like a bride. Innocent, but unafraid. Whether he wanted it or not, tonight she offered herself to him because she had given him her heart.

For a moment, it was easy to believe that she was his by right, the wife of his heart. There was nothing wrong or sinful about what he wished to do.

He smiled back at her, and said, 'I do not like to think you are cold because of my carelessness. Let us climb beneath the covers and warm you up.' And he pulled back the blanket and climbed into bed beside her. Soon, their mutual fumblings beneath the covers had them laughing, and far more than warm. When she was gasping with pleasure, he wasted no time in coming into her body as though he belonged there. He should not have rushed, for it was over too quickly, and she curled close to him, laying her cheek against the hair on his chest and sighing in contentment.

She'd stayed.

He had told her the truth, which should have been more than enough to send her running back to London. And yet, here she was, at his side.

His actions last night should have been enough to drive her away, if his words had not. He had tricked her out of her maidenhead. For even though she'd shown no sign of pain, there was nothing to make him believe that he was not her first lover. Tonight, she had been curious, but inexperienced.

He stared down at the top of her head, soft chestnut curls spreading out over the pillow. They looked better that way, and would look better on soft linen instead of the rough cloth here. She should be lying on down, wrapped in silk, with a roaring fire in the grate to chase away the chill.

He could give her that, if he wished. Move her downstairs into a guest bedroom. Dress her in satin, shower her with jewels. Stay in her bed so that he could feed her a breakfast of apricots from the orangery, and make her lick the juice from his fingers. But it would make her position too clearly that of a mistress.

Could he live with himself?

Instead, she was huddled in an attic, and tired from a day of caring for his children. He understood the satisfying feeling of fatigue, after a day's labour. But even at the worst times of his life, it had always been by choice. To be forced to take a position to survive… And to be forced again into the kind of service he required of her. He shook head in disgust at his own hasty actions.

She woke from her nap and looked up at him, smiling.

He gathered her close to him again.

She'd stayed.

When he'd confessed, she'd faced it without flinching. She didn't dance around it, not wanting to hear the truth, as even his dearest friend did. And she must have forgiven him for it, even if he could not forgive himself. It was the first proof he'd got that such was even possible. It gave him hope that there might be a way past what he had done, and a future after it.

And it occurred to him that there was a perfectly good way to keep her safe and warm and at his side for ever, with her honour restored. If she could accept his offer, knowing the villain that he had been, then he would put it behind him and work to be worthy of her love. They need never mention Clare again, or think of the time before Daphne had come into his house.

He could start anew.

She was nestling against him, again, and he felt her head dip as she began to doze.

He kissed her hair. 'You are tired. I should not disturb you.'

'It is nothing.' She yawned. 'The children…'

'Do you like them?' he asked hesitantly, afraid that he was overstepping yet another boundary that an employer should not cross. 'Not just the job, mind. But the children themselves.'

She gave a little start. 'Yes, I do.' She sounded almost surprised by the fact, and he wondered if this were in some way different from her last position. 'There were some difficulties at first. But they are bright and good company. And Sophie is a darling.'

'That is good. I think they like you as well.' There was one hurdle, at least. For he could not very well ask her to make a life with him, if she could not accept another woman's children.

'And how do you like me, Lord Colton?' Her lips teased his chest. Her tone was low and sultry, and went to the very core of him, stirring his body and his mind.

'Very well indeed.' He tipped her chin up, and kissed her properly, tasting her mouth. She returned the kiss, rocking gently against him. He could feel the heat rising in him, the desire to have her again. But he wanted to prolong the play. 'And am I to believe that you are growing to like me in return?'

She was kissing her way down his throat. 'Now that you have stopped trying to frighten me away, I think I like you very much.'

And he saw how much things had changed in a day, for though he had woken wanting nothing more than to be rid of her, it was now of the utmost importance to him, a matter of life and death, that he do nothing that would make her leave. 'Was it so obvious that I was trying to scare you?'

'Of course. You were nearly successful. For I do not want to say the things I thought you capable of, listening to the wind howl while lying in this bed, night after night.' Her hands were stroking his sides now, and it was only a matter of time before she touched him as he longed to be touched, and then conversation would be impossible.

'Say them, all the same. For I wish to know.'

'I thought you were a violent brute who cared for nothing but his own pleasure.' And she laughed softly.

He remembered the way he'd come to her, ready for sex but barely able to think of her by name. And lust for her mingled with a kind of sick dread.

'I thought that you would hurt me, if I opposed you.' She looked up into his eyes, and hers were as green as a cat's in the darkness. 'But now that I see the real you, the one that you hide from the world, I think my fears were quite ridiculous.'

The apprehension in him grew. And she continued,

'You are no more capable of hurting me, or anyone else, than you are of hurting the plants in your garden.'

She did not believe him.

'But…but I told you… You understand what happened here…'

She smiled her satisfied cat's smile. 'I understand what you think happened here. You feel responsible for your wife's death.'

He grabbed her hands, and held them so that she would stop tormenting his body. Then he said slowly, so that she could not doubt his meaning, 'I killed Clarissa. This is not just guilt over an accidental fall. I murdered my wife. She had preceded me to Wales. And I knew it was to be with her lover, a man I thought to be a friend. I followed. I arrived at the house. And through the windows I saw her in the drawing room, entertaining him. I went to my study and poured a brandy, even though it was still morning. Then I went to Bellston to talk to the Duchess. Adam arrived and we fought. He sent me away.'

His face tightened. 'And then I came home to my darling wife. The house was in chaos. The coach with the children had arrived, maids and nurses, bags and baggage, everywhere. So much noise, and so many people. It made my head ache, and so I had more brandy. I found Clare and we argued. On and off it went, all day and night for the better part of a week. I threatened divorce. She threatened to leave and take the children with her.' He shook his head. 'I don't know what she meant by it, other than to hurt me, for they did not mean a jot to her.'

He rubbed his temple, for his head ached at the memory. 'There was so much alcohol, and servants constantly interrupting, and the children were crying. Then there was even more brandy. And it ended with Clare, broken at the foot of the stairs.'

'That is all you remember?'

'It is enough.'

'What were you thinking, as you stood at the top of the stairs? What did she say to you, before you pushed her? What did you feel, when you saw her begin to fall? Triumph? Joy? Fear?'

'Stop!' He had spoken too loudly; for a moment he feared someone below them might have heard a man's voice coming from this room, where it had no right to be. He calmed himself, and continued. 'I know what happened. I do not need to remember the act. I remember my anger plain enough and my hatred of her. And telling her I would see her dead before I let her leave the house with the children. The next morning, I woke in my clothes in the study to the sound of more crying and the servants shouting. And there was Clare, on the floor of the hall.'

'That does not mean you killed her. It was a fall, nothing more.'

'She fell backwards, not forwards. It was plain by her injuries that she had been pushed. I was the only one in the house, Daphne.' He put his hand under her chin, and forced her eyes to meet his. 'I know the effect that strong spirits have upon me. I become violent, unreasonable. It is why I avoid them. And yet I kept taking them. I knew all along what I meant to do, and I drank until I could not stop myself.'

'No,' she said again. She refused to see the truth in his eyes: that he was capable of murder.

So he smiled and told her the real truth. 'And there is worse to come.'

'It does not matter,' she whispered.

'You are the only one who thinks I am innocent. Everyone knows what I have done. Adam is magistrate. He saw the evidence, as did Penny. He took one look, and then he ordered Penny to sit with the children. He had the body taken away and prepared for burial, and the floor and stairs scrubbed clean. He looked at me with such pity. And then he declared it an accident.'

Tim's voice broke on the last word. 'I begged him to take me to London to stand trial. I want to see justice served. If I do not pay for what I have done, I am damned for sure. But he kept repeating that it was an unfortunate accident. All for the best. And that no one blamed me.' He squeezed her hands tightly in his. 'But I blame me. The children blame me. You have seen them. The way they look at me. They know what happened. They saw too much that day for it to be otherwise.

'I must be punished for what I did to the children, even if the law will not punish me. Once I am sure that they are away to school, I will take care of it myself. They are better without parents than with the ones they were born to.' And then he began to shake. He sobbed like a damned soul, ashamed that she saw.

She reached for him, gathering his face in her hands to lay it upon her breast, stroking his hair as though he were a lost child. 'It is all right. It will be all right. What happened that day cannot be changed. And the Duke and Duchess are right as well. You are not to blame for it.'

His shaking subsided. 'And now you know why I wished the children out of this house. Even if they cannot love me, I meant to see that they were gone, and that their futures were secure before—'

'No,' she said again. 'You will not do what you are thinking. Ending yourself will leave the children in a worse state than ever. They cannot afford to lose more. They simply cannot.'

'They need to go away from this poisonous place. They are old enough to go to school, and I mean to send them.' He laughed softly. 'I told you that I was opposed to this scheme of a governess. It only prolongs the inevitable.'

'I need you.'

He shook his head. 'I have nothing to give you. If you are imagining some happy scenario, where we are together, perhaps as a family?' He shook his head. She had not forgiven him, because she believed there was nothing to forgive. And without her forgiveness, he felt his future begin to unravel again. 'Then you are more foolish than I imagined.' Just as he had been.

'I am not a fool. And I will prove it. I will uncover the truth, and set you free of your fears. There is another answer, Tim. There has to be.' It was the first time she had used his given name, and the familiarity was both startling and disturbing. It meant she thought she knew him. But really, she did not know him at all.

The time would come when she would admit that his answer was the only logical one. She would begin to doubt. And then she would run, or he would send her away.

He leaned forwards and kissed her, long and slow, but without heat. Then he escaped from her arms and her body, and sat up on the edge of the bed.

'You are going?' She stretched out an arm to him in an attempt to draw him back. The gesture was as languid and sensual as a trained courtesan's, and he wondered at how quickly she had fallen.

'It would not do for the children to see me coming down the stairs in the morning.'

She smiled. 'There are hours yet before we must worry.'

She was right, of course. He could stay as long as he liked. He could stay all night, and be damned to her reputation. He had already damned his own, by his actions. He swallowed. 'You are tired and need your rest. And there is always tomorrow.'

She yawned, and smiled. 'Tomorrow, then?'

'Of course.' He kissed her again, ignoring her hands, as they played upon his body. In time, she would see the truth, as he did. And then, when all hope for his innocence was gone, he would ask her if she still wished to make a life with the shell of a man.

Chapter Fourteen

Daphne swung her feet to the floor, as the first rays of dawn hit the tiny window. He had not stayed the night with her. But he had been with her longer than on the previous night. For a moment she feared that someone might meet him on the back stairs from her room. In any other house, it would have been most unusual to find the master creeping down the back stairs. But for once, the curious behaviour might be explained. Tim's habit of turning up in unexpected corners of the house was a change in habit, but typical eccentricity.

She smiled at the thought of him, in shirtsleeves, on his way to a cold breakfast in the conservatory. Then she reached for her sketchbook and her charcoals. She worked quickly, for her day must start soon, and there was no time for daydreaming over the master of the house.

At least not in such an obvious way as to sketch him.

In her mind he was just as he had been, cravat missing and shirt open, revealing a V of bare skin. She let her fingers linger on the place as she smudged the hollow in his throat, the shadows of muscle and bone on his chest as they disappeared behind the linen. She did the eyes next, with their sparkle of intelligence and the faint sadness that never seemed to leave them. And his smile, slightly higher at one side than the other, as though he were continually surprised by her, though delighted.

A few minutes later, she paused to admire her work. She felt she had done rather well in capturing the way his brown hair fell into his eyes as he leaned towards her, the faint dimple in his cheek as he smiled and the soft but mobile mouth. The whole demonstrated his gentleness, as well as his intelligence. In looking at the face she had drawn, she wondered how she had ever thought him capable of cruelty, much less murder. This was a portrait of a man who would be at home bent over his books, or working in his glasshouse, hands deep in earth.

She frowned. He and Clare must have known from the first that they would not suit. He would be uncomfortable in the excitement of the city, at the parties she craved. And she would be bored to tears at the estate in Wales, unimpressed by the beauty of the garden, and uninterested in her husband's discoveries. She would remain in town without him, telling all and sundry that he was a dullard and a burden, and that she had married beneath her.

It was embarrassing to admit how far she had been misled by her glamorous cousin. But it meant that she owed an even greater debt to Tim and his family for doubting them. So she rose from the bed and prepared to see to the children.

Later, Tim summoned her to the study. She was surprised to see the butler, cook and housekeeper as well. Apparently, she was there as governess, and it had nothing to do with her new, less official capacity.

Tim looked up at the servants with an air of suppressed agitation. 'I have received a letter in today's post. It seems Bellston has decided to come to dinner. He says he must take matters into his own hands, since an invitation was not forthcoming from me.' She could see by the crook of his mouth that Colton seemed both annoyed and amused by the turn of events.

'Unfortunately, I am unsure how ready the common rooms are for visitors. Can the dining room be prepared for this evening?'

The housekeeper assured him that all would be in readiness.

'And the menu?' He gave a vague wave of his hand. 'It matters not to me. He is bringing the Duchess, of course. If they mean to treat themselves as family, then they'd best not be expecting me to serve a peer. Give us whatever can be got together with a minimum of fuss. We will be retiring to the drawing room for cards, after.' He raised his head to her, as though just noticing her presence. 'And since her Grace is so fond of the children, I expect them to be dressed and present at table, and after.'

'Sir.' She tried to make the warning implicit in the single word.

'Very well, then.' He nodded, as if all were in agreement. 'You are dismissed.'

She lingered and closed the door after the others had gone.

Without looking up, he said, 'Miss Collins, do you have a problem with my request?'

'Are you sure it is wise for the children to dine with you?' she said, remembering the long uncomfortable meal of a few days ago. 'They are likely to be a nuisance.'

'And that is why their governess will be there, to prevent any problems.'

'I am to dine with you? And the Duke of Bellston?'

'And the duchess, as well,' Tim reminded her. 'These evenings always go better if there are an equal number of ladies.'

'But I am not—' She stopped herself. Of course, she was a lady. When she was in London, at least. But she could not exactly explain herself. 'It will insult them greatly, if you mean to seat a servant at the table.'

'If the Duke and his wife are bothered by the presence of a servant at table, that the Duchess herself hired, then they'd best return to their own home.'

He saw her hesitation, and added, 'My other servants know better than to cross me, when I have made up my mind. You should learn it as well.' There was something about the set of his mouth that was different from the last time he had tried to order her about like help. She suspected that he was laughing at her.

Then, for just a moment, he gazed at her as he had on the previous night. 'Wear your finest gown, with none of that muslin nonsense tucked into the bodice. Dress as a lady and preside at my table.' The last words were soft, coaxing, as though her presence was an honour to him that had nothing to do with expedience. Then his brusque manner returned. 'Do not think you can hide from me, Miss Collins. Be downstairs with the children at six sharp. Obey or be gone.' And once again he gave the invisible shifting of attention that told her she was no longer required.

Later as she was preparing herself for the ordeal ahead, she tried to quell the nervous butterflies that had taken residence in her stomach. It was aggravating of him to even suggest this, for so many reasons. She could barely stand to think what her mother would say, if she knew that Daphne was to have dinner at the very same table as a duke and duchess. The poor woman would be in alt. Considering the minor social set in which they travelled, the chances were better that she would go dancing on the moon than dining with the peerage.

But if her mother were to find that she was doing it as a servant? The horrors. She faced herself in the tiny mirror, and set about trying to do up her hair in a fashion that might match the gold satin gown she had chosen from her luggage. It was far too modest for an evening with the Duke and Duchess of Bellston, and yet too daring for a governess. And what was she to do about her manners?

It would be difficult enough to speak to the couple,

especially considering what she suspected about his Grace and the parentage of little Sophie. But though she was dressed as a lady, she must also remember to speak like a servant when spoken to, and no more than that. And to watch over the children as well. She must let nothing slip, that she was anything more to the host of the house than a loyal servant. The whole evening would be like trying to take tea on a tightrope.

But it would give her the opportunity to observe the Duke and his behaviour towards Sophie. Perhaps he would turn out to be the villain she suspected, and she could persuade Tim that his supposed old friend meant him ill by the visit. Her life would be much simpler tomorrow, if tonight she could prove the Duke of Bellston was a murderer.

The children were to be no help in the matter of decorum. For when they heard that it was 'Uncle Adam and Aunt Penny' who were visiting, they were quite beyond her control. When the time finally came to lead them downstairs, it was all she could do to keep them from running on ahead of her. As it was, they burst into the drawing room with shouts of delight. Before she was able to gather them up again, they had launched themselves upon the couple and greeted them with exuberant hugs.

As she watched, the Duke greeted each in turn, bowing to the older girl, shaking the hand of the boy and lifting little Sophie high into the air and tossing her until she laughed. As she compared the two, she could see no resemblance and no hesitation on the part of the Duke that might indicate he felt more strongly attracted or repelled by the youngest child than he did with either of the others.

When he put the little girl back down to earth, he turned his attention to their governess.

And for a moment Daphne was quite taken aback. He was the handsomest man she had ever seen, with fine pale features, black hair and sooty lashes covering deep blue eyes. And it was most affecting as he returned her gaze. It was as though she were the centre of attention, and not an invisible thing placed in the room to maintain peace during the meal. 'So this is the new governess that I have heard so much about. My wife feels that you are just what the family needs, my dear. I can only hope she speaks the truth.' He said the last too quietly for his host to hear.

And then Tim stepped forward, and offered introductions. 'Adam, this is Daphne Collins. May I present the Duke of Bellston. And, of course, you're already familiar with his wife.' He gestured in the direction of the Duchess, who had busied herself greeting the children.

She dropped a deep curtsy, and murmured, 'Your Grace', in a tone that she hoped was sufficiently subservient.

The Duke glanced at her for a moment, and then at his friend, and there was a momentary hesitation as he seemed to gather some bit of information from the silence. Then he said, 'Airs and graces are hardly necessary tonight. Please, if you are to dine with us, you must call me Adam. And my wife's name is Penny. Penny loathes formality, and will be quite out of sorts if you curtsy to her again.'

He went on for a bit about the quality of Tim's table and how he had missed it over the past months as though nothing unusual had happened between them, either before or after Clarissa's death.

Daphne had the brief, horrifying feeling that in the moment of silence, the Duke had formed the opinion that her relationship with her employer was rather closer than was normal. She turned and looked at Tim, hoping that he would give her some clue as to what was going on, and saw the look in his eyes.

He was admiring her as he might a woman of quality. As though he wished to gain and keep her approval by his actions. She had expected him to treat her as he had in the study: as a servant, to be tolerated only as long as she fulfilled her duties. And that had been at best. At worst, she expected him to do something to betray her status as his mistress. A lasciviousness of expression or a familiar touch that might indicate their intimacy.

But instead he smiled at her in a way that was encouraging, and almost shy. And when his guests were distracted by the children, he came to her side and murmured, 'See. There is nothing to be concerned about. Adam has been a dear friend to me for most of my life.' His face darkened for a moment. 'Although there has been an estrangement, of late. I did him a wrong.'

'You did him—' She shut her mouth quickly, for she was unsure how much he understood of her knowledge of the affair.

Tim was glancing at the Duke. 'But it appears that he

has decided to forgive it. And we are to go on as if nothing has happened.' He smiled sadly. 'I find that to be a great relief. Although I do not know her nearly so well, I expect you will find the Duchess to be a refreshing change from what you expected. She was the daughter of a printer, before marrying.'

'Her family was in trade?' She hoped the snobbishness did not show too clearly in her voice, for her mother would be just as shocked to hear that she had dined with a printer's daughter as she would a duke.

'Yes.' He smiled encouragingly again. 'If it gives you any comfort to know the fact, she was not born to this life. She was frightfully rich, of course. But she is not one to put on airs or think less of a person because of their birth or a need to take employment.'

'Oh. That is good.' For she remembered, after a moment, that this would have been a comfort to a true governess. But what would her mother have made of the situation now? There would have been much bowing and scraping, while at table. But when they got home, there would be a stern lecture on the tendency of great men to marry beneath themselves while gently raised ladies of a better class, ladies such as Daphne, for instance, went unclaimed.

'And I am sure she will be interested in your progress with the children's education. She is frightfully intelligent as well. She is just finished with her own translation of Homer.'

'Are you speaking of my wife's book?' The Duke's ears seemed to prick from across the room, to catch the mention. He turned from the children, and reached into his pocket. 'I have brought a copy for you, since I knew you would appreciate it. It is an early printing, of course. A proof from Penny's brother. The man still has no understanding of the material, but I must admit he has done a good job with the setting and binding.'

'Do you really think so?' The Duchess looked eagerly at Tim. 'What is your opinion? I thought, if I was seeking a more accessible translation of the story, perhaps it would do to have some illustrations, but I have not the slightest idea of how to go about getting them. I suppose I must hire an artist.'

'Oh, Miss Collins. Have Miss Collins do them.' All three of the children were chorusing the suggestion enthusiastically.

Daphne took a step back, wishing there were a way to withdraw from the room without notice. But the children did not cease their clamour.

'Could you?' The Duchess looked hopefully at her.

'Oh, I don't know. I doubt I would be good enough.' And it would be incredibly complicated to explain, once she had completed her task here and returned to her old life. Especially if she accused the Duchess's husband of murder.

'No. You must. It would be wonderful. Come and see her sketches, Uncle Adam. Come and see.' Sophie had opened like a flower in the presence of company, talking non-stop and showing no sign of shyness. She grabbed the duke by the hand and was pulling him from the room.

Too late, Daphne remembered that it was her job as governess to prevent just such an embarrassing occurrence. 'Sophie. That is quite enough. You must return to your seat, immediately.'

The Duke smiled at her. 'Do not mind her. It is quite all right, really. I have not seen Sophie in a very long time. And if this gives her pleasure?' He smiled down at the girl and gave a courtly bow. 'I am at your command, my dear. Where are these sketches? If you would like to show them to me, I would very much like to see.'

'In the nursery.' She had tugged him out into the hall before Daphne realised the girl's intent. And they had headed up the stairs.

'Do not concern yourself, Miss Collins.' The Duke tossed the phrase over his shoulder. 'She is not the least bit of a bother. We will return shortly.'

So she stood in the entry and watched. It took only a few steps for Sophie to recover from her hesitation over taking the main stairs. She gripped the Duke's hand tightly, and started up them.

The Duke showed no hesitation at all. He was smiling down at the girl, holding the banister with relaxed fingers, proceeding at an orderly pace towards the first floor, and chatting as he went.

It was a stark contrast to the way Tim approached the same stairs. There was no guilt in this man's posture at all. Perhaps her suspicions were wrong. He did not behave as if there was a reason to fear discovery. And while some might be so duplicitous as to disguise a murder, would it not have been easier to avoid the Colton family altogether, if the object was to hide an illegitimate child?

And with man and girl, side by side, she could see

no resemblance at all. Surely there would be something alike in the two, if he were Sophie's father?

But if it was not the Duke? She looked back over her shoulder at her employer, who was glancing at the stairs with the same trepidation as always.

If the Duke was not a murderer, then she was left with her original suspect, whether she wanted him or not.

The Duchess was looking over her shoulder at the retreating pair. 'My word. You have been here less than two weeks and already I see a substantial change in Sophie's behaviour.'

'Well, I…' She struggled, unable to come up with an explanation for it.

Tim had come to her side, to answer for her. 'It is all up to Miss Collins, Penny. And I must apologise for the way I treated you, when you insisted on hiring her. You were right and I was wrong. The children needed someone sensible to look after them.'

Daphne was stunned. For when had anyone ever used the term *sensible* to refer to her?

Tim was smiling at her, as though she had hung the moon and stars. 'We needed someone who could look at the situation with a head unclouded by previous events, and come up with solutions to our problems. And Miss Collins has been a godsend.'

The Duchess was staring at Tim, who hardly seemed to notice her scrutiny, for all his attention was focused on Daphne. 'I can see that.'

Oh, dear. By the look in her eyes, the Duchess could see far more. Sophie was not the only one who had been transformed since her last visit. Tim was behaving in a manner that would be most ordinary in any drawing room. The saturnine man who had been forced into hiring her had disappeared. This man was gazing upon her with the same doting pride that the Duke lavished on his own wife.

Daphne would have found it quite flattering and a sure sign of strong admiration and attraction had they met under ordinary circumstances. But to bestow such lingering gazes on one's children's governess must seem almost as mad as his earlier storming. She dipped her head in subservience, and muttered, 'Lord Colton is too kind.'

The Duke and Sophie returned to the main floor a short time later, with her sketchbook under his arm. She had a brief, irrational desire to snatch the thing away from him and argue that it was none of his affair what she might draw, or whether she displayed any skill while doing it. But it would not do to insult a peer. Her mother would be horrified that she would even consider it.

And as a governess? She should be doubly honoured that he took any notice at all.

He set the book before his wife, and opened it to the odd landscape she had drawn. Then he cocked his head and looked at her. 'I must say, the work is most singular. But I do not recognise the location.'

She cleared her throat. 'It is all of my imagination, I fear.'

'All the better, for you would have to use imagination

freely, to render the scenes from my wife's book.' He smiled proudly at Penny. 'Although she has a most vivid turn of phrase. If she can make me read Homer, then think what she will do to you.' He flipped a few more pages, to see how she had rendered the plants in the garden and the statuary there. 'And I trust you can draw people as well?'

And it was then that she remembered the sketch she'd done of Tim. Her hand was halfway to reaching for the book when he flipped the page and stared down at the image.

Tim was across the room, seeing to the children, and did not notice the sudden silence from the group standing over the sketchbook. The light in the drawing was obviously from a breaking dawn. It was soft and flattering, as was his expression. His cravat was missing, and his shirt undone. It was a view that no decent woman should have seen, much less committed to paper. What must they think of her?

Perhaps she should protest that it had been a passing fancy, and not drawn from life at all. But would it be any better that they believed she was in some way obsessed with a glimpse of her employer's bare chest? And how would the Duchess react, knowing that she had hired such a person to care for children?

But it was even worse that they think she had drawn the picture from memory of an actual event. If that was the case, it was plain what was going on in the house. And that Tim would entertain the Duke and, worse yet, his Duchess, while his mistress sat at table with them, was the gravest possible insult. She swallowed, trying to come up with some explanation that would make him turn the page.

And he said suddenly, 'It is a very good likeness, is it not, Penny?'

She adjusted her spectacles in a way that might have implied disapproval. But then it became clear that she was only wishing to get a better look at the picture. The Duchess responded, 'Most well drawn.' When she glanced away from the sketch, there was a faint hint of colour in her cheek as evidence that she had seen, understood and been amused by the subject matter. But however she might look, when she spoke to Daphne she made it clear that there was nothing worth acknowledging about the picture. 'I would be most flattered to have you accept a copy of my work, and see what you might make of it. I have ideas, of course. But I would welcome the advice of so talented an artist.' And then she smiled warmly. 'I suspect that you will be with us for quite some time, and we will be able to discuss this again.'

Daphne expelled the breath she had been holding, and murmured, 'Thank you, your Grace.'

And the Duchess reached out to touch her hand, giving it a small, affectionate squeeze. 'Please. You must call me Penny. And my husband is Adam. All the titles can get so tiresome, at times. It is good to be able to relax.'

Then her husband shut the book quietly and looked back toward his host.

Tim was giving him a curious look in response, as though he waited on an answer.

The Duke called, 'Where is the dinner you have promised us, Tim? And the wine. I have quite missed the access to your fine cellars.'

Apparently, the answer had been given, for Tim grinned back at them. 'As though you cannot afford to stock your own. I had hoped, Adam, that since you had found a wife with more sense than you possess, you'd have let her take on the accounts.'

'That is just what I have done. And now she will not let me spend on such foolishness as decent brandy. So I have come to drink yours. Gather your children.' He held out an arm to his wife and the other to Daphne. 'And I will see to it that the ladies arrive safely in the dining room.'

Daphne gingerly accepted his offer of escort. So he chose to think of her as a lady, even after the damning evidence of the drawing?

He saw her hesitation and glanced in the direction of his friend. 'It is good to see Tim so happy. I was worried that he would not recover from his wife's death.' He looked at her pointedly. 'It was very difficult for him. Almost more so than the time before her death, which was very bad indeed. And I feared for the children as well, to be raised in such a household. In your short stay here, the mood of the house is returning to what we hoped it might be. Our friend Tim deserves an end to strife, for he has suffered long enough.' Then he smiled in her direction. 'If you are the cause of it, then you are a most welcome addition to his table, and to our little circle. Tell me, my dear, do you enjoy cards? For it would be pleasant to have a fourth…'

Dinner had been delightful, as had the cards and games afterwards. And it was only when Sophie had begun to nod over the drawing she was making by the fire, and the older children yawned into the books they were reading, that the adults decided it was time to end the evening.

When Daphne made to excuse herself to help them to bed, Lily fixed her with a curious look, as though reassessing her place in the family, and offered to tend to her sister herself, so that Miss Collins could stay a while longer with the adults. Tim smiled to himself. It did his daughter credit that she could interpret the situation so quickly, without him having to enlist her help.

He could see Daphne opening her mouth to refuse, and moved quickly to speak ahead of her. 'Thank you, Lily. That is most considerate of you and very helpful.' And when he was sure no one was looking, he winked at his older daughter and she smiled back at him.

It felt natural to have Daphne there, sharing a final glass of wine before Adam and Penny departed. And even more so to have her standing at his side, as he bid adieu to his guests. His friends reached out to her with warmth, eager to put her at ease. Both the Duke and Duchess took her by the hands and kissed her cheeks, as though she was more sister than servant. Although she was still too shy to return the gesture, he felt that it would not be too long before she treated them just as warmly as they did her.

When the Bellstons were safely on their way home to the grand estate just a few miles away, he shut the door and smiled down at her, laying a hand on her shoulder in a gesture of casual affection. 'Did you enjoy the evening?'

She smiled. 'Very much so. At first, I did not think...'

'That it was appropriate?' He smiled in return. 'I saw the look in your eyes when you came downstairs. Full of doubt. It was most unusual for you.'

'Well, it is rather unusual to seat the governess down next to a duke. And given the rather unique nature of my position here...' She took a deep breath.

'You were worried that they would learn the truth?' He laughed. 'I am sure they surmised the truth, even before they arrived. Adam is not the idiot he might pretend to be. He had it all worked out before he stepped over the threshold. His wife as well. I fought and complained over you, and made no secret of the fact that I did not want or need you. And then, two days ago, I stopped complaining. Perhaps they came to make sure that I had not pushed you down the stairs.'

'Do not joke over such things.' She'd gone deathly white at his words.

'Why?' He smiled at her, the wine and good company leaving him reckless. 'It may very well be true, you know. They had reason to be worried. I have lost the right to expect full trust, even from those who admired me in the past.'

'If they do not trust you, then they are not truly your friends, Tim.'

He laughed softly to himself. 'It is flattering to have such blind devotion from you, my love. No matter how unwarranted.'

She reached out and touched him lightly on the cheek. 'I see no reason to doubt.'

He kissed her palm and then reached to catch her about the waist, pulling her close to take her lips. This was as it should be. A beautiful woman who trusted him against all reason and loved his children. And whose lips were sweeter than after-dinner port.

For a moment, she was kissing him as ardently as he did her. But then she stopped, and struggled in his arms. 'Lord Colton. Stop it this instant.'

'Lord Colton, am I? You were not nearly so formal last night. I did not think you would mind a few kisses overmuch.'

'That was last night. And this is here and now, in an entryway, where anyone might see.'

'Are you afraid to have others know the truth about what is going on between us?'

'The Duke, Adam, and his wife might know already. But the servants do not.'

'It is my house, and I will behave how I wish.' He tipped her chin up and kissed her again, open mouthed, so there would be no question of his feelings should they be discovered. 'And I wish to do this. As often as possible.' He kissed her again and again, until she forgot all arguments. When he released her mouth so that she might catch her breath, he ran a finger along the neckline of her gown, and sighed in contentment. 'You look lovely tonight. But I imagine you in satin and lace, every night. With diamonds, here and here.' He nibbled on her ear, as his fingers stroked her throat. 'Sharing my table and my bed.' She tensed at his touch, and he whispered, 'Tell me you want me as much as I want you.'

There was a pause, and then she whispered, 'I do. But…'

'But…' He nodded, for her hesitance confirmed his fears.

'It is not about you,' she insisted. 'It is all much more complicated than that. We are not married. Not even betrothed.'

It stung him to think she might reject him, and he struck back with words meant to wound. 'If suddenly your honour matters so much, I will marry you. Only to see you forfeit it again, by your association with me.'

He could see that he had hurt her, for her green eyes grew large and sparkled with tears. But when she spoke, her voice was clear. 'I regret that I cannot accept your kind offer. And before you suggest it, my reasons have very little to do with what happened to your late wife. You talk of marriage. And yet you know nothing about me, nor do you seem to care about that fact. Though you will continue to enjoy my physical company, it would be very foolish of me to expect that you will change your mind about the rest of me, and suddenly begin to care once we wed.'

And with that, she stalked up the main stairs, so fast that she was gone before he could follow.

Chapter Fifteen

Daphne pounded her pillow in frustration. It had been three days since she had left him in the hall, and it was obvious she had offended him so greatly that he did not mean to visit her again. The whole thing was grossly unfair. If she'd claimed that she could no longer bear the shame of lying with a murderer, she suspected he would have been apologetic and perfectly understanding of it. It would have appealed to his sense of tragedy.

But he could not seem to fathom that someone might have feelings to be hurt, just as he had. He supposed he could marry her, if honour mattered…

She punched her pillow again. He was not a murderer, and hardly worth saving, if that was the best he could do. Timothy Colton was a selfish lout, no better than the men she had known in London. Just like the faithless cads whose attentions Clare had trained her to encourage. It served her right that when she met someone who mattered to her, and tried to learn from her mistakes and not be a public embarrassment, it would mean nothing to him.

And yet, she could not leave. There were the children, who needed her so much more than their father did. And she had not been paying attention to them, too focused on the needs of their father. The older children were all right, for they seemed to thrive, no matter what mistakes she made.

But she had not been tending to Sophie's lessons, since the girl was happy to entertain herself, now that she had paper and pens. And Daphne had been rewarded with just the sort of pictures she should have expected when the girl had nothing specific to occupy her mind. Endless sketches of Clare, all curiously misshapen, so oddly angled and disturbing that it gave her vertigo to look at them.

She set the girl to drawing pictures of her brother and sister, of the furniture in the room, and the marble busts in the front hall. And all of them came out properly formed and natural, with nothing the least bit alarming. It was only when the little girl attempted to draw Clare that the results were wrong. Perhaps it was the fading memory that caused it. If that was true, they would run their course and stop altogether one day, once the memories held no more fear for her.

So Daphne had bundled up the pictures and stuffed them into her trunk where none might come upon them by accident. Perhaps she should simply throw them on the fire, but she could not bring herself to do it. They were Sophie's memories. It would be unfair to take all she had of her mother, no matter how horrible that might be.

Below her, she thought she heard a tread on the stairs. There was only one person who would come to her at this time of night. And without meaning to, she hoped.

It was galling to know that she could forget so easily how angry she was with him. Now that he was near, she'd managed to convince herself that the differences between them could be solved. Tomorrow, perhaps. Or at least, later this evening.

He must feel it too, for his step sounded hesitant, as though he could not help but go forward, but was not sure it was wise to continue.

He'd reached the top of the stairs now, and stopped. He did not open the door, but neither did he knock. And refusing to make it easier on him than it needed to be, she did not call out.

And then, the footsteps shuffled on the landing, turned and retreated.

She lay upon her bed, angry and frustrated. She heard the steps going down one flight, and then another, until the sound faded. He was going? Without a word of apology. Not even a whisper. No note slipped under the door. Just a pause at the head of the stairs, and that was all?

Perhaps not all. She took up her candle and opened the door, holding it low so she could see the floor in front of her. Small purple flowers, scattered like wishes at her feet. She scooped them up, into a lopsided bunch.

No book was necessary to interpret the message. They were forget-me-nots.

She gave it not another thought, running down the stairs in her bare feet, as silently as she could. She hesitated only a moment at the door that would lead her to the bedrooms. They did not matter, for she knew that she would not find him there.

Down another flight, then, as she forced all thoughts of their argument from her mind. She must believe, in her heart, that what they were doing meant as much to him as it did to her. Or how could she bear to live?

When she reached the downstairs hall, a faint light was shining from the glass doors at the end, which stood partly ajar.

She smiled. It was just as she'd suspected. He'd brought the flowers and returned to the safety of the conservatory. It was where he always came when he was unsure of himself. And it was the place where he was most like the Tim Colton that she admired. He claimed he did not mind visitors. Now was an excellent chance to put his statement to the test. She slipped into the room with him, and closed the doors behind herself with a soft click.

At first, she saw nothing but the shadows of the plants, but there was a faint glow coming from the back of the room. The stoves were lit, but there was only a single candle, near the work table. She could see Tim moving from place to place, familiar in the darkness.

He looked up as she approached, freezing in place as he watched her. 'I did not expect you.'

'You did not?'

'I was caught up in work.' He gave a shadowy gesture to the table before him. 'Some say that it is better to plant at the dark of the moon. I doubt it will make a difference. Although there is a pull on the tides. But in the seeds and the earth, it would be so small that it shouldn't matter. Still, it may be that the wisdom of those that till the earth is greater than mine...'

She crooked her head to the side, and set the flowers upon the table beside him. 'What utter fustian. You brought these to me. What do you mean by them? You cannot think that I would forget so soon?'

He wiped his hands upon his apron, in a nervous gesture. 'They mean that I am out of hyacinths. Hyacinths are better for a proper apology. I suspect that I shall continually be forcing bulbs, if I can persuade you to remain with me. I cannot help making a muddle whenever I talk to you.'

He had made her smile, and she bit her lip, trying to hide the fact. 'When you say remain, what do you mean by it? Remain in the conservatory? For though it is quite nice by day, it is well past time for us to be in bed.' Three days past time. She smiled again, at what a wicked thought that was.

He gave her an odd look. 'I often sleep here, nights. I find it more peaceful.'

'You sleep here.' Again, she feared her amazement would offend him. 'It cannot be particularly comfortable.'

'I have seen where you sleep, my dear. You must understand that comfort is hardly an issue, if one is tired enough.'

'So you work yourself to exhaustion, and then sleep in the conservatory to avoid going up the stairs.'

She saw his reaction, and knew that she had guessed correctly. 'Not every night,' he hedged.

'But often.'

'It is not so uncomfortable. There is a *chaise* near the stove. You were sitting on it yesterday.'

She walked to the back of the room, behind the screen of palm trees, and sat down upon it again. 'Here? This is your bed?'

He was obviously embarrassed, now, and went to the stone basin in the corner, carefully washing the soil off his hands. 'Silly of me, I suppose. It is really quite pleasant, once you get used to it.'

'Compared to a fine bed upstairs, with silk hangings and a warm fire. And a valet to look after your every need.'

'It is more than I deserve,' he muttered, and she could feel the darkness stealing in on him again.

'Then share the space in my bed, under the eaves. There is not much room, but you are welcome there,' she said softly. 'Use the back stairs, if the main ones trouble you so.'

'You would allow me more freedom than my own children? For you have trained them to go up and down the main stairs again, as though nothing is wrong with them. Just like they used to.'

'They are young. They can heal from anything, given the chance. And perhaps a gentle nudge such as I gave them.'

'But I am old?' He smiled sadly. 'Older than you, certainly. Thirty-three.'

'That is not so very old. And age does not signify. You are merely set in your ways. And harder to persuade than the children. Stubborn.'

She had made him smile.

'But if you are a scientist, then you must have a rational mind. When the time is right, you will abandon your fear.'

He shook his head in amazement. 'You are a nine-days' wonder, Daphne Collins. You give me too much credit. And you still treat Clare's death as though it were some sort of unfortunate accident. Can you not see that what I did was wrong? And what I have done to you is just as bad. You should not be encouraging me to continue.'

Perhaps it was true. She would have been sure, at one time. But now that she had known him, she could not manage to give him up. 'I only know that it feels very right when you are with me, and very wrong when you are not. Whatever happened, I do not believe you can be blamed for it. And if this is where you wish to be, then I would be here as well.'

She leaned back, and stretched out upon the *chaise*. When she opened her eyes, and looked up, she gasped in wonder. 'The stars.' For there, stretched out before her on the other side of the glass roof, was the night sky.

He laughed softly. 'You have discovered my secret. And I needn't feel guilty for the pleasure it brings me.

For it is available to saints and sinners alike, if they take the time to look.'

She could feel him sitting down beside her, but was unable to tear her eyes away from the sky to look at him. 'It is amazing. So dark. The stars are like diamonds. And there are so many. I have never seen a sky like this in London.'

'Because the smoke in the air spoils the view. Only when you are deep in the country and the moon is new can you see a night as black as this. And that is the best time to see stars.'

He blew out the candle that sat nearby. And as the room became darker, the stars seemed to pop from the sky in relief. She imagined she could see the distances between them, and that some were far closer than others. She reached out a hand to them. For a moment, she had been tricked into thinking she could pluck them from their places.

She could feel his hands, moving to the ties of her robe. 'I meant to resist. But I cannot help myself. Let me see you by starlight.'

And she felt the lascivious urge to feel the light upon her bare skin, as though it were sunlight after a storm. She heard him sigh, as the cold air touched her naked body, and she arched her back to let her breasts point up to the heavens. She stared up at the stars again. 'So many. And they all have names.'

'The stars?' He laughed. 'You must know that as well as I, for you are a teacher.'

She squirmed slightly against the couch. 'Well,

I know the Plough, of course. And Polaris.' She pointed.

He leaned down and turned, to follow the line of her finger. Then he took her hand and moved it. 'There is Polaris. You are pointing at Sirius, my dear.'

'Oh, my. Well, they seem very different in the sky than they do in books.'

'Do they now?' He did not believe her in the least. But he did not seem to mind it, overly. 'It appears I must teach you astronomy.' He released her hand, and reached out again to touch her shoulder. 'If you look above where you are pointing, you will see a great W in the sky.'

She furrowed her brow, wondering whether she should pretend it was clear or admit defeat.

He touched her body lightly with his fingers, at the navel. 'If this is Polaris, then...' he traced his fingers from shoulder to breast to throat, to breast, and then the opposite shoulder '...there is Cassiopeia.'

He traced it again, and again, lingering over the tips of her breasts. She shuddered at his touch and closed her eyes.

He took his hand away. 'There, now. You will never learn the stars by keeping your eyes closed. Open them again.'

She did as she was bade.

'Do you see them, now?' His lips replaced his hand, travelling gently over the path of the stars. For a moment, she was lost between pushing him away so she could concentrate, and pulling him closer, never mind the stars.

And then it was as though the great W over her head leapt into sight, so clear and bright that it was a wonder she had not noticed it before. 'I see it.'

'Very good.' He dropped another kiss into the hollow of her throat, as though to reward her. And then to her mouth, kissing slowly. She could feel the smile upon his lips. 'Now that you have found that, lower your eyes to Polaris.' His lips travelled down her body to her belly. 'And you can find Ursa Major.'

'What?' For a moment, she lost all sense of the stars, and could think only of his tongue on her body.

'The Plough.' His fingers were tracing the bowl of the dipper on her skin, curving with the handle to go lower on her body.

His touch was so gentle, it felt as though he were drawing the design on her skin with a feather. As he passed, each nerve awakened, singing for more stimulation. When she looked down, he was staring at her face, watching her reaction. 'Can you see it?'

When she looked puzzled, he pointed up towards the sky.

And she glanced up to find the brightest star, and let her eyes wander the path that his fingers had taken, feeling the skin heat as she looked at the stars. She gave a trembling sigh. 'Yes.'

'Very good.' There was amusement in his voice. 'Now let us find something else. Orion. The hunter. His arm is like so, with sword raised.' He took her right hand and raised it over her head, trailing his fingers along the skin. 'And Betelgeuse is here.' He settled his lips upon her right shoulder, sucking gently upon the skin, until she felt her breasts tingling in response. 'His throat.' He moved to demonstrate, licking at the hollow of her throat, until she twisted, trying to catch his lips with her own.

So he moved to her other shoulder, kissing it, and stroking down her arm. 'His bow arm, outstretched.' He twined his fingers with hers until she stilled.

And then he slid lower on her body. 'And the stars of the belt.'

She had been waiting, breath held, for the feel of his lips upon her breasts, but he had gone lower, and was circling her waist with kisses. And when she looked into the sky, to the stars that he had described, she could find them all. There were the lower stars, just there, where his hands were resting on her knees.

And the stars that made up the sheath. She felt her body give a shudder, as she understood where the lesson was likely to end.

For he had settled there, where there were many stars, clustered together, and kissed her as though he knew the position of each one.

She stared up into the night sky. And it was as if she could see the lights turning above her, spinning around Polaris to mark the time. He kissed, lightly at first, and then more boldly, tracing designs upon her with his tongue, sucking upon the tender flesh, delving deep, his hands stroking her thighs, and parting them wide. He held her tight against his mouth, as his tongue dipped into her, and then returned to work magic.

The sky was spinning madly now and she bit at her lip to hold back the scream she felt was coming. Her body pulsed in rhythm with the touch of his tongue and clenched to each brush of his lips. And then his fingers came into her, and the stars came unfixed and flashed before her in a jumble of brilliant sparks.

He shed his clothes then, and came to her as she trembled in anticipation, finding his place inside her as surely as if he'd never left. She touched his body, which was hard and real, moving with him and against him, staring up into the fathomless night sky as she felt him find release. Then he reached for the thin blanket that was thrown over the end of their substitute bed, and pulled it up over them. And she settled into the small space between the couch and his body, wrapped her arms around his neck and they slept.

She awoke tangled in her lover's arms, still balanced precariously with him on the *chaise*. As she moved, he rolled with her, slipped out from under the blanket and dropped bare on to the stone floor of the conservatory.

And he laughed. He looked up at her, from his seat on the floor, rested his elbows beside her on the makeshift bed and kissed her.

'What time is it?' She whispered the words, and wondered why it had taken her so long to realise the risk.

'After six, I expect. The sun is up.'

'Oh, dear.' Suddenly, her voice sounded very much the offended schoolteacher. She reached for her wrapper, quickly pulling herself back into respectability. 'I must get back to my room, before I am missed.'

'If you leave me, I assure you, you shall be missed.' He reached out to stroke her hair. 'Stay.'

'Do not be a fool. You know I cannot. I have stayed too long already. It is light. The servants will be up. And someone is sure to see me on the stairs.'

He seemed only mildly affronted by her tone. 'You needn't worry. I doubt that it is still possible to shock the occupants of this house, after what has occurred already.'

'But none of that pertained to me.'

His face quirked in an ironic smile. 'And the fact that I have borne shame means nothing to you?'

'Only because you refuse to look for the truth.' She put her hands on her linen-clad hips. 'You are innocent of what happened. And I will never believe otherwise. Never.'

'Then though you are beautiful, you are also a fool.'

The words stung, for she had feared he thought thus. 'And you do not wish a fool for a wife, so you won't have me.'

'That is not what I said,' he corrected hastily.

'Do you mean to offer for me? Answer truthfully.'

And he hesitated. But then he said, 'In the hallway, when Bellston left, I said it badly, for I made it sound as if I didn't care about you. I am sorry for that. I wish very much to offer for you. But I want you to face the facts of the marriage you will be making. If you wish to be the wife of a murderer, then I shall be happier than I deserve if you will take me as your husband.'

'I do not wish to marry a murderer. I wish to marry you. I love you, Tim. And I will not change.'

'Then we are at an impasse, Daphne. I love you as well. More than ever I believed I could. And I will live a long and full life if you will admit my crime and forgive me for it. But it will hurt too much for me to bear it, if you believe me innocent. For the day will come when you come to full understanding of the mistake you made.'

She turned and fled, running for the stairs, heedless of her condition, and surroundings.

And there, at the foot of the stairs, was Mrs Sims staring in chilly disapproval.

Chapter Sixteen

In her room, Daphne scrubbed at her face, trying to make the tearstains on her cheeks less visible. She had met the cook on the stairs as well, on her way from bringing the children their breakfast. In a short time, everyone in the household would know what she had done. She would have to face their disapproving looks in the hall and know that they thought her unfit to care for children. And what would they think of their master? Though they could forgive him a murder, there might be a limit beyond which he had travelled that would lose their respect.

No matter how sure she was of the truth, until she could prove it to Tim, there would be no marriage, no chance to redeem her reputation. Her only hope was to slip away, leaving Miss Collins behind, as a crab leaves a shell. She could go back to London, to her old life. And with no likelihood of seeing Tim or the children. For when had she seen them before?

She pulled out the contents of her trunk, ready to repack it, and Sophie's sketches fell in a cascade of horror on to the wooden floor. She could hardly bear to look down. If she left, what was she to tell the children?

She would go to Lily and explain. She would tell her that she had ill family to attend to. The girl was the oldest, and might fill in the details on her own. She suspected something, just as Adam and Penny did. So Daphne would explain, as gently as she could, that Miss Collins could not stay with them. But that they were to be good for their father, and Sophie was to be allowed to draw, no matter what the subject...

She looked down at the sketches. All Clare, all in the same dress. It was the dress she had died in, if Sophie's first sketch was to be believed. And with the toe of her slipper, she rearranged the two papers in front of her. And picked up the first drawing, to put it last.

When viewed thus, in order, the angles came right, and the story fell into place. Clare at the top of the stairs. Clare angry. A hand, holding a bit of torn cloth. Her shocked expression, as she lost her balance. Clare falling.

Clare dead.

Daphne pulled off her wrapper, and washed and dressed quickly. She ignored the breakfast, and the schoolroom, leaving the children alone without explanation. If she took time to explain, someone was sure to convince her that what she was about to do was wrong.

She went straight down to the conservatory, back to Tim.

He was sitting beside his work table, with a light breakfast and tea cup laid on a napkin on the bench beside him. He rose with his tea cup held in a hopeful gesture, as though he had forgotten the way they had parted only a few moments ago, and thought she might have returned to dine with him.

She reached out and caught him by the hand, pulling him off the bench and away from his tea. 'You must come with me. To the children. Right now.'

He rose easily at the mention of the children, obviously worried. 'Is there a problem? An accident?'

'No, they are well. But they *know*, Tim. They know everything.'

His brow furrowed in confusion.

'The night Clare died. They saw it happen.'

The china cup fell from his numb fingers and shattered on the slates. 'God, no.'

'It is true. Sophie saw everything. She has been drawing it, over and over for me. But I did not understand. The others either saw as well, or they know what she has seen. They are afraid to come to you. So you must go to them and ask.'

He looked at her as though she were mad. 'Ask them? They have suffered enough. They should not have to tell what they know. The truth would be enough to hang their father. I can live with the punishment. But I cannot die knowing that they will feel responsible for my end.'

'That is not what will happen. I am sure. If they saw

anything at all, they will be able to tell you that it was an accident, just as Adam decreed.'

He laughed. 'The accident was a polite fiction. We all know that. Adam feels guilty for allowing himself to be seduced by my wife. He thinks he can make things right between us by covering up my crime. It gains nothing to make the children relive a night they would just as soon forget. And if you care at all about my welfare or my sanity, then do not force them to denounce me.' His voice trembled. 'No wonder they could not stand to be with me. I will send them from here, as soon as I am able. And once they are gone, I will see to it, one way or another, that justice is served in the matter of Clare's death. But do not make them play a part in my downfall.'

'That is not what will happen at all. The truth is nothing to be afraid of. I am sure of it. Why are you always so intent upon taking the weight of this upon yourself? Why do you never place the blame upon Sophie's father? For he had as much reason to wish Clare dead as you did. I doubt Penny would be so patient, living next door to her husband's lover.'

'You think Adam did this?' And then Tim let out a bitter laugh. 'What utter nonsense.'

'You are too quick to protect him, after what he did to you. I understand that your friendship is deep, and that he can be a most personable and pleasant man. But that is no reason to let him free of his crime.'

'Crime?' Now Tim was truly laughing. 'Adam is guilty of many things. He has been by turns a drunkard, a rake and a wastrel. He cuckolded me, as did half the men in London. But his respect for the law holds no equal. He would be physically incapable of breaking it to rid the world of my wife. Even if she threatened him with exposure, as I know she did.'

'Did you not read the letters that I stole? She was going to Adam on the night she died, and taking their daughter with her. And he would not have wanted her, now that he was married.'

'Was she now?' He shook his head. 'Then, obviously, you are mistaken. For he had no daughter by her, nor was he likely to get one. She was not pregnant when she died. At least not by him, for they had not been together for several months.'

'But Sophie…'

He laid a hand upon her arm. 'Was another man's child. I suspect she belongs to a drawing master, if such talents are a thing that can be inherited.' He laughed again, and for a moment, he seemed sincerely light-hearted. 'Clare must have been quite angry with me if she was threatening to go to him at the end. The man was penniless, and ran like the wind when it became apparent that he might have fathered a child. From time to time, Clare made such idle threats and left the letters around to frighten me. She knew how much I loved the girl. But the idea that she might leave the comfort of our home to live as a Bohemian, with her artist…' He laughed. Then he sighed, as if he was trying to expel all the grief in his body in one great breath. 'Daphne. If the circumstances were otherwise, I would be grateful for your naïve trust in my character. If only I had met you twelve years ago, before I met Clare. I would gladly trade the wealth I gained from my first marriage for a chance to have a love such as yours, willing to put such blind faith in me. But I swear to you on all that is holy, I was the only one in the house on the night she died. The servants would have noticed had there been a guest and remarked on it. They might have cared enough for her not to reveal the names of her lovers. But they care enough for me not to hide the identity of a murderer.'

'All you have are guesses and assumptions. The children have the truth,' she said.

'It does not matter to me if they do. I forbid you from talking to them on the matter of their mother's death. If not for my sake, then for theirs. Let them forget.'

'Forget?' She laughed in his miserable face. 'Now you are the one who is being naïve. They are not going to forget, Tim. It does not matter what I say or do, they are still living the night their mother died. Sophie especially. Have you seen her drawings? Blood and death. It has taken weeks to get her to draw anything but her mother's corpse. Would you have me take her pens away, or punish her as the last governess did?'

'No!'

'Then let them tell you what they saw. Even if it is bad, at least it will be honest. They should not have to go through life afraid of stairs and watercolours, and strangers. For God's sake, Tim, they should not have to be afraid of you. No matter what they might say, you would never love them less, would you?'

'Of course not.'

'Now, they live in continual fear of your rejection.

They think that you mean to send them away because
you no longer want them.'

'That is not true.'

'But they reason like children. They do not understand that they were not to blame. They think you want
to be rid of them and refuse to believe otherwise. Go to
them. Go now. Tell them it is not so. And ask them for
the truth.'

He wavered.

'We will go together,' she offered, placing her hand
on his shoulder. 'I will be there to help you. But it must
be done, for their sake, for yours, and for ours.'

He stared at her, and his eyes held the same shocked
confusion that the children's did. 'And if helping them
means I lose you?'

She smiled. 'You will not lose me.'

'I will if I hang for murder.' He ran a hand through
his hair and gave a shaky laugh. 'It was all so much
easier to contemplate ending my life, knowing that the
day for the deed had not arrived. But you would have
me do it now, after I have found a reason to survive.'
His face was grey with fear and shock, but he rose from
the desk and squared his shoulders. 'And I am so vain
that I cannot let the woman I love see my cowardice.
You say I am hurting the children by my inaction. And
I must trust you on this, for you are their governess, and
know more than I about the minds of children.'

The truth stuck in her throat. The time was coming
when she would have to admit that she knew far less
about children then he did. But not now. For now, she
only knew what was right. 'They are your children, Tim.

You know what is best for them. In all save this one thing.'

His shoulders slumped, and she knew that she had defeated him. 'Very well, then. Let us go to them and be done with it. If they have been suffering because of my inaction, then I would not have it be for one moment more.' He went to the door, and opened it, waiting politely for her to pass through. She followed him to the main stairs, and he paused at the foot for a moment, just as he always did. Then he offered her his arm, and began the ascent. His steps were steady and unhurried, but she could see in his eye the desire to turn and run, to hurry, or to tarry. It was a struggle for him to make the trip appear ordinary.

At last they reached the top of the stairs and he escorted her down the hall, still holding her arm. And she wondered for a moment if it was for her protection or as a way to gain strength from the contact. She could see the housekeeper approaching from the other end of the hall, and the hitch in her gait as she saw the master arm in arm with the governess, about to talk to the children.

Emotions flickered across the woman's face. Shock, disapproval and then thoughtfulness. She gazed again at her employer, as though considering both the past and the future. And then she gave a small smile of approval, and continued on her way as if nothing unusual had occurred.

If Tim noticed, he made no mention of it. But it set Daphne somewhat at ease to know, if they survived the afternoon, she would not have Mrs Sims as an adversary.

He paused at the door of the schoolroom as though he still considered it possible to turn back. And then he opened the door and stood before the children.

Daphne could see by the looks on their faces that they instinctively sensed the difference in the adults and were confused by it. Without a word, the older children took a half-step towards their little sister.

'Children?' Tim looked at them for a moment as though he had never seen them before. He was staring at the worried looks on their faces, the set lines around their mouths and the frightened look in Sophie's eyes, as though it were all registering on him, fresh. Then he dropped Daphne's hand and went to them, down on one knee so that he might not be over-tall for the little one. 'It is time for us to talk.'

'About what, Father?' Edmund was curiously formal. Daphne suspected it was a ruse to buy time, for it was apparent that he knew exactly what the subject was to be.

'About the night…' Tim swallowed. 'The night your mother died. Daphne seems to think that you saw the… when I…when she fell.'

She looked at them all, her eyes travelling from face to face. Giving them a look that was all kindness and implacability. 'Tell your father.'

'If you have a secret?' Tim smiled down at them, as if to reassure them, but there were lines of strain around his mouth. 'Whatever you are concealing, I am sure it will be better if we face it together.'

'Don't send Sophie away,' Lily blurted, and then silenced herself after a glare from Edmund.

'And why would I do that?' Tim smiled again, this time with incredulity.

Sophie took a step away from him, as though afraid, and said, 'Mama fell.'

His smile became a rictus, and he flinched. 'Yes, little one. I know. And I am very sorry.' He said it carefully, not knowing how to proceed. 'But because Mama…fell…it does not mean that I am angry with you, or that you are in any danger from me. Or that I do not love you very, very much. I just think that you would be better off if you were in school, and away from here. You will find, once you try it, that it is very pleasant. And you will have such fun that you will not miss this house, or your old father, very much at all.' The last words rang false, as did his smile. For it appeared that it was difficult for him to hold even the sad parody of a grin that he had managed before.

Sophie's lip began to tremble.

'Do not punish her,' Lily blurted again, and reached to gather her little sister to her. 'Send us away, but let her stay. She is so small. And she did not know. It will not happen again. She knows better now.'

'This is not meant as a punishment,' Tim said hopelessly. 'When you are older, you will see. It is for the best. There are people better suited to take care of you than I, darling Sophie.'

Sophie was crying in earnest now, large tears sliding silently over her round cheeks. Daphne reached to comfort her, but the children closed ranks, just as they had from the first. Lily hugged her little sister and Edmund stepped between father and sisters to protect them, as though he were already the man he would become, and a match for his father. He squared his shoulders and shouted, 'Just because she is not yours, does not mean that you should not care for her.'

'Who told you that?' Tim demanded. But Daphne was sure that she knew. Where else would they have got the truth, but from their mother?

'She is not yours,' Edmund repeated. 'And so you mean to punish her, even though it is no fault of hers how our mother behaved.'

Tim took a deep, shaky breath. 'I do not blame you, any of you, for the problems between your mother and myself. And I am sorry you had to witness what you did, at the end. It was wrong to subject you to that. I think, in sending you to school, that it would be better if you were removed to an atmosphere that would be less unhealthy.'

'School?' Edmund said bitterly. 'We know the sort of school you want to send Sophie to. A madhouse is no place for a little girl.'

'Madhouse?' Tim said, helpless. 'When did I ever…?'

'Let us take care of her,' Lily pleaded. 'She is no trouble. She doesn't eat much and she's not a bother at all. And she will never hurt anyone again.'

'Again?' Now Tim was truly puzzled. 'Children. No more games. And no more nonsense about the madhouse, not even in jest. I never meant to send Sophie there. You must tell me what has frightened you so. Tell me exactly. For I truly do not understand.'

'Mama fell,' Sophie said again. And the two children looked at her in horror, as though she were not stating the obvious.

And suddenly, the meaning of the pictures became clear. And the strange angles of the drawings, as though they were from the perspective of a small child who was only drawing what she had seen right in front of her.

'Tell your father what happened that night,' Daphne prompted. 'For he knows less about it than you think he does.'

Tim flinched again, as though he did not want to know the truth, after all this time. And then he said, 'Tell me. I need to know what happened, children. I need to know the truth.'

Edmund looked at him, sullen and in challenge. 'After you fought, Mother was angry. She said that you had sent her to pack her things and get out of your sight. And she came here and told Lily and me that she wanted no part of us any more. We were our father's children, and you could keep us. But that Sophie was none of yours, and so she must go as well. Because you would not want her, once Mother had gone.'

Tim took a deep breath. 'I did not mean for her to do that. She was being hurtful.'

Lily gave a small nod. 'We did not want her to take Sophie and we called for you, but you did not come.'

Their father let out a small moan of pain.

'And she took Sophie by the arm, and dragged her out onto the landing.'

'It was hurting her,' Edmund said quietly. 'So she cried and fought.'

'Mama fell,' Sophie said again.

And Daphne could see the scene in her mind, in horrible clarity. The children crying, and mother and daughter struggling at the top of the stairs. Clare's dress ripping. And the horrible moment when she knew that she could not stop herself from falling.

She turned to Tim. And she could see the moment when he understood, as something inside him released that had been held tense since the moment of his wife's death. His features struggled between relief for himself and agony for his children. He reached forwards and pulled Sophie into his arms. 'It was an accident,' he murmured. 'Only an accident. And no one's fault at all. Is this what you have been afraid of, all this time?' He hugged her tight and murmured into her hair, 'I am so sorry, little one. So sorry.' He looked over her head, to the other children. 'I did not understand.'

'I don't want to go,' whispered Sophie.

'And you will not, sweetheart. You will stay safe and happy, right here. Isn't that so, Miss Collins?' He looked to her for confirmation, for she could see that the little girl had turned her worried expression to her, probably fearing her response.

'Of course that is so, little one.' And she smiled encouragement, although the truth was horrible. 'Where else would you belong but in your home?'

Sophie seemed to slump a little, to become even smaller than she was, as though she wanted to climb into her father's lap and stay for a very long time. But there was a hesitant smile upon her face, as though the worst had happened, and she had begun to suspect it might be all right, after all.

'And you will always be my little girl.' He looked up to his other children, and opened his arms wide to encompass them. 'You are all mine. It does not matter where you go. I am your father, and this is your home. And always will be.'

And, hesitantly, the other children stepped into his arms as well. And suddenly it was a tangle of arms and legs, and laughter and tears. And Daphne looked around, feeling lost and out of place.

And Tim looked up, over the heads of all his children, and said, 'Miss Collins?', holding his arms even wider.

And the children laughed, and turned to her as well, calling, 'Miss Collins?', and holding out their arms as well.

She froze for a moment, and then she laughed, and stepped in, joining the family. And she understood what had been lacking in the house, for the warmth and love in the hug seemed to pervade her very soul.

And Tim's eyes met hers, and he gave an incredulous little shake of his head. 'It was an accident,' he whispered again. 'A terrible accident. No one's fault at all.' And while she could feel the concern for his daughter emanating from him like a warm glow, he seemed a totally different person than the dark, tortured soul she had first met.

Chapter Seventeen

After what seemed like a long time he released them, and reached for a handkerchief to wipe his eyes and his brow.

Edmund looked at him, with sudden shyness, and said, 'Must we still go to school, then?'

Tim sighed. 'We will talk of that later, I think. The revelations of the day have given me much to think on. Perhaps next term…'

The boy seemed to sag in relief. 'And Sophie? Mother said—'

Tim stopped him. 'I would not put too much weight on anything that happened on those last days. Your mother and I were very angry at one another. What was said then changes nothing. We will not speak of it again.'

Lily smiled in understanding, and hugged her father all the harder.

'And Miss Collins will stay as well,' Sophie announced, and gave her father a hug.

And she could feel the awkwardness, coming from Tim, just as the love and protection had before. 'I think that is something I must discuss with Miss Collins,' he said.

'Yes,' she said softly, in answer. 'But now, children, you must get ready for lessons.'

'Lessons?' Tim laughed out loud. 'No lessons today. No work. We will go for a walk in the woods. And visit the orangery to see how the trees are faring.'

The children's faces shone with anticipation. Daphne looked at each in turn. 'There is a chill in the air. Go to your rooms and change into clothing that is sensible for the weather. And wash the breakfast from your hands and faces. Take care with your nails...' She let the familiarity of the routine take her, blunting out the question in the back of her mind. What would become of her, now? She had done what she had come to do, and satisfied herself as to the details of Clarissa's death.

And she could hardly fault the family, if she had been foolish enough to lose her heart as well. The man standing before her now was nothing like the dark lord who had come to her rooms. That man was gone, and in his place was a respectable father who would never have taken such liberties.

And it suddenly occurred to her that what her mother had always told her about the value of reputation might be true. She might have been able to hold his desire, but would he respect her, now that he could have any woman he wanted?

As the children moved off to care for themselves, she heard him behind her. 'Daphne?' His voice was soft, the question in the name surprisingly gentle.

'Yes?' She turned to face him.

He paused again, unsure of how to continue. And then he said, 'We have to talk.'

'We are talking now.'

'In private. After the children have gone to bed, about what will happen next between us.'

She glanced at the children, walking down the hall together. 'It would be best, if the news is bad, to inform me of it, quickly. To prevent any nonsense and false assumptions on my part.'

He gave a dry little laugh. 'How like a governess you sound, all of a sudden. Very prim and proper.'

'Perhaps it is about time for me to do so.' She frowned, thinking of Sophie's obvious attachment to her. 'I never gave thought to them, and what might happen after, even though it was my job. That should have been my first priority.'

When she looked at him, he was smiling at her, in a way she had never seen before. It was strange and soft and warm, and it made her blush. 'You honour my family with your concern. And you have given a great gift to us, with what I thought was meddling and snooping and a far from healthy curiosity about Clare. If it were not for your persistence, I would never have known the truth.'

And another flash of guilt caught her. Her motives had been just as bad as he'd thought, even if the results had been in his favour.

'And I must apologise for my treatment of you, which was coloured by my fears of the truth, and was not as respectful as it should have been.'

An odd apology. She brushed it away with a wave of her hand.

'And I would like to take the opportunity to start again, and to treat you as you deserve, as one who holds my affection, and that of my children.'

It sounded almost like he meant to pay court to her, and pretend that nothing had happened between them. And to prevent the awkwardness, she dropped a small curtsy, and said, 'Thank you, my lord,' averting her eyes and easily becoming the servant she had never thought to be.

'Oh, bloody hell.' And, for a moment, the old Tim was back. He seized her by the arms and pulled her lips to his. 'I meant to start fresh with you, now that I am free. But I cannot manage it, if you mean to change as well.' He kissed her with such force that she could hardly breathe, his hands twisting in her hair, her crisp gown rumpling under his touch, and she said, 'Lord Colton, please. The children.'

'Oh, what nonsense. The children will best get used to the way I feel about you. You have given me my life back, and my family as well. I am not going to let you drift away from me, now that everything is finally right.'

'Right?' Didn't he understand it was all wrong? For she had done wrong in coming here, even if the results were right.

He held her hand, and dropped to his knees before

her. 'I love you.' He gave a great breath, as though a weight had been lifted from his chest, and grinned up at her. And it was happy and relaxed and open. 'I have loved you for some time. But I was afraid to act. You are too good to tie yourself to a wreck such as I was. A murderer. A man with no future. I wanted better for you than I could ever give. But now?' He spread his arms wide. 'Now, it is all changed. I can be happy without guilt. And I can make you happy as well. Or, at least, I would like to try.' A shadow passed over his face. 'It will be difficult, of course. There are the children to think of. They have been through hell over this, and it will take time to recover. But you know better than anyone that what happened was an accident. You can help them see that, now that they no longer fear the discovery.'

That was true, at least.

'They are very fond of you. And now that you know the truth, there is nothing to stand between us.'

'Nothing,' she said softly, her own motives in coming there, and her real name and family, rising like ghosts from the mist.

'Is that a yes?' he asked hopefully. And then muttered, 'Or have I forgotten the proposal? Because I fully intended to ask. And it has been so strange between us. All the wrong way round. Not the normal thing at all. Perhaps you misunderstood.' He cleared his throat, and said, in a formal tone that was quite spoiled by his grinning, 'Miss Collins, it would do me a great honour if you would give me your hand in marriage.'

And once again, there was the little break in her

mind, as she recognised her alias. It occurred to her too late that Tim should really be speaking to her father over this. But he did not even know that she had a father, since the Duchess believed that Miss Collins had no family. Which meant that there was even more to explain than she thought. And she found that she could not meet his gaze. 'This is very sudden. I will have to think on it.'

'Of course.' She could hear his optimism faltering in his voice. 'It is rather out of the blue. And I meant to do it differently. Better. It is rather unfair of me to present it so.' He reached out and touched her hand. 'But I am so…happy. You cannot begin to understand. I am overcome.' And now there was a break in his voice, which was quickly mastered. 'Please, take as much time as you need. For we will have a lifetime.' He released her hand.

And when she looked into his eyes, she saw such hope, such confidence in her and in their future, that it was even more difficult to blurt the truth.

'I must go and see that the children are ready for your walk.'

'And you?'

Where was she to go? It was not really her place to walk with the family. And she was not sure if it would ever be. But she knew that the idea of a day with Tim and the children would be intensely painful to her, until she could find the right words to explain things to him. 'Today, I think it should be just you and your children. You have much to learn about each other, and it is not the place for a servant to intrude.'

He looked puzzled, as though he could not understand why her joy did not match his own. 'You know I do not think of you in that way.'

'Still, you need time alone with each other. You can manage without me, for a few hours. I will be here tonight.' She almost had to convince herself of the fact, for there was some panicked portion of her that wanted to rush to her room, gather her belongings and flee.

He nodded in regret. 'I suppose it is true. There is much we have not discussed, as a family. They have lived in needless fear for months, and I was too blind to see it.' His lips tightened for a moment, in resolution. 'I must undo any nonsense instilled by Clare, at the end. It has festered too long.'

She had a fleeting image of her dear cousin, so happy, so pleasant, and yet so vain. And so very thoughtless of those around her. 'They will be all right now that they know they have your love.'

He stared at her again. And then he smiled. 'As do you. And thank you for your confidence in me. Now go, if you must. Or I will hold you here until you say the things I wish to hear.'

Where she once might have been terrified by the threat, his words came as gentle as a caress. Without thinking, she dropped a curtsy and exited as his governess, not his lover.

It was no easier, waiting in her room. She had hoped that the things she must say would come to her, once she was alone. But her mind was a whirl of beginnings, and no clear ending. She was sorry, of course. But when he came to her tonight, would an apology be sufficient?

* * *

When at last she heard the footsteps on her stairs, she took a deep breath and sat up, still not ready to meet him.

It came as a surprise when there was an unfamiliar rap upon the door, rather than his hand upon the knob. 'Miss Collins?'

'Yes.' It was Willoby, the footman.

'I have a letter for you. From the master.'

'Slip it under the door, please.' She pulled the covers up to her chin.

She suspected he was disappointed that she did not open for him and take the letter herself. The communication was unusual, and he no doubt wanted some scrap of gossip to take below stairs. But instead there was the scratch of paper on wood as the letter appeared, and the somewhat dejected sound of Willoby's retreating steps.

When she was sure that he had gone, she got out of bed and hurried across the floor to pick up the paper. The seal was unbroken, thank God. The contents were still private. She snapped the wax and unfolded it, turning to the candle so that she could read the words.

My darling Daphne,
While I want nothing more in life than to be at your side this night, I cannot allow myself to come to you, until I am sure of your response to my question. Should it be no, I could not in good conscience share your bed. For what would it say of

my motives, or the respect and esteem I have for you, to treat you in so common a way?

You will probably think it quite foolish that I have found the value of your honour so late in our acquaintance. And perhaps it is. But I find that life was much simpler when I had no hope in the future. In my despair, I took without thinking of the consequences, for they did not matter to me. I was completely sure of myself, in thought and action. Once a man realises he is damned, he has nothing more to fear.

I am immeasurably happier than I was, just a day ago. But I find that with renewed hope, comes doubt. Did I force you to do something which you now regret? Did you only agree to save your job, or my feelings? Now that the way is clear for us to be together, are your feelings less fixed than mine?

If I have done anything that makes you unable to answer yes, with your whole heart, then please forgive me for it. If there is a way to mend the problem, if there is anything at all that I can do so that we may begin fresh, tell me it, and I will give it you.

I want nothing more than that you might know me for the man I truly am, and not the demon that possessed me for so long. My heart, my mind, all I have, I will lay at your feet. You have but to accept it to make me the happiest man in Wales.

If you will have me, then I shall always be,

Your Tim.

She climbed into bed, clutching the paper tight to her breast, the words still echoing in her head. She wanted them to make her happy, and wished to make him happy as well. But how could he not realise that it was her unworthiness, and not his, that created the rift?

After a sleepless night she decided that the problem was all hers. She wished to soften the blow, when nothing but the whole truth would do. She arose when it was barely light, and pulled her finest day dress from the portmanteau, doing her best to shake the wrinkles from it. It was a beautiful thing of deep blue silk, embroidered all about the hem with tiny flowers. Far too impractical for a servant, which was the reason it had lain unworn for all these weeks.

She washed carefully and dressed herself. And she could see in the small scrap of mirror that already she looked different. Then, with many pins and much fussing, she managed to do her hair up in a fashion much more in tune with the way she used to wear it, when she'd had a ladies' maid and time for a proper *toilette*. With each stroke of the brush she felt a little more her old self, and a little less like Miss Collins the governess.

And she was prettier, of course. Tim deserved no less than that. But more confident, entitled to speak freely to a man who was within her social set.

A man very much to her tastes. She smiled. She suspected her father would approve as well. Tim's intelligence and good sense fairly shone from him, now that he was feeling better. He was rich enough, but not frivolous. He had a fine house, and a title as well. She suspected that, when the time came for the two to meet, his suit would be received with as much relief as joy.

And that he loved her, and she loved him in return, was almost too much to hope for. She had imagined that marriage would be as Clare had assured her, an impediment to happiness, rather than the beginning of true joy. Which proved again how little Clare knew on the subject. It appeared she was likely to have everything she might want: a man who suited her temper, and a husband to suit her family. And a family of her own, ready made—if she could make it over the difficult hurdle of revealing her true name and her reasons for coming here.

She would go to him this morning, first thing, full of humility. She would suggest that they take breakfast in the conservatory, just the two of them. The presence of his plants relaxed him, and he would be in the best frame of mind for unfortunate truths. She would tell all, and give what sorry explanations she could manage. And she would swear that there would be no more falsehoods or deceptions from her. He would have nothing but fidelity, honesty and obedience from his wife, if he wished to make the offer in his letter again, in person. She took a deep breath, and set off down the stairs to find the man she loved.

When she arrived in the drawing room, she found Tim waiting in attendance upon a guest.

It was her father.

Chapter Eighteen

She stopped in the doorway, listening to the two men, who had not yet noticed her. 'The London Collinghams,' Tim said in a stunned voice.

'I was Clarissa's uncle. Her father's brother. I assumed your late wife must have mentioned our daughter to you, for they spent much time together, when Clare was in London.'

'Of course.' His voice was faint, as though he were trying to hide the fact that he had no idea what his wife did when she was away from him. There were so many things he did not wish to hear in detail that innocent family visits must have fallen by the wayside.

'It came as a great surprise that she should be eager to visit here. She did not tell us of her intentions, when she set out. It was only when she did not arrive at her aunt's that we set about inquiring. And then, of course, we received Daphne's letter of explanation, delayed due to a blurred address.'

'Oh.' Tim's voice was still faint. Perhaps he had begun to understand, or was still merely confused by her father's strange, disapproving tone.

She stepped fully into the room, before it became any worse than it was.

'There you are.' Her father's voice held the same exasperated tone she had grown used to in London. As though whatever she had done it was faintly disappointing and not at all the course he would have chosen for her.

He beetled his brows and gave her a half-hearted glare. 'If you wished to visit a different branch of the family, I would not have objected, for I must say that Wales is remote enough to put you out of scandal's way. And one cousin is very like the next. But it is most rude of you to have given us no notice. And careless of you to send a letter that could not be read.' He glared again, as though he meant to say 'suspiciously careless'. Then he went on with his gentle harangue. 'Your mother is beside herself with worry. And I have had to track you across Wales like a wounded stag.'

She swallowed and said softly, 'I am sorry. I did not think.'

'You rarely do.' Her father shot a glance at Tim, smiling to mitigate some of the gall. 'I swear, if the girl was not so sweet natured, we'd never put up with the mischief. I hope she has not given you too much bother, in her time here.'

Tim's face was frozen as though carved in stone. At last, he managed, 'She has made up for some of the bother, and been a great help to the children.'

'Daphne helping with children?' Her father laughed then, unable to contain himself. 'What a ludicrous idea. You must have been bored out of your senses, Daphne darling, to succumb to the charms of little ones.'

'They are most exceptional children, Father. All three of them…'

But he'd turned back to Tim and was confiding, 'She really is the most selfish creature on some subjects. My wife and I have been long resigned to the fact that when she settles, any grandchildren we are likely to have from her will be raised by the nanny. If it is left to my daughter, the first handprint left on a gown, and she will put the poor mites outside with the dogs.'

'Really.' It was impossible to read the meaning in a single word. But she suspected that Tim meant to let her father ramble, just to see where the path of the conversation went.

Her father was laughing as though it were the most wonderful diversion that he had raised his daughter to be so insensible to the needs of others. And Tim was staring at her as though she were a monster. She could feel her cheeks, hot with embarrassment.

Her father ceased his laughing, and dipped his head in apology. 'I can't think what has got into the girl. We sent her to Wales as a punishment. She was nothing but trouble while in London. And, until recently, I had no idea that she had not followed instruction and gone directly to her aunt's.'

'I see.' Tim's face was deathly white, and still devoid of expression.

'I really cannot understand young women nowadays. Not even the ones in my own family. For they seem to know no bounds of decorum.' It was then that her father realised that he was speaking ill of the former lady of the house, and his tone moderated. 'But lovely, of course. Your wife was a great beauty.'

Tim nodded, giving the man nothing to rescue himself.

'And a particular friend of Daphne's. I suspect that is why she came here.'

'I had no idea that you and Clare were so close. You never said.' If possible, Tim's complexion went even whiter. And his face twisted in a sickly smile. 'Had you not heard that Clarissa was no longer living?'

'I had.' Her answer was barely a whisper.

'Oh, yes,' her father announced. 'She was most affected by it. She grieved for days about the unfairness, the strangeness that one so young, without a trace of infirmity, should die in a fall.'

Daphne touched a hand to her throbbing temple, as her father all but explained her suspicions, and the way she had declared to all in the family that it was likely to be the work of that horrible Timothy Colton.

And then, her father stopped just short of the truth, and said, 'But the children... I expect that was what drew Daphne here, and it explains her sudden change of heart. It was all out of a desire to see that they were well. I am sure that Clarissa would have wished it.'

'You are sure, are you?' Tim's smile had changed to a grimace. And for a moment, she was afraid that he would reveal all. Then he seemed to gain mastery over himself, and returned to the reliable lie. 'That is it, certainly.' He turned to her, then, speaking formally. 'Well, Miss Collingham. As you can see, after staying with us, you have nothing to fear for the sake of the children. I am quite able to care for them, from this time forth. I trust I have been able to set your mind at rest on the subject.'

'Yes.' She choked out the word, and her answering smile was as false as his. But it seemed to reassure her father that, at least this time, there would be no scandal. She had not made as complete a cake of herself as he feared.

'While I appreciate your concern, you had but to ask and I could have invited you formally to stay as a guest. Your treatment would have been much less haphazard, had we been better prepared for your visit.'

Her father accepted it as an apology, and nodded again. But she knew the truth of the words. Had he known who she was, he'd never have touched her, or trusted her with the care of his children. And he certainly would not have been fool enough to love her.

'I'm sorry.'

Her father glared again. 'As well you should be, for causing the man so much trouble.'

Tim waved his hand. 'We will not speak of it again.'

And again, her father accepted it, as a gentlemanly dismissal of the mess she had caused with her foolishness. But she suspected that the words were directed to her, and meant *I will not speak to you again.*

'I appreciate your understanding. And now, if the servants will finish packing your things, the carriage is waiting.' Father gave her a significant look.

'If I could speak to Mr. Colton for a moment, before departing?'

Her father gave an impatient sigh. 'This was not sufficient farewell?'

'In private, Father.'

Her father looked to Tim, who looked back, still impassive, and gave the slightest of nods.

'Very well, then. I will await you in the carriage.'

She waited for a moment, as her father left the room, until she was sure that he was out of earshot. And then she spoke. 'Tim, I must explain.' She reached out to touch his sleeve.

He shook off her hand and stepped clear of her grasp. 'Further explanation is not necessary. I already knew you thought me a murderer.'

'As you did yourself. But you are not. We both know that now.'

'It must have disappointed you to discover the fact. I had no idea the lengths you would go to, to prove my guilt. And I thought it was I who dragged you to do what you did.'

'Do not speak of it so,' she moaned. 'As though what we did was foul and base.'

'It was,' he said firmly. 'But now that I know of your relationship to my wife, it makes much more sense. You were not without guilt, or your parents would never have sent you from London.' He laughed. 'And I tortured myself with the notion that I had debauched an innocent. It appears that I am the more naïve of the two of us.'

'That is not true. I never… There was no one before you.'

He shrugged. 'Perhaps not. But you gave your virtue up fast enough, once you could find a reason to. You let me use you, to gain the information you craved. And you used me as well.'

Tears were stinging in her eyes to hear what had happened between them relegated to a transaction. 'It was more than that, I swear. I love you.'

'If you are a protégée of Clare's, then you are no more capable of love than she was.'

'That is not true. Perhaps once it might have been. But she was wrong. I do love you, Tim. And I love the children.'

'Do not speak of them!' His eyes narrowed. 'If I can do nothing else, I will see to it that you never bother them again. You know what I am capable of, with regards to them. Do not cross me. And do not think, for even a moment, that I will let you become a part of their lives.'

'Have you forgotten so quickly what we were talking about last night?' she argued. 'I am already a part of their lives, just as they are a part of mine. And I am a part of your life, as well.' She held her hand out to him again.

He ignored it. 'No longer.'

'You cannot send me away so easily. They need me, Tim. You need me.'

'They do not need another Clarissa. They need a

mother. Or perhaps, they need better than that. A true governess, and not some ignorant, lying sham.' He looked at her, slowly, up and down. 'And if I wish to replace what you have been to me? To find a pretty woman, to share my bed and tell me lies? Then I will find a whore. Good day to you, madam.'

And he turned and left her alone in the room, ignoring the tears in her eyes.

Chapter Nineteen

'Vouchers!' Her mother fairly sang the word. 'The patronesses have seen fit to forgive you, my dear. We are going to Almack's.' She waved the letter over her head in triumph. 'A few months away was all that was necessary. The disasters of last Season are forgotten.'

'Much has changed,' Daphne said, without much enthusiasm.

'I should say so.' Her mother nodded in approval. 'For you turned down a chance to go to Vauxhall Gardens last night, and Covent Garden the night before. And bless my eyes if I did not see you reading before the fire.'

Daphne shrugged. 'It is a quiet way to pass the time. And I have begun to suspect that there are gaps in my education. It would be wise to remedy them, lest I be thought a fool.'

Her mother laughed. 'It certainly did not concern you before. But reading is harmless enough, if not carried to extremes. I would not want to see you wrapped in a book once the Season is full upon us. That would be most unnatural.'

'Of course not.'

'Or dressed in the same gowns that you wore before. I do not wish people to think we have no money to purchase new. It will give the husband-hunt an air of desperation. Or worse yet, it will make your suitors think you do not care enough for them to put on fresh silks. And so we must shop.'

'I suppose, if we must.' She sighed.

Her mother looked at her strangely. 'Are you ill, darling?'

'No. I am fine, really.' She could not help it. She sighed again.

'Well, I think you must be ill, if you are resisting a trip to Bond Street. Your father will be incensed over it, of course. How very like a man not to see the need.'

Daphne glanced at her already too-full wardrobe. In truth, she could not see the need herself. Even her oldest dresses were hardly worn. 'It just seems so wasteful not to manage with the things I've already got.'

Her mother was giving her the look again. 'The scandal of last Season may be behind you, my dear, but I doubt that last Season's dresses will be forgotten so easily. It would never do to have every mother's daughter sniping behind their hands at your finery, in your moment of triumph. If I'd known that a month in the country would give you such bizarre notions... But never mind, it could not be helped. And now we must work to bring you back to the spirited girl you once were. For I swear, while I welcome the moderation in your character, you are most decidedly not yourself since your return.'

'I suppose.' She looked into the mirror at her own reflection, trying to see what her mother saw, and continually surprised at what she did not see. When she looked into her own eyes, the new knowledge in them was plain enough. She had expected, with a single look, that her mother would discern what had happened, and ship her right back into permanent rustication.

But no. While her father and mother had feared for her reputation before she left London, and all society had proclaimed her a hoyden, they now saw a picture of maidenly modesty. And they meant to reward her for it, whether she liked it or no.

The thought would have made her laugh, if she could bring herself to that mood. Instead, she sighed again.

He mother laid a tentative hand upon her shoulder. 'I am sure it is just a matter of re-entering society, and your mood will return to normal. I am sorry that we had to take such drastic action, my dear, and send you far from home. We missed you dreadfully, of course. And it did concern me to learn that you had stayed with Clare's family, instead of the family we had chosen for you. She was dreadfully wild, you know. We did not realise what we had done by encouraging the friendship. But hers was not the influence we sought.'

To be told this now heaped irony upon the situation. 'Oh.'

Her mother smiled. 'But I can see it has done you no real harm, and, in some ways, much good.'

'Lord Colton was most hospitable,' she lied, 'and the children were lovely.' She felt the pang of longing go through her. Did they miss her at all? she wondered. Or had they forgotten?

'And it has put you in an excellent position to receive suitors. To spend time in the country, with a family in need, and in the wilds of the country, instead of gadding about town with your rackety friends, says much about your character that is admirable. In all, we could not have hoped for a better result.'

And now she felt more like crying then ever. Her future required that she pretend she had gone to help, rather than to punish. Her mother was spreading it about that she had spent the last month as an angel of mercy to a broken man and his orphaned children, instead of tangled in the sheets with her lover. She was sure that she would go mad.

Of course, her father suspected that something other than the obvious had gone on. He had lectured her all the way back to London about the dangers of attaching herself to the household of a single man, with no sign of a chaperon. And never mind that he was family.

But her mother cared only about the improvement in her character, and gave little thought to how it might have been wrought. She went blissfully on, not noticing Daphne's melancholy. 'I must send Lord Colton a note of thanks for taking such good care of you.'

'I doubt thanks are necessary,' she said softly. 'I am sure he is too modest to think of it.'

'No thanks after such a long visit?' Her mother's eyebrows arched. 'Well, I suppose, with no woman to head the house, Lord Colton has gone a bit odd about the social niceties. But perhaps we can arrange another visit, next autumn, so that you might see how the children have grown. Or invite them here so that we all might meet them.' She smiled. 'I dare say you will be wedded by then, or at least betrothed. And the Colton family will have an honoured place on the guest list. We owe them much in reforming your character.'

'That would be…lovely. I am sure the girls would like to see a wedding.' She swallowed hard to keep back the rush of tears she felt at the thought of Tim, relegated to a front pew with the family like some sort of doting uncle, holding his tongue while another man met her at the altar.

Her mother was smiling broadly at the image formed in her mind. 'Perhaps it is not too early for me to begin the guest list. Such a large event will require planning. And once the Season is under way, we will not have time to do it justice. It is much more difficult to lay out a proper wedding breakfast than to find a groom.' Her mother exited the room in a haze of fantasy, still clutching the vouchers that were the ticket to all her future hopes and dreams.

Daphne sank back into a chair beside the dressing table, too weak to move. That was her future, and always had been. A proper Season, with no false starts, embarrassments or trips into the bushes. Suitors, an offer and a society marriage. It did not matter that her heart was in Wales. And her true family as well.

For that was how she had begun to feel. It had been such a short time. But she had begun to think of Tim's children as her own. She had helped them, and they had loved her for it. It was not her fault that she had loved in return. And was it really so strange? For little Sophie belonged to no one, and yet Tim knew from her first moment on earth that he was her true father. Perhaps that was the way, with young ones.

They had got so much better, under her care. Had the changes lasted? she wondered. No matter how she felt now, it was a small comfort to think that she had done some permanent good. But what if they felt betrayed by her sudden departure? Had everything gone back to the horrible way it was, before she'd started meddling in it?

At least now Tim knew the truth. He could move on with his life. There was no danger in marrying again. The children needed a mother. And if he had given his heart to a woman who was not worthy of him? The fact was immaterial. He was a handsome man, and wealthy as well. If he wished to remarry, then it would happen soon enough. He might even precede her down the aisle.

What did love have to do with making a future? For either of them? Clare was evidence enough that it need not enter into marriage at all.

She waited until her mother was out of sight, before ringing for her maid.

'Hannah, I need you to pack me a bag.'

'Miss?'

'And dresses, Hannah.' She looked into her closet, at the annoyingly bright array of silks that hung there. 'None of these. Could you find me something simpler?

Borrow from the servants if you must. Or remove the trims from some of my older things. Do any of the dresses remain from my time away? I know that Mother wished them destroyed, but there were a few that I would quite like to take with me. Plain dresses, such as a governess might wear.' And she felt something crack inside her, like ice on a stream in spring.

'You are going in disguise?' The maid brightened at the idea.

'Yes.' Although the way she was now felt more like a disguise than her governess clothes ever had. She shoved her lovely gowns to the side, searching the back of the wardrobe for the clothes she had borrowed from the real Miss Collins.

'And it is to be a secret. You must wait as long as you are able before giving my parents the letter that I will leave for them. Can I trust you to help me?'

The girl hesitated for a moment, and then smiled. 'Will you need a lady's maid, miss, once you get to the place you are going?'

Daphne grinned. 'If I am successful in what I mean to do? Then I certainly hope so, Hannah.'

'Then you must be sure to succeed. For your father will throw me out once he realises that I have helped you get away again. And I will be needing a position.'

Chapter Twenty

Tim threw more coal into the stove and held his hands out to the metal. Would he never stop being cold? The thermometer said that the conservatory was warm enough. Almost too warm, if he was to be honest. The air was dry. If he was not careful, the excessive heat would damage the plants.

But he was cold. He ached with it. And there was no warming.

He rubbed at the skin of his bare neck, thinking perhaps a coat and a cravat were in order, as protection if nothing else. But he hardly left the conservatory now, other than to see the children. And while surrounded by the plants, anything more than shirtsleeves and apron seemed excessive. He sat down on the *chaise* again and leaned back, pushing his face deep into the cushions. Sometimes, he thought he could catch a whiff of her perfume. Perhaps it was an orchid coming into bloom, or merely his imagination. But it was something, at any rate. And there was the vague sense that warmth lingered on the bed they had once shared.

He laughed to himself, wishing that he had taken her to his room while he'd had the chance. At least then he would be sleeping in his own bed. It would be less worrisome for his valet if he moved back upstairs.

But when he went above stairs, he found himself wandering to the end of the hall and looking up at the narrow passage that led to the attic bedroom. It would look even stranger to all concerned if he took to sleeping in a narrow bedstead, under the eaves.

He heard a rustling in the leaves by the door, and sat up quickly, before Sophie could catch him trying to sleep during the day again. The older children could see something was wrong. But they did their best to ignore it, giving him hugs, and trying to joke him out of his bad humor.

It was easier, now that they knew there was no risk to their sister. Edmund had even been talking, tentatively at least, of going to school for the spring term.

But although Sophie was better than she had been, he dare not frighten her too much with his strange behaviour, lest she relapse.

She came around the palms to where he sat, and he patted the seat beside him, and held out his arms for a hug.

In response, she climbed up beside him, and put her arms around his neck for a small wet kiss. 'Papa, are you sad?'

'Not now you are here, little one.' He smiled down at her and patted her curls.

'I am sad.'

'You are?' It was better than frightened, he supposed. And after all she had been through, he could not blame her.

'I miss her.'

He had done his best not to speak of her mother. But Clare would always be a part of their lives, and he must accept the fact. 'I know, darling.' And then he hazarded what he suspected was a bold-faced lie. 'But she has gone to a better place.'

'London is a better place?' Sophie tugged at his coat, and smiled hopefully. 'Then can we go there, too? We could visit her. I want to show her my pictures.'

'London? Visit…' He shook his head, and looked down at her again. 'We are talking of Miss Collins again?'

Sophie's hopeful smile increased, and she nodded until her curls bobbed. 'Or you could go to fetch her back.'

This was even harder to answer. For at least with Clare he could assure himself that there was an end to the conversation, and no way to bring her back. There was also no way that she could hurt them further.

But what was he to tell the girl about Daphne? 'I think she is probably happier where she is now. It was not very exciting here, I am sure. And her father said she liked the parties and balls.' It was probably true. She must have a coterie of admirers. And if he had given her a taste for carnality?

He swallowed hard, fighting the shame of what he had done. And then he had turned her off, to fend for herself against the machinations of the rakes in London. Suppose she came to harm because of him?

But he could not have kept her. His children did not need another mother like that. What proof did he have, really, that she would not have fallen to another?

Sophie tugged at his sleeve again. 'Tell her we have oranges. And strawberries. They do not have those in London, I'll wager.' She began bold enough, but her eyes had gone wide and watery at the thought of her missing friend, and her tone was softer, more hesitant. If he was not careful, she would become the little ghost she had been before Miss Collins had come into the house, convinced that her actions were the cause of Daphne's rejection.

'Would you like a strawberry, then?' He seized at the distraction. For anything was better than further questions.

Sophie smiled and nodded.

He went to the plant, and picked a handful, placing them in a handkerchief. 'There you are. Take some to your sister and brother, as well.'

Sophie took them carefully from him, and scampered out of the room, Daphne temporarily forgotten.

He would have to deal with it again tomorrow, he suspected. And at some point, he would need to explain that Miss Collins was really Miss Collingham and she was not coming back from London at all. And then he must make the child believe that it was for her own good he had sent Daphne away, and not as a punishment.

He stared at the fruit in front of him. If only it were so easy to get the memory of her from his own mind. Or to convince himself that she had forgotten him already, or been as bad as he suspected: another Clarissa ready to sink her fangs into his heart like a viper.

At least, if he could believe that the children were better off, then his own misery might not be so acute. But the house, although changed for the better, was growing just as strangely quiet as it had been before Daphne had arrived. His own sense of loss showed no sign of abating with the passage of time. And while the older children might be able to hide their displeasure for his sake, Sophie seemed to alternate between puzzled sadness and optimism that Miss Collins would be returning at any moment. While Edmund and Lily seemed resigned to the fact that they would see her no more, Sophie could not be persuaded. He dreaded to think what would happen when she finally came to realise that it was over.

Another chill went through him, and he allowed himself the luxury of a memory. Her body, pressed tight to his, as it had been on the *chaise*. How could he have sent her away?

He tried to reassure himself again that it had been for the good of the children. But what harm had she done them, in the time she'd resided under his roof? She had shown more compassion and love for them in a few short weeks than Clare had in a lifetime. They had grown, blooming like roses in the sunlight.

And he had ignored the successes and taken her

away from them, because he was angry that she had lied to him.

In her absence, he was lying to himself. It was his own heart that he feared for. She was of Clare's blood. Suppose she was more like her cousin than she appeared? She'd lied to gain entrance to his house, with the express plan of destroying him.

Instead, she'd helped him to face his fears and had healed the children. And when she had discovered the truth? She had been as eager to hide it again as he had.

Being with her felt nothing like it had been with Clarissa. He could not remember ever loving his late wife. Polite apathy and a vague sense of lust had quickly turned to loathing on both their parts, and a low-banked desire for escape. That he should be so frightened of his reaction to Daphne could mean only one thing: that he had a heart to be broken, after all this time of believing himself without one.

It was an exhilarating thought, and a terrifying one. To open himself to the woman could mean great joy, or greater heartache than he had known in his miserable life. And it might already be too late, for he had treated her abominably. She might have gone back to London, to the suitors she had left there, and chosen one who appreciated her charms. It had been weeks. For all he knew, she could be betrothed, or even married.

Or she would be, if he did not do something quickly. If he sat here brooding over her loss he would never learn the truth. He would be trapped in a limbo of unknowing, halfway between happiness and sadness, and too afraid to move in either direction.

Being without her would be no different than being with Clare.

He would go to her, and throw himself on her mercy. Or better yet, he would seize her, drag her back to Wales and force her to finish what she had begun. For whether she intended it or not, she had been well on the way to becoming wife to him and mother to his children. She had made him love her, with her sweetness and her willingness to give. If she meant to deny them, just to engage in London foolishness, then it was time for her to grow up and take responsibility for her life.

The thought appealed to him. He reached a hand to touch his face, felt the stubble on his chin and saw dirt under his fingernails. She would not want him in this condition. And he did not want to let her see what a few weeks without her had done to him, or how quickly the gains of the last month had been undone. A wash, a shave and a clean shirt would do wonders. His best coat, and a properly tied cravat. He was not the handsomest man in London, at least not compared to Adam. But when properly turned out, he had nothing to be ashamed of.

So he would clean up, and then he would head to London. He would claim it was on business, for it would not do to raise the hopes of the children if the errand proved fruitless. And he would find Daphne and bring her home.

There was a soft rapping on the panes of the door,

and the sound of his butler's shuffling footsteps as the man sought to gain his attention. 'My lord?'

He looked up, and smiled.

'A visitor.'

He cast another quick glance over his appearance. 'Stow whoever it is in the drawing room, and I will go and make myself presentable.'

'She wishes to see you immediately, and says it is most urgent.'

'She.' All his plans collapsed in a puddle of trembling hope, and then coalesced, as he realised that it could not possibly be what he was hoping for. 'Here then, and right now. Bring her to me.'

The butler stepped out of the way, evaporating into the hall. And the object of his desire stepped into the conservatory and closed the door behind her. She looked pale, and much as he felt, as though sleep had been elusive, and happiness impossible. Everything about her was more subdued than he remembered. Her hair was more controlled, her dress starched and sensible. It was a dark colour that would not show wear and would be undamaged by grubby palms. And her expression was that of a woman unsure of her position.

She dropped a curtsy that had none of the hidden arrogance of her first attempts at subservience. 'Sir?'

'Miss Collins?' And then he corrected himself, for it was not her name. 'Miss Collingham.' He wanted nothing more than to gather her into his arms. But he hesitated, just as she was doing. 'You have returned to us, against my wishes?'

'Yes.' She said it softly. 'I was hoping that during

my time away, perhaps your feelings on the subject had changed. If my old position is still open, I would very much like to have it back.'

'Your position.' Now this was an unexpected turn. 'I was under the impression, when we parted, that you did not actually need employment.'

'Not when I first came here, my lord. But now that I have left you, I find that there is not as much joy in my old life as I once felt, or as much purpose. It was an endless circle of false friends and foolishness. And if, at the end of it, the best I can hope for is an offer from a man as foolish as myself, then I think I would much prefer to forgo marriage and find some way to be of use.

'I have no references to offer.' She smiled. 'At least none that are actually mine. For those I offered you from the first were forgeries. And you have witnessed the fact that my knowledge of geography, geometry and languages are not what they should be. But the children…' She shook her head, and her eyes seemed to grow large and wavered behind unshed tears. 'Your children need a governess, just as much as they did before.'

But what of their father? 'So you need purpose, and the children need someone to watch over them. And we both know that is not the only thing that happened, when you were last here.'

'You need someone to watch over you as well.' She looked up at him, with a sad smile. 'For you are not as I remember you, Lord Colton.'

He looked down at the floor and muttered, 'Gone to seed. Just like the plants. I should take better care.'

She rushed on. 'And I would understand, if you needed to marry. For it is only right that you should have someone. Someone you could trust, who would not lie to you, or bring you unhappy memories. But if I could only have my little room under the eaves, and see the children sometimes, and bring them down to the conservatory to see you on occasion?' She swallowed. 'Then I think I should be quite content.'

'Content?' The idea was madness, and he would show her so. He closed the distance between them in an instant, and pulled her off balance and into his arms, kissing her in a way that cut off the flow of foolish words. Her mouth was as soft as he remembered, and as sweet, and her body yielding beneath the unyielding fabric of her governess dress. 'It is small comfort to offer me contentment, after what you have already given. Now that you have crossed my threshold I want you, all and unreserved, at my side in the day, and in my bed at night. I want a wife, and the children want a mother. I want a woman who I can love with all my heart, who will love me in return. If you can give me that, then stay. If you offer less, then for God's sake, Daphne, leave and give me peace. For I will go mad if I can see you each day, but cannot touch you.'

'Your offer stands, then?' She sighed into his mouth, and he could feel the spirit returning to her.

'I was horrible to you.'

'And I to you.'

'Because I hurt you.'

'But I will be better.'

'It does not matter.' He kissed her again.

She tilted her head away, not yet willing to surrender. 'And Clare. She was my cousin and my friend. And although she was not the woman I thought she was, I cannot change the happy memories of the past. Nor do I wish to. But she is gone now, for me, and for you as well.' There was a trace of question in her statement.

'She is gone. She cannot hurt me further, and I do not begrudge you your happiness. What she was to either of us does not change what we are to each other.' And she was truly gone, for when he kissed the woman in his arms, there was no shadow of the past in the bright future before him.

'I wanted to tell you, that day. After I got your letter. For I knew what my answer must be. But I could not say the words until you knew the truth. I had believed the most horrible things about you, even worse than you thought of yourself. But I had been terribly wrong, and was terribly sorry. And I wished to beg for your forgiveness, because I had come to love you more than life, and would never wish to see you hurt again.' Her words were like a balm on the old wounds, easing the ache of the past. 'But then Father came, and it was too late to explain.'

'Your father.' And he remembered that they were not the last two people on the earth together. 'Does he know that you have come back to me?'

She looked sheepish. 'I left him a note. I expect, after what has already occurred, that he will be twice as angry as he was the last time. And he was very angry with me, and none too happy with you. He will be coming along shortly, I expect. And you might be receiving a visit from my brothers, as well.'

'Brothers.'

'Three.' She smiled wickedly. 'All very large. They are rather protective, when it comes to me. They spoil me terribly, and give me my way in all things. And I am sure that they would want me to be treated honourably.'

'Then I had best work fast, if I am to deserve the thrashing they are likely to give me.' He kissed her throat. 'If it were just we two, I should rush you off to Scotland today. But I expect we shall have to read the banns in St George's in London, or some other grand church, and do this properly for the sake of your family.'

'And yours,' she reminded him. 'The children might quite like to see a wedding.' She considered. 'Although I think it is far too much bother to go back to London. If there is a small church nearby, it would suit me well. For I have grown quite fond of Wales.'

He laughed and held her close. For if there was any proof that his second marriage would be different from the first, he had heard it from her very lips. 'As long as it is soon, I do not care where. For I must have you, my love. It has been too long.'

'Then take me. For I would not wish otherwise.'

He kissed her in earnest, and she answered him with kisses of her own, her hands stroking his hair, his shoulders and his chest, until he felt the desire rising in him. The linen of his shirt was thin and her touch seemed to burn through it. She was his and his alone, warm and willing, arrayed in starched cotton like some carefully wrapped package, so many layers of cloth between him and what he wanted. He fumbled for the closures at the back of her dress.

'She is *heeeeeeere*. She is, she is, she is!' Sophie pelted into their knees like a bullet, and clung to them so that they could not part if they had wanted to. 'And Papa is kissing her!'

Daphne looked down in obvious amusement. 'Do not shout so, Sophie. While it is very good to hear you talking again, perhaps it would be better if it were not so loud. I fear you will scare your father's plants.'

The girl giggled. 'They are not like animals. I cannot scare them, see?' She ran over to the nearest orchid and cried, 'Boo!'

He used the opportunity to put distance between them, and to hide the embarrassing evidence of his desire. Focusing his mind on his responsibilities as a father, he turned to the nearby basin to plunge his hands into the icy water, scrubbing at the nails furiously with the brush and hoping that he had not left proof of his intentions as hand prints on his beloved. 'Actually, there are plants that will wilt in fear from a single touch. Now that Daphne has returned, I will find some. And perhaps she will help you to paint a picture.' He saw his two other children, hovering in the doorway, old enough to realise that they had interrupted something, but still unsure what it had been. 'Come in, you two, and say hello. For I think we all have a great deal to discuss today.'

And they ran across the threshold, obviously in no

mood to discuss anything, launching themselves on their former governess, and enveloping her in a mutual hug.

Daphne's eyes met his, over the tangle of children, and she smiled, as if to apologise for the interruption. But she seemed supremely happy to be welcomed so. She looked down at the children, smiling at them as though the separation from them had been as difficult for her as it had been for them.

They made a beautiful picture, gathered together under the leaves, the varying reds of their hair contrasting with the green and blending into each other. Some day soon he would have them painted together, just like that. His family. And he felt a completeness that he had never felt before as he put down the brush, wiped his hands on a cloth and went to join them.

* * * * *

COMING NEXT MONTH FROM

HARLEQUIN®
HISTORICAL

Available July 26, 2011

- **THE GUNFIGHTER AND THE HEIRESS**
  by **Carol Finch**
  (Western)

- **PRACTICAL WIDOW TO PASSIONATE MISTRESS**
  by **Louise Allen**
  (Regency)
  (First in *The Transformation of the Shelley Sisters* trilogy)

- **THE GOVERNESS AND THE SHEIKH**
  by **Marguerite Kaye**
  (Regency)
  (Second in *Princes of the Desert* duet)

- **SEDUCED BY HER HIGHLAND WARRIOR**
  by **Michelle Willingham**
  (Medieval)
  (Second in *The MacKinloch Clan* family saga)

HHCNM0711

REQUEST YOUR FREE BOOKS!

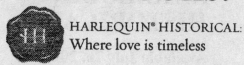

HARLEQUIN® HISTORICAL:
Where love is timeless

2 FREE NOVELS PLUS 2 FREE GIFTS!

HHIIB

*Once bitten, twice shy. That's Gabby Wade's motto—
especially when it comes to Adamson men.
And the moment she meets Jon Adamson her theory
is confirmed. But with each encounter a little something
sparks between them, making her wonder if she's been
too hasty to dismiss this one!*

*Enjoy this sneak peek from ONE GOOD REASON
by Sarah Mayberry, available August 2011
from Harlequin® Superromance®.*

Gabby Wade's heartbeat thumped in her ears as she marched
to her office. She wanted to pretend it was because of her
brisk pace returning from the file room, but she wasn't that
good a liar.

Her heart was beating like a tom-tom because Jon Adamson had touched her. In a very male, very possessive way.
She could still feel the heat of his big hand burning through
the seat of her khakis as he'd steadied her on the ladder.

It had taken every ounce of self-control to tell him to
unhand her. What she'd really wanted was to grab him by
his shirt and, well, explore all those urges his touch had
instantly brought to life.

While she might not like him, she was wise enough to
understand that it wasn't always about liking the other person. Sometimes it was about pure animal attraction.

Refusing to think about it, she turned to work. When
she'd typed in the wrong figures three times, Gabby admitted she was too tired and too distracted. Time to call it a
day.

As she was leaving, she spied Jon at his workbench in
the shop. His head was propped on his hand as he studied
blueprints. It wasn't until she got closer that she saw his

eyes were shut.

He looked oddly boyish. There was something innocent and unguarded in his expression. She felt a weakening in her resistance to him.

"Jon." She put her hand on his shoulder, intending to shake him awake. Instead, it rested there like a caress.

His eyes snapped open.

"You were asleep."

"No, I was, uh, visualizing something on this design." He gestured to the blueprint in front of him then rubbed his eyes.

That gesture dealt a bigger blow to her resistance. She realized it wasn't only animal attraction pulling them together. She took a step backward as if to get away from the knowledge.

She cleared her throat. "I'm heading off now."

He gave her a smile, and she could see his exhaustion.

"Yeah, I should, too." He stood and stretched. The hem of his T-shirt rose as he arched his back and she caught a flash of hard male belly. She looked away, but it was too late. Her mind had committed the image to permanent memory.

And suddenly she knew, for good or bad, she'd never look at Jon the same way again.

Find out what happens next in ONE GOOD REASON, available August 2011 from Harlequin® Superromance®!

Celebrating
Blaze 10 *years of*
red-hot reads

Featuring a special August author lineup of
six fan-favorite authors who have written
for Blaze™ from the beginning!

The Original Sexy Six:

Vicki Lewis Thompson
Tori Carrington
Kimberly Raye
Debbi Rawlins
Julie Leto
Jo Leigh

Pick up all six Blaze™
Special Collectors' Edition titles!

August 2011

Plus visit
HarlequinInsideRomance.com
and click on the Series Excitement Tab
for exclusive Blaze™ 10th Anniversary content!

USA TODAY *bestselling author*
Lynne Graham
introduces her new Epic Duet

THE VOLAKIS VOW
A marriage made of secrets…

Tally Spencer, an ordinary girl with no experience of
relationships… Sander Volakis, an impossibly rich and
handsome Greek entrepreneur. Sander is expecting to
love her and leave her, but for Tally this is love at first
sight. Little does he know that Tally is expecting his
baby…and blackmailing him to marry her!

PART ONE:
THE MARRIAGE BETRAYAL
Available August 2011

PART TWO:
BRIDE FOR REAL
Available September 2011

Available only from Harlequin Presents®.

❦™ Harlequin®

SPECIAL EDITION

Life, Love, Family and Top Authors!

IN AUGUST, HARLEQUIN SPECIAL EDITION FEATURES
USA TODAY BESTSELLING AUTHORS
MARIE FERRARELLA AND *ALLISON LEIGH.*

THE BABY WORE A BADGE
BY *MARIE FERRARELLA*

The second title in the **Montana Mavericks:
The Texans Are Coming!** miniseries....

Suddenly single father Jake Castro has his hands full with
the baby he never expected—and with a beautiful young
woman too wise for her years.

COURTNEY'S BABY PLAN
BY *ALLISON LEIGH*

The third title in the **Return to the Double C** miniseries....

Tired of waiting for Mr. Right, nurse Courtney Clay takes
matters into her own hands to create the family she's
always wanted— but her surly patient may just be
the Mr. Right she's been searching for all along.

**Look for these titles and others in August 2011
from Harlequin Special Edition wherever books are sold.**

BIG SKY BRIDE, BE MINE! *(Northridge Nuptials)* by *VICTORIA PADE*
THE MOMMY MIRACLE by *LILIAN DARCY*
THE MOGUL'S MAYBE MARRIAGE by *MINDY KLASKY*
LIAM'S PERFECT WOMAN by *BETH KERY*

www.Harlequin.com

SE 15A08